TROWEL
AND ERROR

THE ENGLISH COTTAGE GARDEN MYSTERIES
BOOK FOUR

H.Y. HANNA

DEDICATION

To Billy and Theresa
– for their wonderful friendship and support.

CONTENTS

CHAPTER ONE

Poppy Lancaster had never been so wet and miserable in her life. Her fingers, jammed inside unwieldy rubber gloves, were numb and stiff with cold, and her clothes were soaked through and clinging to her unpleasantly. Water had even somehow seeped into her Wellington boots and her feet squelched inside wet socks, making her grimace with every step.

Raising her head, she looked in despair at the enormous pane of glass in front of her. She felt like she had been soaping and scrubbing for hours... and yet still, there were so many more panes waiting for her: endless expanses of dusty glass, smeared with dirt and grime, bordered with cobwebs and edged with algae. They stretched around her and over her head, forming the walls and the slanted roof of the large greenhouse that was attached to the rear of her grandmother's cottage.

I'm never going to finish cleaning this place, she thought with a sinking heart as she eyed the structure around her. She was beginning to regret following the advice of several well-meaning villagers who had suggested that autumn was the perfect time to give one's greenhouse a much-needed clean. The mild forecast had lulled her into thinking she had a comfortable stretch of warm weather to accomplish the job. Unfortunately, she should have remembered that the only thing you could rely on weathermen for was to get the forecast wrong, and the dry, sunny day she had been promised had quickly morphed into a chilly, grey drizzlefest. In fact, it was only mid-afternoon, and Poppy noted worriedly that the light was already fading as she gazed through the streaked glass at the surrounding garden outside.

It had seemed like a dream come true when she had been told at the start of summer—just a few months ago—that she had inherited a cottage and large garden from the estranged grandmother she had never known. Poppy had left her life in London without a backward glance and eagerly settled at Hollyhock Cottage, determined to follow in her grandmother's footsteps and continue the plant nursery business which had been in the family for generations. True, she'd no horticultural experience, could barely tell one end of a trowel from the other, and had always killed any green thing she touched (yes, including that plastic plant from IKEA) but Poppy had been undaunted. After all, both her mother and grandmother had been brilliant plantswomen, so she was sure that the green fingers were in her genes... somewhere. She just had to find them.

And during the glorious months of summer, when the cottage garden had been at its most beautiful—with billowing roses everywhere, elegant spires of foxgloves swaying in the breeze, and fragrant climbers like honeysuckle scrambling up the walls—Poppy had been full of hope and delight. But with the coming of autumn and darker, colder days, the garden had lost some of its romantic appeal and Poppy had begun to realise that gardening wasn't all roses and sunshine. There was an unpleasant side too, like endless weeding to do, slimy slugs to trap, dead leaves to rake... *And greenhouses to clean*, she thought with a sigh, looking around her once more.

Her grandmother's long illness before her death had meant that the greenhouse had become as neglected as the cottage garden outside, filled with broken terracotta pots and dusty seed trays, faded plant labels and discarded bags of compost and potting mix. The cracked floor was littered with dead leaves, and an army of creepy-crawlies had taken up residence in seams and corners. Up until recently, Poppy had been too preoccupied with the garden outside to give the greenhouse much thought. But with the weather cooling and the new gardening knowledge she had gained, she had soon begun to realise that she would have to find somewhere to shelter the "tender" plants from the cold if they were to survive the winter. She would also need a warm, bright place where she could nurture seedlings so that they would get a head start and grow to a good enough size to sell when spring arrived.

The greenhouse was the answer—or at least, it would be, once it was cleaned. So that morning, Poppy had grabbed her brushes, sponges, and buckets of soapy water, and set out to tackle the multitude of nooks and crannies filled with dirt, moss, slime... and several other things she didn't want to know about. It had seemed fun at first, even therapeutic, as she swept and scrubbed, sponged and scoured, but now, several hours of hard scrubbing later, the whole project was rapidly losing its charm.

Still, it's not as if there's anything else I could be doing, she reminded herself with a sigh. The usual rush of worries flooded over her and Poppy wondered once again how she was going to manage in the months ahead. Her batch of perennial seedlings wouldn't grow big enough to be ready for sale until spring; the winter bedding plants she had ordered from wholesale suppliers were bringing in a few customers, but selling little pots of pansies and primroses could only produce a small income. Her popular home-made flower arrangements, which had been a welcome side business through the summer, were no longer an option now that the cottage garden was fading and looking barer each day.

Most of all, the nagging voice telling her that she had bitten off more than she could chew when she'd decided to take on her grandmother's cottage garden nursery was growing louder and harder to ignore. Still, Poppy didn't regret her decision. She loved Hollyhock Cottage and already saw it as the home she'd never had, the kind of home she had always dreamt of during her turbulent childhood drifting around the country with her hapless, nomadic mother.

And I've got big plans, she reminded herself. *Plans to expand the nursery, open the garden to the public, and develop my unique flower arrangements...*

Of course, that was all in the future. Meanwhile, there were more practical things to consider, like putting food on the table and paying the bills. Poppy gave a rueful smile. *It's all very well having grand schemes for the future but how am I going to find the money for necessities—*

"*N-ow?*" said a voice by her ankles.

Poppy laughed as she looked down at the enormous ginger tom rubbing himself against her leg. "You took the words right out of my mouth, Oren."

The big tomcat jumped nimbly onto the wooden workbench in the centre of the room and weaved his way between the trays of seedlings laid out. Poppy watched him apprehensively; Oren moved very delicately for such a big cat, lifting his paws and stepping between the trays, his long tail waving for balance. Poppy began to relax, then she saw him stroll down to the other end of the workbench, where a lone potted plant sat. Oren bent to sniff it curiously, then rubbed his chin against the side of the pot, causing the plant to teeter precariously.

"Careful!" Poppy yelped, diving across and grabbing the potted plant just in time.

"*N-ow?*" said Oren, looking at her with a mischievous gleam in his big yellow eyes.

Poppy gave him a mock glare, then turned and carefully carried the pot to the other side of the greenhouse. Setting it down on a shelf, she stood back and gazed lovingly at the small cluster of stems and leaves protruding from the blue porcelain pot. Everyone had told her that it was impossible to grow gardenias in England, that it was just too cold for these natives of tropical Asia to thrive and flower well. But when she had seen the little potted *Gardenia jasminoides* offered for sale a few weeks ago, she had been unable to resist. With its richly fragrant, creamy-white flowers set against the glossy green leaves, it had been one of the most beautiful things she had ever seen.

Since bringing it home, she had treated the little potted gardenia like a pampered pet, giving it pride of place in the greenhouse, carefully rotating it each day so that it would receive even light from all sides, and watering it with meticulous care. She had been disappointed when the beautiful flowers had faded soon after she'd brought the plant home, but she had been excited to see that there were several more unopened buds. Poppy leaned over the plant now, eagerly checking to see if any of the buds had started to unfurl. To her dismay, she found that instead of opening, several of the buds had dropped off and lay shrivelled on the soil beneath.

"Oh!" she cried, frowning as she picked up a bud and looked at it more closely. Why were they dropping off? Was it something she had done?

She looked back up at the plant and was even more worried to see that several of the lower leaves had started to yellow. Gingerly, she took hold of a leaf and turned it over, looking for parasites or signs of a fungal infection, but she saw nothing. The waxy surface was clean and unblemished, and the leaves weren't shrivelled or wilted in any way. And yet they were definitely taking on a sickly yellow tinge.

Poppy sighed. It had all looked so promising! Maybe she should have heeded the advice about gardenias; maybe she had been silly and naïve to think that she could succeed where more experienced gardeners had failed. She wondered if she needed to water the plant but when she prodded the soil in the pot with a finger, she found it still damp. If there was one thing she had learnt in gardening so far, it was that over-watering killed more plants than anything else. So she refrained from grabbing the watering can. Instead, she set the gardenia on a ledge right next to one of the glass panes, where it would get maximum sunlight, and hoped that it would look better when she checked on it tomorrow.

"*N-ow? N-owww?*"

Poppy glanced back across the greenhouse to see Oren sitting by the bucket of soapy water, regarding her with his big yellow eyes. She went over to him and said with a wry smile: "Yes, you're right, Oren—I'd better get back to work now."

She had barely started again, though, when her phone rang. Dropping the sponge back into the bucket, Poppy fumbled with wet fingers to pull the phone out of her pocket. Her heart sank as she glanced at the screen and saw the Caller ID. Hubert Leach was one member of her long-lost family that she could have done without finding again. Her cousin was brash and vulgar, with a deceitful manner and greedy attitude. Besides, she had a suspicion that she knew what the call would be about: Hubert was probably calling to claim his pound of flesh.

"Cousin Poppy!" came Hubert's unctuous voice. "How are we today?"

"I'm fine, Hubert. How are you?" asked Poppy cautiously.

"Oh, you know... busy... busy... Life as a property agent is always interesting. We've had a flood of new commercial lease properties come on the market recently, which has kept us on our toes—but I expect your friend Nell has told you all about that, since she has been given the cleaning contracts for all of them. How is she enjoying her new job with us?"

"Er... she's very happy."

"I'm glad to hear it. It is so hard to find a good job nowadays, especially when one is a bit—*ahem*—older, like your dear friend, so I was delighted to be able to help her find stable work."

Poppy squirmed at Hubert's meaningful tone. "Yes, she's very grateful to you for employing her—"

"Ah, well, of course, there was a little *quid pro quo* involved, as you'll probably recall...?"

Poppy winced. *Here it comes.* She wondered again if she had done the right thing when she had blithely agreed to her cousin's request of an unnamed future favour, in return for providing a job for her friend Nell. At the time, she hadn't even hesitated; Nell had practically been a surrogate mother and Poppy had been willing to do anything to help, after her old friend had been made redundant from her cleaning job in London. It had been wonderful to see Nell settling in as her housemate at Hollyhock Cottage and to watch Nell making friends in the village of Bunnington, as well as enjoying her new work... but Poppy had quietly dreaded this call from Hubert for a long time.

"Yes, of course, I remember," she said. "What is it you want, Hubert?"

He twittered. "Oh, nothing much, nothing much. Just a tiny favour, really. You see, I've been invited to a party being given by David Nowak tomorrow night—you do know David Nowak?"

"Yes, of course. He owns the Róża Garden Centres chain—one of the biggest in the country," said Poppy, unable to keep the envy and resentment out of her voice. She might not have been in the horticultural business long, but already she could sympathise with the many small, independent nurseries who were being out-competed by the big garden centres. "He's some local-boy-made-good, isn't he? Grew up in Bunnington, from a poor immigrant Polish family, didn't have much schooling but managed to build a multi-billion-pound company—"

"Bloody hell, he's much more than that! The man's on the Sunday Times Rich List! He won the Top Brit Entrepreneur Award two years running and he's probably got his fingers in all the local businesses in Oxfordshire. He bought a manor house just outside Bunnington last year. Could have had his pick of properties in London but he said he wanted to come back to his roots."

"Well, that's nice of him—"

"Nice had nothing to do with it," scoffed Hubert. "Very astute chap, that Nowak: got the property at a knock-down price because the previous owners couldn't afford to keep up the maintenance on the place, and it has since doubled in value already with the improvements and renovations he's put in..."

Poppy could practically see Hubert rubbing his hands and she wondered if her cousin was hoping

Nowak would sell his new property, and hire Leach Properties to conduct the negotiations.

"...it's called Chatswood House," Hubert continued. "And it's famous for its beautiful old orangery, attached to the rear of the manor."

"Orangery? That's like a greenhouse where you keep oranges, isn't it?"

"Oh, much more than a greenhouse and much more than just oranges!" said Hubert with a patronising laugh. "An orangery is like a big, fancy conservatory; they were originally built to house all types of citrus plants during the winter. The Italians invented them in the seventeenth century. The royal family loved 'em. Put them up everywhere. You been to the Orangery at Kensington Palace? Or the one at the Royal Botanic Gardens?"

"No," said Poppy regretfully. "They're on my bucket list, though."

"Well, this one at Chatswood House could give any of those famous orangeries a run for their money. Oh, it's not as big but it's pretty fancy. Of course, it had fallen into complete disrepair and needed serious work, and Nowak has spent a ton on restoring it. That's the official reason for the party: they've just finished the renovations and he wants to celebrate. If you ask me, though, I think it's also a clever fundraiser. I'll bet he's thinking of his election campaign next year—you know he's running for local MP? A party is a good way to hobnob with all the local VIPs—"

"And you've been invited to this party?" said Poppy, wishing that Hubert would get to the point.

"Naturally," said Hubert smugly. "As one of the leading property agents in Oxfordshire, I'm top of the guestlist."

More likely you weaselled your way onto it, thought Poppy. Then she nearly dropped the phone in surprise as Hubert added smoothly:

"And I'd like you to go with me as my date."

"Me?" said Poppy, dumbfounded.

"Yes, I need you to pretend to be my girlfriend for the evening."

"What? Why?"

"Well, you see, when I met Nowak recently, I sort of implied that... well... that I had a girlfriend—a serious girlfriend. You know how it is, everyone was standing around, talking about their wives or partners, and I didn't want to look bad..."

Poppy could just imagine how her cousin's love of bragging and one-upmanship would have prompted him to make up an imaginary girlfriend, just to look good in front of his peers. Still, she couldn't understand why he would ask her to be his date. She and Hubert were hardly close—in fact, they'd barely seen each other more than a handful of times since she'd moved to Oxfordshire—and surely even her slimy cousin could find a woman from his own social circle who would be willing to hang on his arm for one night?

"There's something you're not telling me," she

said.

Hubert laughed quickly. "Nonsense! All I'm asking you is to get dolled up and come along for some cocktails and canapés... surely that's not too much to ask for?"

Poppy hesitated. The last thing she wanted to do was go anywhere as Hubert's date. On the other hand, if this was all he was asking for as his favour, then it was a huge relief and an easy way to fulfil her obligation to him.

"What's the dress code? If it's very formal, I don't have anything posh to wear—"

"Oh, no problem! It's actually a sort of fancy dress. Hang on a sec..." There was a rustle of paper. "Here it is—the invite says the dress code is 'Vintage Cocktail'. I'll tell you what, why don't you come up to Oxford and visit the Ballroom Emporium on Cowley Road? They're famous for stocking vintage gear— they even supply costumes for TV productions, you know. You can hire some glad rags from there. It'll be my treat."

Poppy wondered if she'd heard right. Since when did her stingy cousin offer to pay for anything? "You're going to an awful lot of expense and trouble, just to convince Nowak you have a girlfriend. Wouldn't it be easier to tell him that you broke up or something? What aren't you telling me?" she asked suspiciously.

"Nothing!" protested Hubert. "Look, all the men always come to these things with some totty on their arm and I don't want to be the only one who turns up alone, okay?" His voice wobbled slightly. "I... I don't want them to think that I'm some sad git who can't even get a girl."

Poppy softened. Maybe she was being paranoid and unfair. After all, for all his faults, Hubert was still human and he must have felt loneliness and rejection too.

"All right," she said with a sigh.

"Fantastic!" said Hubert, instantly recovering his good mood. "The party starts at six so I'll come and pick you up around five-thirty."

"Okay, I'll be ready." Poppy hung up and looked down at her phone. In spite of everything, she had a bad feeling that she had just made a very big mistake...

CHAPTER TWO

"Ooh, did you find something nice, Poppy? Let's see what you've got! I hope you didn't pick a boring black dress—not that they aren't very practical, of course, and I know they're supposed to flatter your figure... but really, a young girl like you needs to wear pretty colours and frills and sparkles—how will you ever find a man otherwise? They say that men are attracted to bright colours, especially red. Yes, they did some research, you know, on online dating sites, and they found that women who wore red in their photos were contacted far more than those who wore drab colours..."

Poppy shut the front door of Hollyhock Cottage and smiled at the grey-haired, middle-aged woman who had come out of the kitchen to greet her. She had met Nell Hopkins when the cleaning lady had offered to sublet rooms in her small London townhouse and Poppy had been grateful, not only for the cheap accommodation, but also for Nell's support during her mother's illness. The kindly landlady had cared for Holly Lancaster as if she had been her own daughter and, after Holly's death, Nell's warm, maternal presence had been a huge comfort to Poppy, who was suddenly alone in the world.

Now, she laughed and said, "Don't worry, Nell, I didn't get a black dress. I'm only hiring something for one night—and besides, Hubert's footing the bill—so I didn't have to worry about buying something sensible and good value! I found a gorgeous 1920s cocktail dress in a sort of champagne-gold colour, and some matching shoes."

"Well, go and put them on and let's see!" Nell urged, her round apple cheeks flushed with excitement.

A few minutes later, Poppy stood in the middle of her bedroom and pirouetted around for her old friend to admire.

"Oh my lordy Lord, Poppy... you look beautiful!" cried Nell, her eyes bright with delight.

"Yes, it really is lovely, isn't it?" said Poppy, smoothing her skirt down and eyeing her reflection in the full-length mirror propped up against the wall. She gave a wistful sigh. "I wish I didn't have to return it. I've never owned a dress like this..."

"Do you have some nice jewellery you could wear with it? A pearl necklace or maybe some dangling earrings would look lovely with that scooped neckline."

Poppy shook her head and laughed. "Nell! Where would I get a pearl necklace from? No, I don't have anything like that—I'll have to make do with the small gold studs that Mum used to wear." She peered at herself in the mirror again and rubbed her bare arms with a frown. "I wish I'd remembered to get a matching wrap from the Ballroom Emporium... I can wear my coat to get there, but I'd have to take that off once I'm inside, and the only cardigan I have is a bit tattered and the wrong colour."

"Yes, it does look a bit unfinished, especially with that sleeveless design... There's something missing..." said Nell, tilting her head to one side. Then she snapped her fingers. "I know just what you need! Wait there!" She disappeared from the room and Poppy heard her rummaging in her own bedroom down the corridor. A few minutes later, Nell returned carrying something pale and silky in her hands.

"Here—these will complete the look perfectly and keep your arms warm too. Go on, put them on!" said Nell, thrusting the item at her.

Poppy looked down at the pair of satin, elbow-length evening gloves. They had probably once been white but had since aged to ivory, and the edges were slightly frayed, but nevertheless there was a timeless elegance to them.

Poppy stroked them reverently. "They're

gorgeous," she breathed.

"They belonged to my mother," said Nell with a fond smile. "She gave them to me when I was a young woman, but I've never had a chance to wear them—"

"Oh, I can't—"

"Rubbish! It will be lovely to see them used at last. Go on, put them on," urged Nell again.

Carefully, Poppy pulled the satin gloves on, then looked at herself in the mirror once more. Nell was right: the gloves were the perfect accessory to complete the outfit.

"Do you think I'll look odd, though?" she asked worriedly. "I mean, gloves are so old-fashioned. No one ever wears them anymore, except maybe to a really formal 'white-tie' event. What if I look ridiculous and everyone laughs at me?"

"The invitation said the dress code was 'Vintage Cocktail', didn't it?" said Nell. "I'll bet you lots of ladies will be wearing gloves. It's the easiest way to look 'vintage'. Oh, I can't wait to hear how it goes tomorrow night! It was so nice of Hubert to invite you. I must say, dear—I didn't like to say it before, seeing as he's your cousin and all—but I'd never really cared for Hubert. I know it was very kind of him to offer me a job, but I always thought that he was a bit... well, never mind. Obviously I was wrong and he's a kind soul."

Poppy bit back the words that rose to her lips and gave Nell a wan smile instead.

"And just think! You might meet someone at the

party! A nice boy from a wealthy family, perhaps, who will sweep you off your feet and take you on a romantic weekend to Paris... and then maybe he'll propose under the Eiffel Tower—I've heard that's *so* romantic—and then you can have your honeymoon in Italy—"

"Nell!" said Poppy with an exasperated laugh. Really, sometimes Nell's obsession with romance novels got a bit out of hand. No matter how much Poppy protested about modern womanhood and female independence, her old friend was convinced that Poppy couldn't really be happy until she had found her soulmate. Still, she could hardly tell Nell the truth—that she was unlikely to meet any romantic prospects when she was attending the party as Hubert Leach's "girlfriend"—so the best thing was to say nothing and to change the subject.

"Thank you for the gloves," she said, taking them off carefully and laying them on the bed. "I'll take very good care of them."

"And what about your handbag?" asked Nell, picking up Poppy's battered leather tote from the chair by the bed. "You can't be thinking of carrying this old thing?"

The bag tipped sideways as Nell picked it up and a rolled-up magazine fell out. Nell made a tutting sound as she saw the cover, which displayed the latest gossip on Hollywood actors, rock stars, and other celebrities.

"Poppy! Have you been wasting money buying

magazines again?"

"It… it was on special offer," Poppy lied, snatching the magazine out of Nell's hands.

"Poppy, dear…" The older woman sighed and looked at her sadly. "You're not going to find him that way, you know."

"Find who?" said Poppy, feigning ignorance.

"Your father."

Poppy flushed. "Who said I was looking for him? I… uh… just happened to be interested in some of the stories." Hurriedly, she rolled the magazine up and stuffed it back into her handbag.

"Poppy…" Nell looked at her sadly. "Is it really so important?"

Poppy bit her lip. "I… I can't explain it, Nell… but I feel like if I could just find him, then… then everything will be okay, you know? Like I'll be able to deal with things better and—"

"Nonsense! Your father has never been in your life and you've managed fine up to now without him."

"But it's different now! Up until recently, I've always had Mum with me… and she… she sort of defined me, you know? I was 'Holly Lancaster's daughter'. My life revolved around her. She was always coming up with crazy new ideas—she was so creative, such a carefree spirit, whereas I was the ordinary one, the one with plain brown hair instead of beautiful honey-blonde; the boring, sensible, practical—"

"Oh rubbish!" scoffed Nell. "You know I loved your

mother, dear, but I wasn't blind to her faults. Creative and carefree is another way of saying impulsive and irresponsible. I know she thought she was doing the best for you, but really, it was no way to bring up a child, dragging you from place to place, all over the country, whenever she got bored and wanted a change of scene; never giving you a chance to put down roots and make friends; refusing to swallow her pride and reconcile with your grandmother so you could have some family—"

"Oh, I didn't mind," said Poppy quickly. "I mean, life with Mum was always so exciting. She was so... so much larger than life! She always said we never needed anyone else and when she was around, it really felt like that." Poppy paused, then said in a small voice, "But now that she's gone... Well, I feel sort of lost. Most people have things to help them define themselves. They know who their parents are, what their background is... How can I figure out who *I* am unless I find out—"

"You are who you make yourself to be," said Nell with an emphatic nod. "You don't need your family history or anything else to know what kind of person you want to be. There are loads of people out there, you know, who throw their pasts away and invent themselves as a new person." She reached out and patted Poppy's hand. "You just have to have faith in yourself, dear, and—What's that?"

Startled, Poppy turned to look at the window ledge that Nell was staring at. "What's what? Oh, that? I think it's just a speck of dust."

"*A speck of dust?*" Nell bridled at the thought of any dirt daring to invade her spotless domain. She frowned and ran a finger along the offending ledge. "I only dusted it this morning! I must switch to another brand of duster. I'll go and get a cloth, and give it another wipe."

As her friend bustled out, muttering to herself, Poppy looked guiltily at the magazine that was half-protruding from her bag. She knew it was silly to spend hours poring over those magazines, scanning the faces of the ageing rock stars and hoping against hope to find one who bore more than a passing resemblance to her own features... but she couldn't seem to help herself. She just couldn't give up the hope that if she kept looking, some day she just might find him...

CHAPTER THREE

Poppy looked nervously around as she alighted from the taxi in the wide circular driveway before an imposing country manor. A series of other cars were disgorging their passengers and everywhere she looked there were couples dressed in outfits from various historical eras. There were cloche hats and 1920s "flapper" dresses, Victorian lace ruffles and skirt bustles, 70s bell-bottom pants and disco shirts, and even Regency-era empire-waist gowns and gentlemen's silk breeches. The women all seemed incredibly glamorous and sophisticated, decked out in velvets and satins, and sparkling with jewellery, as they sashayed towards the manor house. Poppy felt suddenly very gauche and out of her depth. She fidgeted with the edge of her satin gloves, tugging them higher, then was relieved to see that Nell had been right: most of the other women were wearing gloves too—and even some of the men. It gave her a little spurt of confidence and, taking a deep breath, she took Hubert's arm and started across the driveway.

They followed the other guests who were not entering through the front door but rather heading down a path that curved around the side of the house. Fairy lights had been strung overhead, lighting the way, and making it look like an enchanted pathway through the grounds. The faint sound of a string quartet could be heard in the distance, as well as the hubbub of voices and laughter. As Poppy started up the path, she caught sight of someone coming in the opposite direction and nearly stopped in surprise.

It was Joe Fabbri, the local handyman who had become an unlikely friend and mentor in the months since she'd arrived at Hollyhock Cottage. When she had first met Joe, Poppy had been taken aback and even intimidated by his taciturn manner. But she had soon learned that the handyman's brusque demeanour belied a kind heart. It was Joe who had patiently shown her how to use each rusty garden tool in her grandmother's greenhouse, Joe who had helped her cut back and tame the overgrown cottage garden, Joe who had listened, without blame or criticism, each time she'd come to him with a horticultural woe, and Joe who had quietly encouraged her growing confidence with seedlings, cuttings, and flowers. As someone who had lacked a paternal figure all her life, Poppy had quickly started to see Joe as a surrogate for the uncle, or even father, that she'd never had growing up—even if he wasn't exactly the chatty, cuddly sort!

Now, as he walked towards her—with his tanned leathery face, grey ponytail, and paint-splattered overalls—Joe looked strangely incongruous amongst the glamorous guests. He was carrying a bag of tools and a stepladder, expertly balancing it against one shoulder as he passed the guests going in the opposite direction. Poppy wondered what Joe was doing there and was just about to call out to him, when a dark-haired woman appeared behind him. She looked to be in her fifties, with high arched brows and a narrow, thin face, and was dressed in a lavishly beaded velvet gown, its rich emerald colour glowing against her pale skin. Diamonds glittered at her ears and throat, and she looked like she should have been dancing a waltz at a royal reception, not chasing a handyman down a garden path.

"Mr Fabbri! Mr Fabbri!"

She caught up with Joe just as Poppy neared him.

"Mr Fabbri, are you sure you've fixed that trellis? It still looks slightly crooked to me—what if it falls down when a guest is standing nearby and injures them badly? I really don't know *what* Dawn was thinking! She should have double-checked *everything* when the event organisers installed the decorations!" The woman huffed irritably. "David always says I worry too much but really, nothing gets done properly if you don't do it yourself. Staff always assure you that everything is safe and secure but I know better than to trust their word... and look how right I was! People always try to cut corners. If I hadn't gone around checking just before the party started, imagine what might have happened!" She looked Joe up and down. "I hear you're the best handyman in Bunnington—I hope your reputation is well-deserved. Are you sure it's fixed now? I can't afford to have any of the guests injured. I warn you, Mr Fabbri, I always insist on getting my money's worth and I won't hesitate to call you back if things aren't up to scratch. But you were fairly quick; I suppose it wasn't a complicated repair?"

She paused at last for a breath and looked expectantly at Joe.

"Screw loose," he said.

It wasn't clear if he was talking about the trellis or the woman, and Poppy grinned. The woman looked bewildered by Joe's laconic reply and Poppy started to say something to help, but Hubert clamped a hand on her arm and dragged her swiftly past. As he propelled her up the path, he leaned close and said in a low voice:

"By the way, your name isn't Poppy tonight, it's Christelle."

Poppy turned to look at him. "I'm sorry?"

"That's the name I told Nowak when I was telling him about my girlfriend."

"You didn't tell me I had to use a fake name," said

Poppy, frowning.

"It doesn't matter, does it? It's only for tonight—and tonight you're not Poppy Lancaster, you're Christelle Bellini, my girlfriend."

"What? *Bellini*?" spluttered Poppy. "What kind of name is that?"

"What do you mean? It's a very pretty name," said Hubert defensively.

"It's also a famous cocktail! Couldn't you think of something that didn't involve Prosecco and peaches?"

"Look, I wanted something sexy and Italian, and that was what popped into my head, okay?"

Poppy sighed. She supposed she should have been grateful that it hadn't been Ferrari or Versace. Smoothing down her dress, she took a deep breath and followed Hubert up the path. It led out through a row of neatly clipped shrubs and opened at last onto a wide stone terrace. Poppy caught her breath as they stepped out. On one side, the terrace looked down into a walled garden, filled with Mediterranean-style plantings of fragrant herbs, gnarled olive trees, climbing bougainvillea, and brightly coloured geraniums in terracotta pots.

On the opposite side, the terrace was flanked by what Poppy thought at first to be the rear of the manor house—then she realised that it was, in fact, a long building attached to the main house. It was the orangery. Poppy looked at it in awe. Despite the gathering dusk, the lights from the building itself lit it with a brilliant golden glow, making it easy for her to admire its elegant grandeur. Built in the English Baroque style, with huge arched windows spanning the walls and a high lantern roof made entirely of glass, the orangery had been lovingly restored and now looked more like a magnificent ballroom than a fancy greenhouse.

When Poppy stepped inside, however, she was delighted to find that it *was* filled with plants. She thought the event organisers had done a wonderful job, decorating the interior of the orangery in such a way as to recreate a tranquil, green oasis while also providing the luxurious setting needed for a high-society party. She completely forgot about the autumn chill and grey skies outside as she admired the row of beautifully clipped miniature orange trees standing in terracotta pots beside the windows, and the lush greenery bursting out of containers artistically grouped together at intervals around the room. There were even a few small troughs of climbing vines trained up wooden trellises attached to the orangery walls. No doubt one of these had been the reason for Joe Fabbri's hasty visit, although they all looked stable and secure enough to Poppy's eye.

A string quartet played a series of classical favourites at one end of the long room, whilst a mixologist presided over a cocktail bar that had been set up at the other. The centre had been left clear as a space for guests to mingle, and there were clusters of people congregating there, helping themselves to champagne and canapés from the trays being offered by uniformed waiters.

Poppy had never attended such a beautiful and glamorous event before, and for a moment she felt like Cinderella arriving at the ball. Then she came back down to earth with a thump when Hubert linked her arm in his. Her cousin was certainly no Prince Charming! He dragged her over to join the nearest group of guests and she couldn't help squirming as he smugly introduced her as "Christelle Bellini". When she had agreed to the favour, it had seemed fairly innocuous to take on an alias and pretend to be Hubert's girlfriend, but now that she was here, she found that the deception made her very uncomfortable.

Still, it's just for one evening, she reminded herself. *And nobody here knows the real me anyway—*

Then her heart gave a lurch as she heard an incredulous chuckle followed by a deep male voice she recognised:

"I'm delighted to make your acquaintance, Christelle. D'you know, I have the strangest feeling that we've met before?"

Poppy looked up in dismay as a tall, dark-haired man stepped forwards from the back of the group and held a hand out to her, a gleam of amusement in his eyes. It was Nick Forrest, bestselling crime author... and mercurial neighbour, who lived right next door to Hollyhock Cottage and who owned a big orange tomcat named Oren.

CHAPTER FOUR

Poppy stared at Nick, wondering how to reply. He was wearing a Victorian-style frock coat with a cravat and top hat. Hubert was wearing something similar and Poppy had secretly thought that her cousin looked rather silly, but now she had to admit that Nick somehow managed to make the period ensemble look suave and dashing. It was easy to see why he had been labelled "the sexy face of crime-writing"—although privately, Poppy thought his moody aura had more to do with his perpetual bad temper than anything else! Tonight, though, the crime author seemed to be in a rare good humour and he grinned wickedly as he waited for her answer.

"I... um..." Poppy stammered. "I—"

"Hullo Nick, great to see you here... and who's this lovely young lady that you're monopolising?"

Poppy turned to see a small, balding man in his mid-fifties approach them. He was dressed in a pinstriped suit from the Edwardian era, and carried a gentleman's cane. She recognised David Nowak from the photos she'd seen in the media. The businessman had an earnest, kindly face and a quiet, almost diffident manner, which made him seem more like a friendly librarian than a billionaire entrepreneur. He held a hand out to Poppy, looking at her curiously, and said:

"Welcome to my party. I'm David Nowak. I don't believe we've been introduced?"

Poppy found herself even more tongue-tied now, torn between wanting to blurt out the truth and feeling obliged to keep her word to Hubert and maintain the deception. She glanced at Nick; for a moment, she thought that he was going to expose her and a part of her was almost glad—it would have been a relief to stop the ridiculous charade—but after a barely perceptible moment of hesitation, Nick smiled and said smoothly:

"I don't believe you have. I was only just becoming acquainted with... Christelle myself."

"Christelle? That's an unusual name," said Nowak, shaking Poppy's hand with a smile.

"Yes, Christelle Bellini! Remember, I told you about her?" cried Hubert, thrusting himself forwards and grabbing Nowak's hand, pumping it up and down vigorously. "Hubert Leach... we chatted at the last business association meeting... I own a property agency in Oxford and I specialise in development projects—"

"Ah, yes... I remember," said Nowak, looking less than enthusiastic as he tried to extricate his hand from Hubert's grasp.

"Christelle is here as my date," added Hubert, beaming.

Poppy saw Nick raise his eyebrows, but he made no comment and, a moment later, his attention was claimed by a couple gushing about his books.

Nowak turned pointedly back to Poppy. "Er... yes, I remember now. Mr Leach has told me a lot about you. Our backgrounds seem to align in many ways: you're a self-made woman too, aren't you, Miss Bellini? Mr Leach says that you purchased your first property at nineteen and were negotiating multiple development contracts within two years. Quite an accomplishment, I must say." He looked at her with admiration. "It's very impressive to find such a young woman handling such a large property portfolio. Hubert says you have a string of properties around the south-east of England."

Poppy's mouth fell open. Hubert gave a nervous, high-pitched laugh and said quickly:

"Ah... ha-ha-ha... I did say she's remarkable, didn't I?"

"So tell me, Christelle, what strategy did you favour when you were starting out? Did you take more of a 'buy to lease' or 'buy to sell' approach?" asked Nowak earnestly. "I've always favoured 'buy to sell' myself—but of course, in a volatile market, especially in a recession, that can be disastrous. On the other hand, with leasing, you have the thorny problem of rental yields... although you only have to get to ten percent with rentals, of course, whereas I always aim for thirty percent with sales..."

Poppy felt her eyes glazing over and she sent Hubert a dirty look. What had her cousin been saying to Nowak about her? Hubert swallowed audibly and hastily tried to change the subject.

"Oh, I'm sure Christelle's portfolio is nothing compared to yours, Mr Nowak." Hubert made a sweeping gesture with his hand. "And this must be the finest property of all. Magnificent, what you've done!"

"Thank you. Yes, this has been a project very close to my heart," said Nowak, looking around and smiling. "In fact, it was seeing the orangery that made me decide to buy this place, in spite of the state that it was in."

"You've done an amazing job restoring it," said Poppy with genuine admiration, forgetting about Hubert for a moment. "I never really knew what an orangery was—I'd never been to one before—and this is one of the most beautiful places I have ever seen!"

Nowak laughed, looking pleased. "I'm glad you think so, Miss Bellini. I was very keen for the orangery to be restored to working order. So many of them are converted into wedding venues and restaurants these days... I think it's a great shame.

You know orangeries were originally built to house citrus plants in the winter and shelter them from the cold? That's where they got the name from."

"This looks far too grand to be somewhere to put orange trees in winter!"

Nowak laughed again. "It's true, that's what they were originally built for in Italy. But they were also a symbol of prestige and wealth, so that the rich and powerful could show that they could entertain their guests in a beautiful garden environment—even in the depths of winter. In fact, a lot of them were designed more with aesthetics than horticulture in mind, so they weren't that great for housing plants at all. Not enough light, you see." He gestured to the solid walls and pillars around them. "One side of an orangery usually attaches to the main house and the remaining walls aren't made of glass, like they would be in a greenhouse or conservatory, plus the roof often doesn't let enough light in. That's why I haven't actually done a completely faithful restoration; for example, I've had the original lantern roof extended, so that more light comes in. I'm hoping these changes will allow me to grow some tender plants in here permanently, such as my collection of gardenias."

"Oh my God—have you got gardenias?" gasped Poppy.

"Yes, there are some in the tubs over there," said Nowak, turning and gesturing to a group of containers behind them.

Poppy looked enviously at the glossy green leaves on the plants, some of which were also displaying snowy white flowers. "Ohhh... they look so healthy and they're even blooming! Everyone told me that you can't grow gardenias in the UK, but obviously that's not true."

"Well, it *can* be very difficult," admitted Nowak. "Gardenias aren't really hardy enough for our winters, despite what many nurseries claim. A lot of people seem to buy them as disposable indoor plants, like poinsettias, which is a real shame, although I can see why." He chuckled. "Gardenias are known as 'plant divas'. You really need to grow them in a warm greenhouse or conservatory, and even then, they need perfect conditions to thrive. It's a very tricky balance to get right."

"Yes, I've been struggling with it myself!" said Poppy. "I got a little potted gardenia a couple of weeks ago and I've been following the advice in the books to the letter, like giving it rich, acidic soil and bright light, but no strong direct sun... but it's still dropping its flower buds and the leaves are turning yellow!"

Nowak gave a rueful smile. "Ah, that's a typical problem with gardenias. They're such finicky plants. You've done all the right things, my dear, but you also need to maintain high constant humidity, free airflow with no draughts, and definitely no fluctuations in temperature. If temperatures suddenly drop, for example, gardenias will just drop their buds. It's one of the most frustrating things about them because you can be waiting ages for them to flower and then—"

"Yes, that's exactly what happened to me!" Poppy exclaimed. "There were so many big, fat buds just about to open, but then this morning they'd all fallen off. I was really gutted."

"Did you check the moisture in the soil? Gardenias don't like to be too wet, but they'll also throw a tantrum if they are allowed to dry out too much."

"Oh no, I've been checking every day and making sure that the soil is consistently moist, and I've also made sure that the pot had very good drainage—"

"You seem to know an awful lot about growing plants," said Nowak with a surprised laugh. "Are you sure you're a property developer? You sound almost like someone in the nursery trade!"

"But I'm not a property dev—"

"Oh, Christelle has always been interested in gardening... as a *hobby*," Hubert cut in, shooting Poppy an imploring look.

Before she could respond, a woman came up to them. Unlike most of the other guests, she was not in costume, her only concession to the dress code being a skirt with a nipped-in waist that was reminiscent of 1950s fashions, and a pair of short lace gloves. She hovered uncertainly next to them for a moment, then put a hand on Nowak's arm.

"David..." she murmured.

The businessman turned and his expression

became guarded as he saw her.

"Dawn! What are you doing here?" He glanced quickly around, scanning the crowd around them as if looking for someone, then turned back to the woman.

She gave him a bitter look. "I know I'm no longer in your employ, but I would have thought that I could at least have a look at the party I spent so much time and effort organising."

Nowak looked uncomfortable. "Dawn—"

"We need to talk, David."

"Now's not a good time..."

"It's important."

"If this is about making a claim to the employment tribunal, you need to speak to my lawyers—"

Dawn shook her head. "No, I need to speak to *you.*"

"Not now. As you can see, I've got guests..." Nowak glanced at Poppy and Hubert, then turned back to the woman. "Look, why don't you call tomorrow and I'll see if I can set up a time—"

"No, I need to speak to you *now,*" said Dawn, her voice becoming urgent.

Nowak hesitated. Poppy knew that she should have turned tactfully away from the little scene unfolding in front of her, but she was gripped by curiosity. Before she could hear anything else, however, Hubert yanked on her arm. Her cousin pulled her aside and hissed in her ear:

"Why were you rabbiting on about gardenias and

acid soil and stuff? You're going to spoil everything for me! Nowak is going to wonder why you sound like you work with plants—"

"But I *do* work with plants!" said Poppy, shaking his hand off her arm and giving him a disgruntled look. "Why should it matter if Nowak should think that? Come to that, why does he seem to think that I'm a property developer?"

"Oh... uh... well, that's because... I told him that you were," said Hubert, not meeting her eyes.

"What? It's completely untrue! Why would you say that?" Then Poppy's eyes widened as it dawned on her. "You never told him that I was your girlfriend, did you? You told him that I was a *client*. He's probably under the false impression that *you* negotiated all my property deals for me!"

"Look, Nowak didn't seem that impressed with me when we met and I had to get his attention somehow, so I... I just embellished things a little, okay?" said Hubert. "Come on, Poppy—don't tell me you've never talked yourself up a bit when going for a job interview?"

"Not like this! I've never tried to impersonate someone else," Poppy retorted.

"Nowak's company has a big property deal up for grabs and I could be doing the negotiations if they engage me as the agent. The commission would set me up for life! Anyone would have done the same thing in my position," argued Hubert.

"You lied to me—you lied to both of us," said

Poppy angrily. "You knew I would never agree to be a fake client, so you got me here under false pretences. I can't believe I actually felt sorry for you! I came tonight because I wanted to help bolster your male ego a bit but I'm not going to lie for you and help you cheat—"

"Keep your voice down, for God's sake!" hissed Hubert, glancing around them. "Who said anything about cheating? You're getting a bit melodramatic, aren't you? It's not as if we're trying to perpetrate fraud—"

"It's just as bad! It's completely dishonest; it's like putting false information in your CV. I won't—"

She broke off as a sudden commotion made everyone turn around.

The double doors to the orangery burst open and a middle-aged man swaggered into the room. He was lean and wiry, and wearing black jeans, boots, and a leather waistcoat which left his arms bare to the shoulders, showing off several tattoos encircling his biceps. His receding grey hair was held off his face by a bandana tied around his head, and an ostentatious silver earring shone in one earlobe.

There was a ripple of excitement through the crowd as he came forwards and stood, hands on hips, in the centre of the room. Nowak had broken off his argument with Dawn and stepped forwards. The newcomer turned towards him and smiled slowly, showing white teeth that gleamed in his tanned face.

"Hello, David... nice party you've got here. Shame I never got the invite... I assume it must have got lost in the post, eh? Because surely you can't have forgotten one of your oldest friends? Or maybe, now that you're so rich and important, you don't feel like you need to bother?"

David's Nowak's eyes bulged as the other man suddenly drew a gun from inside his waistcoat and pointed it at his host, drawling:

"Maybe this will remind you to be more polite next time."

CHAPTER FIVE

There was a moment of stunned silence, then people began shouting and screaming, pushing each other in panic as they tried to get out of the way. A young man shoved Poppy aside and grabbed Nowak's arm, all whilst yelling: "Security! Get security!"

Then suddenly the gatecrasher burst out laughing and pressed the trigger on the gun. There was a loud snapping sound, followed by a piece of red fabric unfurling beneath the gun barrel. It dropped down to display the word "*BANG!*" just as he roared with laughter again and said:

"Got you!"

It's a stupid toy gun, Poppy realised, relaxing. All around her, she saw angry faces as the other guests realised that they had been the victims of a practical joke.

"That's... that's not funny!" spluttered the young man standing next to Nowak, and several other guests began shouting in agreement.

"How dare you!"

"My wife could have had a heart attack!"

"Guns aren't anything to joke around with!"

"Someone could have been hurt!"

The clamour of angry voices rose in the room, until Nowak put his hands up.

"Ladies and gentlemen... please! I'm really sorry about what happened and for causing you distress. I'm sure my friend didn't mean any harm..." He glanced at the man in front of him and compressed his lips. "It was a silly joke to play, but I hope you will forgive his prank and take it in the spirit of fun that was intended."

The shouting settled down to a grumble and people looked slightly mollified. Nowak signalled urgently to the waiters to bring out more champagne, and order and good humour were slowly restored to the room. The string quartet began a tentative rendition of Vivaldi's *Four Seasons* and people started to mingle and chat once more.

The young man beside Nowak didn't look appeased, however. He beckoned to the two burly security guards who'd appeared in the orangery and pointed to the man with the toy gun.

"That's him! I want him thrown off the premises—"

"No, wait," said Nowak, holding up a hand. He

turned to the young man. "It's all right, Stuart. This isn't a gatecrasher—it's my old friend Rick Zova. You might be too young to remember but he used to front a rock band in the Eighties and Nineties."

The young man sniffed. "I don't listen to rock music or pop or anything like that. I prefer Classic FM."

"Ah, right..." said Nowak, looking slightly taken aback. "Well... er... I'll take care of Mr Zova now. Perhaps you'd like to check on Mrs Nowak? I know she was worrying about a broken trellis... perhaps she's still with the handyman?"

The young man gave another disapproving sniff, then turned and walked away, his back ramrod straight. Rick Zova gave a low whistle as he watched the younger man leave, then he grinned at Nowak and said:

"I suppose I should be grateful you didn't let your puppy dog throw me out."

Nowak sighed. "Stuart is my executive secretary. And Rick... that really wasn't a nice thing to do."

Zova rolled his eyes. "Oh, lighten up, for God's sake! It was just a joke!"

"There are some things you just don't joke about."

"Bollocks! What's happened to you, David? You used to be fun. You used to do all sorts of crazy things! Yeah, that important businessman act might fool others but it won't work with me... We were lads together, remember? I know about all the things you used to get up to."

"That... that was a long time ago," said Nowak stiffly. "Things are very different now."

"Yeah, I can see that... so different that you didn't even invite one of your oldest friends to your party," said Zova caustically.

"I didn't realise you were in the country. I thought you were overseas."

"Oh, I come and go. I've been in London for a while now, and I've been meaning to come up to these parts. It's a funny thing, getting older. You start to get homesick for all sorts of things from your younger years—"

Zova broke off as his gaze went beyond Nowak to another middle-aged man who had just stepped out of the crowd. He was weedy, with pale-blue eyes and a wispy beard, and was the bland sort of man you would never normally notice... but now he was approaching them with an expression of fury. He stopped in front of Rick Zova, his eyes blazing with hatred.

Zova didn't seem to be daunted. "Geoff! You're here too!" he said with a laugh. "Well, isn't this the perfect reunion? The old threesome together again, just like it used to be—"

"You... you sodding bastard!" burst out Geoff. "I can't believe you have the nerve to show up here!" He turned to Nowak, his face livid. "And I can't believe that you let him in!"

Nowak put out a placating hand. "Geoff—"

Geoff made an inarticulate sound of fury, then

turned and stormed away. Rick Zova raised his eyebrows, then said: "Bloody hell, what's got into him?"

Nowak gave him an impatient look. "You *know* what's got into him, Rick. He's never forgiven you for what you did—"

"Hey, the courts found me innocent, remember?" Zova held both hands up, palms out. "And that was, like, twenty years ago! Don't tell me Geoff's still sulking? I always said he was an old woman."

"It was very important to him," said Nowak.

"Yeah, well, it was very important to me too," cut in Zova, his voice suddenly hard. "And I'm not going to go around feeling bad for something I didn't do."

Nowak sighed and made a visible attempt to change the subject. "Did you come straight up from London?"

"Yeah, came up on my old Harley. Still rides like a dream, even after all these years in the garage! I thought I might spend a couple of days in Oxfordshire—check out some of our old haunts..." He grinned at Nowak. "Don't suppose you want to join me?"

"I'm sorry, I'm busy. There's a fundraiser for my Beneficium Foundation next week and I'm also just about to start planning my campaign—"

Zova snapped his fingers. "Of course! You're running for Parliament in the next election, aren't you?" He whistled again. "Who would have thought little David Nowak would end up as an MP one day, eh? And a bigwig philanthropist too, I hear. Your Beneficium Foundation—is that the one that helps ex-drug addicts get back on their feet? Education programmes for stoners and halfway houses for junkies..." He roared with laughter. "Pretty ironic, isn't it?"

Nowak flushed. "Some of us decided to grow up, Rick." He glanced across the room. "Now... er... if you'll excuse me, I'd better go and see if Geoff is all right."

"Nothing changes, does it?" said Zova with a jeering laugh. "You might say things are different now, but Geoff is still flouncing off like some bloody prima donna and you're still running after him like an anxious mother hen—"

"And you're still arsing around without any thought as to who you might hurt in the process," Nowak shot back.

Rick Zova shrugged and turned away towards the cocktail bar. Nowak stared after him for a moment, then sighed and began to leave. He paused as he realised suddenly that Poppy was still standing next to him. She blushed, embarrassed to have been caught unabashedly listening to their conversation. Nowak hesitated and seemed about to say something to her, then he changed his mind and hurried away.

Poppy watched him go, wondering about what she had just overheard. Then she remembered Hubert and looked around for her cousin. She was annoyed to see that he seemed to have used the distraction from Rick Zova's arrival to slip away.

Where is the rotter? I'm not going to let him wriggle off the hook, thought Poppy, scanning the room.

She began to move through the crowds, searching for her cousin. She spotted him across the room, shaking hands and smiling fatuously at a couple of Asian businessmen. Hubert looked up and caught sight of her, and an expression of dismay crossed his face. She waved to him, but Hubert didn't acknowledge her. Instead, he bade his companions a hasty goodbye, then turned and ducked into the surrounding crowds.

"Hubert—wait!" Poppy called, annoyed.

She rushed after him, weaving and swerving through the crush of people. When she arrived at the other end of the room, however, Hubert was nowhere in sight. Poppy paused and looked around in frustration. *How had he disappeared so fast?*

Then she spied a man in a green frock coat moving swiftly away from her. She could only see his back, but she thought he looked like Hubert. She dived after him. He ducked behind a group of people standing near a large, multi-panelled, lacquered Chinese screen. A waiter carrying a tray of wine was just rounding the group of people at the same time and Poppy nearly collided with him.

"Oh! I'm so sorry, miss!" cried the waiter as red wine sloshed out of several glasses.

Poppy flinched and jerked out of the way, then winced as she saw that some of the red liquid had splashed onto her gloves.

"Oh no..." she murmured in dismay, looking down at the beautiful ivory silk which was now marred by red splotches. She felt terrible. She had promised Nell that she would look after the gloves!

"Can you tell me where the toilets are?" she asked the waiter. "I might be able to get the stains out if I flush them with water immediately."

"There are guest toilets at the other end of the orangery, miss," said the waiter, pointing to the other end of the long room. He saw Poppy's face sink as she eyed the crowds that she would have to push her way through to get to the other side and he added confidentially, "But there's also a toilet just at the end of the corridor that connects the orangery to the main house. It's not officially for the use of the guests but I'm sure Mr Nowak won't mind if you pop down there." He turned and pointed to the Chinese screen. "If you go behind that, you'll find a doorway that leads to the corridor."

"Thank you," said Poppy, giving him a grateful look.

She hurried around the screen and through the doorway concealed behind it. She found herself in a short corridor which ended in a large room of the main house, which looked like an art gallery. As the waiter had said, there were a couple of doors that led off the corridor. The first of these was slightly ajar and Poppy pushed it open eagerly. She stepped in, her hand going up automatically to the inside wall to grope for a light switch. Then she gasped as she crashed into a man coming out of the room at the same time. She stumbled back just as her fingers found the switch and light filled the room.

Poppy blinked in surprise. She wasn't in a toilet— she was in a large study. And the man she had crashed into was Rick Zova.

CHAPTER SIX

"Oh!" Poppy stared at the rock star.

He stared back for a second, then his lips stretched into a practised smile and he drawled:

"Well, hel-lo... What's a pretty young thing like you doing in a place like this?"

Poppy was nonplussed. She didn't know whether to respond as if he was joking again or to take him seriously.

"Oh... um... I... er... I was searching for—"

"The loo?" said Zova smoothly. "It's the next door down, I think. Would you like me to show you?" He put a hand under her elbow and began to steer her back out of the room.

Poppy resisted the pressure of his hand and something—she wasn't sure what—made her ask: "Were you looking for the toilets too?"

He laughed easily. "Me? Oh no... I was searching for some matches." He reached into the pocket of his leather waistcoat and pulled out a half-smoked cigar. "Forgot my bloody lighter. I thought David might keep some matches in his study, but of course, he's probably given up smoking and all other vices by now," he said, rolling his eyes. He spoke with a slightly put-on American accent—probably to fit in with his "rocker" image—but it was easy enough to hear the Lancashire tones coming through.

Poppy glanced over Rick Zova's shoulder and saw that the study was beautifully furnished, with bookshelves around the walls and two desks: a large executive one beside the door, and a smaller, more modest one on the other side of the room, beside the window. There was a fireplace set in the wall between them, with a mantlepiece cluttered with framed photos, trophies, and ornaments, plus a series of plant stands and stools in every available corner, each sporting a lush green plant in a pot. Even if she hadn't been told, Poppy could have easily guessed that this was David Nowak's study.

"So how do you know David?" Zova asked casually.

"Oh... um..." Poppy balked at the thought of calling Hubert her boyfriend. "It's actually my... er... friend who knows David; I'm just here as his date."

"You don't look like the kind of girl who would be 'just' anything," said Rick Zova with a smile, eyeing her up and down.

He's flirting with me, Poppy realised, and found to her surprise that she was blushing slightly. *Oh,, for goodness' sake*, she admonished herself. *The man's old enough to be your father!*

Still, in spite of his silver-fox status, she had to admit that Zova was an attractive man. His face might not have been conventionally handsome but it had character and a certain calculating intelligence that was somehow compelling. And his flamboyant clothes, rather than making him a figure of fun, somehow lent him a dashing air. Poppy had thought at first that he was dressed like an 80s rock star cliché because he was in costume for the party, but now she realised that this was how he actually dressed; it was his "look". It should have been pathetic and embarrassing, but somehow Zova had enough charm and attitude to pull off the "ageing rocker" look with panache.

And as he began to chat easily, she found herself laughing at his jokes and funny stories. The man had charisma and she could see how he would have been a star with legions of fans in his younger days. Could he have had a particular fan called Holly Lancaster? Her pulse quickened as she studied the man in front of her. He would be about the right age but no matter how hard she tried, she just couldn't see any resemblance between his features and hers.

"What are you staring at?" asked Zova suddenly.

"Oh… n-nothing," stammered Poppy, blushing. Then, regaining some of her spirit, she said cheekily,

"I would have thought you'd be used to being stared at by girls."

Zova laughed. "You're right there. Ahh... how things have changed with all the PC crap nowadays! I see some of the concerts now and I think, you young blokes now have no idea! You should see what *real* rock stardom was like, back in the Eighties and Nineties, when we had *real* groupies and—"

"Groupies? You had groupies?" Poppy gasped.

Zova shrugged. "Yeah, we all did. There were always girls hanging around backstage or at the various clubs, hoping to latch on to any rock band they could."

"Did you know a girl called Holly Lancaster?" asked Poppy breathlessly.

Zova laughed. "Are you kidding? You expect me to remember the names of the girls? I don't even remember the ones I slept with!"

Poppy recoiled slightly. It was an unpleasant reminder of the world of groupies. She knew her mother had been a groupie in her wild, rebellious teens, but she'd never wanted to believe that her mother might have been the type to sleep around, even if that was the usual behaviour expected at the time.

Seeing her reaction, Zova looked at her curiously. "Why are you so interested? Who's Holly?"

Poppy swallowed. "She... she was my mother. I was hoping... well, I thought you might have known her."

Zova shrugged carelessly. "Maybe I did. What did she look like?"

Poppy described her mother as well as she could, and was disappointed when Zova shrugged again.

"Dunno. Blonde hair, blue eyes? She sounds just like a bunch of other girls. There were so many of them, always hanging around the concerts and tagging along on the tours... They were just pretty things to warm your bed, you know?"

Poppy stared at him, slightly shocked and repulsed. Before she could think how to respond, there was a squeal behind her.

"Rick! Rick, I've found you at last!"

Poppy turned around in surprise to see a woman in the study doorway. She must have been in her late forties at the very least, although she was dressed like someone much younger, in a shimmering Lycra mini-dress and teetering platform shoes. Her hair was an improbable shade of blonde and she was wearing thick false eyelashes which made it look like two enormous spiders had died and got stuck between her eyelids.

Zova looked at her blankly. "Who are you?"

"I'm Bunny—don't you remember me? I'm your greatest fan!" the woman gushed. "I've been to all your concerts—every one! I even flew to New York for one night, just to see you when you were performing in Madison Square Garden! And that time in Birmingham when you did the anniversary show, I was in the front row! I was waving to you the whole time." She giggled and gave him a coy look. "I was the girl who threw the red lace knickers at you... do you remember?"

"That concert was, like, fifteen years ago!" said Zova with a dismissive laugh. "And dozens of girls have thrown their knickers at me. How am I supposed to remember one from any of the others?"

"Because I'm different—I'm your superfan!" said Bunny, her face taking on an earnest, almost evangelical expression. "I'm not like the other girls. I even sneaked backstage once and went into your dressing room—do you remember? I wanted it to be a surprise for you when you finished the concert. I covered my naked body in your favourite shaving cream and I was waiting on your—"

"Oh God, you're *that* crazy cow," said Zova with sudden recognition.

Bunny pouted. "That's not a very nice thing to say, Rick, especially to your number one fan. I've been faithful to you for years! I've cut out every newspaper and magazine piece you've ever been in. I've tattooed your name on both my breasts. I even broke my own arm after you broke yours in a motorbike accident—"

"What? You're off your trolley," said Zova, shaking his head.

"I thought we could be twinsies!" cooed Bunny. "I want to feel everything that you feel, Rick. You know there's nothing I won't do for you!" She flung herself at Zova, throwing her arms around his neck.

"Get off me!" he growled, trying to disentangle himself.

"Don't push me away, Rick!" wailed the woman as tears sprang to her eyes. "Don't reject me! I'll die!"

Zova made a sound of impatience. "Ahh... I've had enough of this bollocks!" He yanked Bunny's arms from his neck, shoved her aside, and stormed from the room.

Bunny staggered back and would have fallen if Poppy hadn't caught her. The woman's handbag dropped on the floor, spilling its contents everywhere, but she barely noticed. Instead, Bunny burst into tears and stood sobbing with her mouth open, like a child who'd had her favourite toy snatched away.

Poppy looked at her helplessly. She had been annoyed at the other woman's interruption and her melodramatic behaviour, but now her resentment faded away as she looked at the tear-streaked face in front of her. Glancing down, she spied a packet of tissues amongst the spilled contents of the handbag; quickly, she bent to retrieve it.

"Here..." she said gently, handing the tissues to Bunny.

"How could he be so cruel?" Bunny sobbed, dabbing her eyes with a tissue. "After all I've done for him... after the way I've followed him... How could he push me away like that?" She sniffed and gulped. "My heart's been broken. No, I'm serious—I can feel it. The pain... it's here, in my heart!" she cried, clutching the wrong side of her chest.

Poppy felt her lips twitch and pressed them together. The poor woman was obviously suffering and it seemed wrong to laugh at her. *Although she is a bit ridiculous*, thought Poppy with exasperation. A lovelorn teenager suffering from her first crush wouldn't be so melodramatic and hysterical!

With a sigh, she crouched down and began helping Bunny pick up the rest of the spilled contents from her handbag. The woman seemed to carry an inordinate amount of junk around with her and even with the two of them, it took quite a while to scoop everything up. When they were finally done, Bunny sagged into the chair behind the large executive desk, clutching the handbag on her lap and looking as if she was likely to burst into tears again at any moment.

"Look... er... would you like me to get you a drink?" Poppy asked.

Bunny nodded. "Ch-ch-champagne," she mumbled.

Poppy gave her an uncertain look, not sure if alcohol would make things even worse, then she hurried out of the study. Back in the orangery again, she saw no sign of Rick Zova anywhere, but she spotted a waiter carrying a tray of drinks almost immediately. Grabbing a glass of champagne, she retraced her route through the doorway behind the Chinese screen, down the corridor and back into the study.

"Here you are!" Poppy said brightly as she stepped back into the room. Then she stopped in confusion. The room was empty. Bunny was gone.

CHAPTER SEVEN

Poppy found the toilet and carefully rinsed the stains in her gloves, then walked slowly back into the orangery. Instead of rejoining the raucous crowds, she found a quiet spot beside one of the potted plants and leaned against the wall. She felt emotionally drained after her encounter with the histrionic Bunny and the thought of having to make small talk—especially if she was obliged to continue the charade of being "Christelle Bellini"—just didn't appeal. Another waiter walked past with a tray and Poppy absently accepted the glass of champagne he handed her. She raised the glass and drained it, feeling slightly giddy as the bubbles went to her head.

"Have you had anything to eat? Champagne on an empty stomach can be deadly."

She turned in surprise to see that Nick Forrest

had materialised beside her. She said, rather shortly, "I'm fine."

He eyed her flushed cheeks and slightly glazed eyes, then turned and beckoned to a waiter with a tray of canapés. Taking a couple of prawn fritters from the tray, Nick thrust them at her and said: "Eat."

She bristled at his tone. "I'm not hungry."

"If you don't like these, I'll get you something else, but you need to eat something."

"Stop treating me like a child!"

"Then stop acting like one," Nick snapped. "Any sensible adult knows not to drink on an empty stomach."

"Oh, fine..."

Poppy grabbed a prawn fritter and popped it into her mouth, chewing mutinously. She knew she was being silly—Nick was right and she should have had something to eat before consuming so much alcohol. It was just... she didn't know why, but Nick Forrest always seemed to rub her up the wrong way. Still, she had to grudgingly admit that the fritters were delicious. And once she started eating, she realised that she was ravenous. She snagged the second fritter from Nick's hands, trying to ignore his smirk, and ate it quickly as she scanned the room.

"Are you looking for someone?" asked Nick, following her gaze.

She started. "Oh... um... yes, have you seen Rick Zova anywhere?"

He raised his eyebrows. "That old rock hippy? I think I saw him around... Why are you looking for him? He didn't seem like the kind of man whose company you'd like to keep."

"No, he's not a very nice guy," Poppy agreed, thinking of the arrogant, callous way Zova had talked about the girls who used to worship him. She hesitated, then added: "But he said he used to know a lot of groupies and I thought... well, I thought he might have known my mother or could at least give me some more information about her... about her life at that time. I know so little. My mother would hardly ever talk about it..."

"Did you ask him about her?"

"Yes, but he... well, he didn't sound like he saw the girls as people." Poppy made a face. Then she brightened. "But the thing is, from what Zova told me, it sounded like the groupies used to spend time with different bands. They weren't exclusive. They just hung around backstage or at the various clubs, hoping to catch the attention of any band. So I was thinking... maybe Zova could tell me about some of the other bands that were around at the same time. Maybe one of the other band members would remember my mother... or they could tell me something about my father... or maybe one of them could even be—"

She broke off suddenly, flushing. Nick looked at her silently for a moment, then he said, his voice deliberately calm and neutral:

"Well, then it would certainly be worth talking to Zova some more. Come on, I'll help you look for him."

Poppy looked at him in surprise. It was the last thing she'd expected Nick to say. Still, she felt strangely glad to have him with her as they began moving through the crowds. There was no sign of the rock star—nor of their host. *Or Geoff*, Poppy thought suddenly. She wondered if the three "old friends" were having another happy reunion and was just about to say something when Nick said:

"Why don't we have a look outside on the terrace? He might have gone out to smoke or something."

"Oh yes—he had a cigar with him," Poppy recalled. "In fact, he was trying to find matches to light it when I met him..."

Nick turned back towards the other side of the orangery, where the main entrance was situated. Poppy started to follow but stopped short as she crashed into a woman coming out from behind a collection of potted plants.

"Oh!" cried the woman, losing her balance and nearly falling over.

Poppy grabbed her hands and caught her just in time.

"Oops! Sorry, I didn't see you," she said, pulling the other woman upright again.

"Th-thanks," said the woman, steadying herself. She seemed to be slightly breathless, as if she had been running, and Poppy noticed that her hands were icily cold.

"Are you all right?" she asked, realising suddenly that the woman also looked familiar. She was the woman called Dawn who had been talking to Nowak earlier.

"Yes, fine... you just took me by surprise, that's all," said the other woman quickly.

Poppy hesitated, then seeing Nick waiting impatiently for her a few feet away, she nodded at Dawn and hurried after him. A minute later, they went out of the large double doors of the orangery entrance. Poppy caught her breath as they stepped outside. The temperature had dropped rapidly in the last few hours, since the sun had set, and the cold stung her skin, making goosebumps appear on her bare arms.

Nick noticed her shivering. "Here..." he said, shrugging out of his frock coat.

"No, I'm fine," she insisted, refusing the coat.

He gave her an exasperated look, then shrugged and left her. Poppy began walking across the terrace, which stretched across the front of the orangery. The light spilling out from the orangery windows cast long oblongs of gold onto the flagstones. The music, talk, and laughter sounded muffled and it felt strangely surreal, watching the guests moving inside the high arched windows.

Poppy walked to the very edge of the terrace, scanning the area around her, but there was no sign of Rick Zova—or anyone else, for that matter. It seemed that the cold and dark outside were making even hardcore smokers think twice about coming out onto the terrace for a nicotine hit. Turning, she saw Nick's tall figure at the other end of the terrace, where steps led down to the walled garden below. She hurried over to join him. He was standing at the top of the steps with his head cocked to one side, as if listening for something.

Poppy looked at him curiously, then descended the stone steps and began to walk down the path which led through the walled garden. She hadn't gone more than a few steps when she noticed a large yew tree beside the path, further ahead of her. It had a thick, gnarled trunk—the kind often seen boasting a hole containing a witch or a monster in fairy tales— and its branches swayed uneasily in the wind, making a strange noise that sounded almost like humming.

Poppy went closer, frowning as she tried to identify the sound. Maybe it wasn't the branches after all? The humming seemed to grow louder as she approached the tree. Something whizzed past her ear... but she barely noticed as she saw the body slumped at the base of the tree.

"Oh my God!" she gasped, rushing forwards.

It was Rick Zova. The distant light from the orangery windows glinted off the ostentatious silver earring in his ear and played across the tattoos on his arms, outlining a large black feather across his bicep. His face seemed to be grossly distorted, though, with one eye swollen shut and angry red welts along his cheeks.

She started to crouch down next to him, then gasped as a cloud of buzzing black insects swarmed suddenly around her. A sharp, burning pain stabbed in her thigh, followed by another in her hand. Poppy yelped and stumbled backwards, waving her arms in front of her face.

"*POPPY!*"

Someone grabbed her arm and jerked her away from the tree. Poppy heard Nick cursing as she lost her balance and nearly fell. He yanked her back to her feet, then hustled her back up the path, towards the steps to the terrace. Behind them, the buzzing became an ominous whine which seemed to drown out all other sound.

"Wait... Rick... Rick Zova..." Poppy gasped, resisting Nick's pushing. "He's—"

"He's dead," said Nick shortly. "And if we don't get out of here, we will be too."

"W-what?" Poppy glanced over her shoulder, then felt her heart clench with fear.

A swarm of wasps rose in the air, filling the night sky.

Nick gave her a violent shove and shouted: "RUN!"

CHAPTER EIGHT

Poppy ran like she had never run before in her life. The swarm was a nightmare come true, savage and relentless behind her, its buzzing a furious roar in her ears. She tripped and stumbled, hampered by the tight skirt of her cocktail dress and her kitten heels, and was grateful once again to Nick as he kept his hand under her elbow, supporting her and urging her along. They ran up the steps and then along the length of the terrace, making for the orangery entrance. Gasping and panting, they burst through the double doors, then turned and yanked the doors shut behind them.

There were exclamations of surprise as the guests all turned around to stare at them, followed by shrieks of fear as the people saw the swarm of insects on the other side of the glass.

"Wasps!" someone screamed.

"So many of them!"

"Oh my God, they're coming in!"

"Noooo!"

Panic filled the orangery for the second time that night as people began pushing and shoving and running in all directions.

"STOP!" shouted Nick above the din. "You're safe! They can't get in the orangery as long as we keep all windows and doors closed!"

He indicated the double doors behind him, which were firmly shut. Poppy saw a few wasps buzzing angrily against the glass but she and Nick had been lucky: they had outrun the swarm far enough that none had come in with them.

People began to calm down again as they saw that Nick was right, although they backed away from the row of windows that lined the front of the orangery and watched fearfully as the wasps surged and whirled against the glass outside.

"What is it? What's going on?" demanded a male voice, and Poppy turned to see Nowak pushing his way through the crowd, followed by his secretary, Stuart. Nowak stopped short and his eyes widened as he saw the swarm of insects outside the orangery windows.

"There must be a wasp nest nearby," someone called out. "They only attack like that when they're defending their queen."

"I've heard that they'll chase you for miles!"

"They say if one stings you, all the others come after you too—"

"Yeah, it's like a stinging frenzy!"

"I was attacked by a wasp once—little bugger stung me eight times in a row!"

"Did you two disturb a nest?" someone shouted, looking accusingly at Poppy and Nick.

"No... but I think your friend Rick Zova did," said Nick, turning to Nowak. "We found his body at the base of the big tree beside the path. He looked like he had been stung pretty badly—"

"Rick? But... but he's allergic!" Nowak cried. "He goes into anaphylactic shock if he's stung—it could kill him! Quick, we've got to go and rescue him—" He started towards the orangery doors.

Nick caught his arm. "No! Anyone who goes out now will walk straight into that swarm."

"David, you can't go out in that!" came another shrill cry.

The woman who had been with Joe Fabbri earlier pushed her way out of the crowd and rushed over to Nowak's side. *She must be his wife*, thought Poppy as she saw Nowak put his arm around her.

"You need an apiarist or pest control expert with a protective suit, and a way to kill all the wasps and destroy the nest," Nick said to Nowak. He turned to Stuart, still standing next to his boss. "I suggest you call the police and ambulance, and emergency pest control immediately."

His voice rang with authority. The crowd, which

had started panicking and shouting at the mention of Zova, slowly calmed down again. Poppy was reminded of Nick's past career in the CID—the Criminal Investigation Department—and caught a glimpse of the detective he must have been as he took charge of the situation, reassuring the guests, checking that no one had been hurt in the recent melee, and signalling the waiters to bring fresh refreshments. Stuart had hurried off to follow Nick's orders but Nowak remained near the orangery doors.

"We can't just sit here waiting while Rick is out there," he protested. "We need to get him to hospital."

"It might be too late for that," said Nick grimly. "I can't be certain because I didn't have time to examine him, but Zova looked like he had been stung all over his face and probably his body too. He was slumped on the ground. Even if he wasn't allergic, an attack like that from a whole swarm could have been too much venom for his body to cope with. And if he did suffer from anaphylaxis..." Nick looked at Nowak's agonised expression and his voice took on a gentler tone. "I know you want to help your friend, but you'd just be putting yourself or someone else at risk. Right now, the best thing we can do is get the professionals here as soon as possible."

"What about the rest of us?" one of the guests demanded. "We want to leave! Are you saying that we're trapped here?"

Nick glanced at his host. "The orangery connects to the main house, I presume?"

Nowak was still staring blindly out the windows and it was his wife who nodded and waved towards the Chinese screen at the far end of the room.

"There's a door behind that screen. It leads to a corridor which connects the orangery to the main house," she said.

Nick turned back to the crowd. "If you want to leave, I'm sure Mr Nowak's staff will be happy to show you the way and you can exit from the front of the manor. There should be no wasps there as the front of the house is a fair distance from the terrace. If you *are* happy to remain, then it would be in everyone's interests if we all remained calm while we wait for the authorities to arrive."

There was a murmur through the crowd and a few people began to drift towards the Chinese screen but, to Poppy's surprise, most of the guests seemed inclined to linger. Now that it was obvious the wasps were safely barred outside, vulgar curiosity was taking over and people were keen to hang around and see what happened next.

It seemed to take forever for help to arrive, although it was probably no longer than ten minutes before wailing sirens reached the front of the estate. Nowak paced restlessly the whole time and the guests milled around in an uneasy manner. It looked like the swarm had started to disperse and return to the tree, but no one was willing to go out on the terrace until the pest control company had subdued the insects and removed the nest.

Poppy barely noticed, though, when the police, pest control, and other reinforcements arrived at last. She had become increasingly aware of a burning pain in her leg and her hand, and she realised with a sinking heart that she must have been stung. The adrenaline that had fuelled her panic-stricken run from the swarm must have numbed all pain and shock, but now that the adrenaline was fading, sensation was coming back with burning intensity. She winced as the two areas throbbed with a hot, stinging pain—it felt as if someone were sticking a red-hot needle into her skin.

"Have you been stung?"

Poppy looked up to see that Nick had returned to her side. He was regarding her with concern.

"Yes, on my hand," she said, shaking her right hand gingerly. "And I think on my leg as well. How come you didn't get stung?"

"I was lucky, although it helped that I'm wearing long trousers, plus long sleeves," said Nick. He didn't add that Poppy might have been more protected if she had been wearing his coat, but the words hung in the air unspoken and she bristled. She knew she had been silly and childish earlier to refuse his offer, and the regret didn't improve her mood now.

"I think the stingers got embedded in my skin," said Poppy, rubbing her thigh through her skirt. "It's hurting like crazy."

"Wasps don't leave stingers behind; only bees do."

"How do you know that?" Poppy demanded.

Nick flashed her a brief grin. "You'd be amazed the things you learn doing book research."

"Well, I think you're wrong," said Poppy fretfully, lifting her skirt and twisting around, trying to see the back of her thigh.

"Here, let me," said Nick, crouching down beside her and lifting her skirt higher.

Poppy flushed and stood still. She felt Nick's cool fingers against her bare skin. She stared ahead, trying to look dignified and ignore the fact that there was a man peering up her bare thigh, with her skirt flipped over his head. The only saving grace was Nick's matter-of-fact, almost clinical manner, which somehow made it less embarrassing.

"There's nothing here, I promise," said Nick at last. He stood up, smoothing her skirt back down. "You should wash the area thoroughly as soon as you get home, though, and put some antiseptic ointment on it. Maybe some ice as well. It'll probably be swollen and painful for a few days, and itch like mad... but you're lucky: you'll live."

As if to underline his words, the paramedics returned from the tree at that moment and walked past the orangery windows, carrying a body on a stretcher. There was a grim silence in the orangery as they all looked at the body. It was covered with a sheet and there was no doubt in anyone's mind that help had come too late for Rick Zova.

After that, the mood was sombre as the orangery began emptying and people started making arrangements for transport home. Poppy glanced at Nowak, wondering if she ought to bid her host goodbye before leaving, but the billionaire businessman was surrounded by his wife, secretary, and several policemen, and she decided not to interrupt. She looked around for Hubert but, to her dismay, her cousin was nowhere to be seen. Had he left without her? *I can't believe that selfish git has abandoned me!* she fumed.

"Do you need a lift?" asked Nick, appearing suddenly at her side again.

Poppy gave him a rueful smile. "Yes, I think so. My date seems to have ditched me. Thanks."

And as she followed him out, she reflected that—brusque and moody as he was—perhaps Nick Forrest wasn't so bad after all.

CHAPTER NINE

"I think I'm going to have nightmares about that swarm for years!" said Poppy, grimacing and rubbing her throbbing hand as she settled into Nick's Jeep. "And Rick Zova... the way he looked... his face, all swollen..." She shuddered at the memory.

"Well, if it's any consolation, he probably had a heart attack from the anaphylactic shock and died instantly."

Poppy sighed, saying wistfully, "I can't believe he's dead. I never got a chance to talk to him again and ask him more about the groupies. He's the best lead I've had in ages..." She glanced Nick. "Did you know him? I'm a bit too young to have known his music, but I suppose since you're so much older—"

"I'm thirty-nine, not Methuselah," said Nick with a grin. "I was only about eight years old when Zova rose to fame in the late Eighties. But, yes, I knew of him, although his music never really appealed to me—alternative rock was more my thing then. I remembered his name, though, when I heard it tonight, because it had been connected with a scandal."

Poppy gave a cynical laugh. "Aren't scandals the norm with rock stars? I thought that was the whole thing with 'sex, drugs, and rock' n' roll'? They're always behaving outrageously and offending people and stuff."

"Yes, but this wasn't the usual kind of scandal about drugs or sex. This was something about IP—"

"IP?"

"Intellectual property. Basically, the rights to any creative property, like a book, song, illustration... It's what allows artists to earn a living. Whoever owns the copyright gets royalties when a copy of a book is sold or a song is played or a painting is reproduced."

"Oh... so you own the copyright to all your books and that's how you make money from them?"

"Well, for an author, the rights are normally sold to a publisher for an advance, and afterwards the publisher keeps most of the book royalties from each sale—the author only gets a small percentage. But you can also keep your copyright and just license it to others for them to use—for example, photographers and artists will often do that with their images."

Nick glanced at Poppy, who still looked slightly

confused. "It's one of those things that's really hard for the average person to understand because IP is intangible; it doesn't really exist in a physical form, like money or gold or real estate, but it can be worth a hell of a lot. Like whoever owns the rights to the Beatles music catalogue would be earning a fortune for doing nothing, since they get paid every time a Beatles song is played on the radio or sold and downloaded."

"Wow…" said Poppy. "And you said Rick Zova was involved in some controversy about IP?"

Nick frowned. "Yes, although I can't remember exactly what. I'll have to do some digging…"

The Jeep drove quietly through the village of Bunnington and entered a cul-de-sac, pulling up in front of a large Georgian house. Just beyond it, Poppy could see a stone wall festooned with climbers, which was the wall that surrounded the gardens of Hollyhock Cottage. As Nick brought the car to a stop, the headlights showed a pair of bright yellow eyes glowing from the shadows beside the front gate. A huge ginger tomcat stalked towards them, tail up and whiskers quivering as he meowed demandingly.

"Hello, Oren," said Poppy, bending down to stroke the silky orange fur. "I think he wants his dinner," she added to Nick.

"*N-OW!*" added Oren, regarding his owner balefully.

Poppy gave Nick an accusing look. "You did feed him before you went to the party?"

"No, I was in a hurry and I forgot," growled Nick. "Anyway, it's not as if he's starving. Look at him!" He pointed to the tomcat's chunky, muscular body. "In fact, the vet thinks that Oren needs to go on a diet—he's put on too much weight recently. I don't understand how, though, since I've been giving him the same food as usual."

Poppy grimaced guiltily and hoped that Nick hadn't noticed. Her neighbour didn't know that Oren often came over to Hollyhock Cottage in the evenings and asked for seconds—and that both she and Nell were total pushovers where the ginger tom was concerned. It wasn't surprising that Oren was putting on weight when he was getting tins of tuna and scraps of steak and kidney pie on demand!

"Well, the vet has prescribed a special diet food now," said Nick. "Oren's not allowed to eat anything else until his weight comes back down."

Yikes. I'd better make sure that I tell Nell that, thought Poppy as she let herself through the front gate of Hollyhock Cottage a few minutes later.

She paused a moment, as she always did whenever she returned to her new home, and looked around the garden. It was too dark now to make out any colours but she could still see the shapes of the flowers and shrubs around her—the sprawling rose bushes and rounded mounds of sedum 'Autumn Joy' contrasting with the spindly frames of Japanese anemones and the tall, swaying fronds of ornamental grasses like *Pennisetum* and *Miscanthus*. Poppy breathed deeply, feeling a sense of peace and contentment settle over her, then walked slowly up the path to the front door of the cottage.

She let herself in and made her way to the kitchen at the rear, where she found Nell sitting at the wooden table, surrounded by various empty pots and pans. There was a strong smell of vinegar and her old friend was busily cleaning the attachment of each pot handle, scraping out the accumulated grease and grime. Nell looked up as she walked in, but her smile faded when she saw Poppy.

"Oh my lordy Lord, Poppy!" she cried, springing up. "What on earth happened to you?"

Poppy caught sight of her reflection in the kitchen windowpane and realised for the first time what a mess she must look, with her hair in disarray, her dress soiled where she had tripped and fallen, her face smudged with dirt, and one of her hands red and swollen. She spent the next ten minutes assuring Nell that she really was fine and hadn't been assaulted and didn't need to go to hospital, whilst her friend fussed around her, putting ice on her stings, helping her clean up, and making her a cup of hot, sweet tea.

"I can't believe it," muttered Nell, shaking her head as Poppy finished her account of the evening. "It's almost like a horror movie! What a terribly tragic accident. And how could Hubert have just abandoned you at the party like that? I thought I was wrong about him, that maybe he was a decent chap after all, but I'm having second thoughts now!"

"It's all right—Nick gave me a lift back."

"Nick?" Nell's voice changed and she looked at Poppy suspiciously. "What was he doing at the party?"

"He was invited—he was one of the guests. David Nowak's a big fan of his books, apparently."

"I don't trust him. There's something very dodgy about crime authors... Why would anyone want to spend their life writing about murders and violent criminals? It's just not normal!" Nell gave an exaggerated shudder. "And besides, Nick is so much older than you. Older men always try to take advantage of young girls—"

"Nell!" Poppy gave an exasperated laugh. "Nick is only fourteen years older than me. And besides, I'm not some naïve young girl; I'm twenty-five. Honestly, I think you've been reading too many of those romantic novels with dangerous, dark, brooding heroes. I mean, Nick's dark and brooding, all right, but he's not dangerous—unless you count his awful temper," she said, chuckling. "Anyway, he's not interested in me romantically—we're just friends. Or friendly neighbours, really."

"Hmm..." said Nell, compressing her lips and not looking convinced. "You know what they say about the lady who protests too much..."

"I'm not protesting—"

"Well, anyway, enough talk about the party!" said Nell briskly, hustling Poppy out of the kitchen. "What you need is a nice hot bath, dear, and then after that, you go to bed. No reading, no messing about on your phone—just straight to bed!"

CHAPTER TEN

Poppy was glad to follow Nell's advice. She felt mentally drained and physically exhausted, and couldn't wait to fall onto her pillow. Her stings were starting to itch horribly by the time she climbed into bed. Despite the recent ice treatment, plus the antiseptic cream she'd applied, they looked even more angry and red than they had earlier, and the burning, itching sensation was driving her mad.

She tossed and turned, trying to resist the urge to scratch, and fell at last into a fitful sleep, where she dreamt that she was being chased by a swarm of wasps. No matter how fast she ran, she could never outrun them and she awoke at last to find herself drenched in sweat. Poppy sat up and looked at her bedside clock, then pulled on her threadbare old dressing gown and wandered, bleary-eyed, into the kitchen to make herself a cup of tea. It was early but Nell was already up, busily dusting the window frames.

"Didn't you clean those last week?" said Poppy, yawning.

"Poppy! I thought you were going to have a lie-in, dear?" Nell said, looking up in concern.

"I was, but I got woken up by a horrible nightmare," said Poppy, yawning again. "And my stings keep bothering me," she added, rubbing the side of her hand against her hip to try and take the edge off the itching, without actually scratching the sting itself. "I applied the antiseptic cream last night but I don't think it's doing much."

"You should get some calamine lotion to put on it," said Nell. "My mother always swore by it for insect bites and stings. Hopefully they'll have some in the village pharmacy, otherwise you might have to go into town."

"I wonder if Bertie might have anything?" Poppy mused. "I should pop next door and ask. He always seems to have amazing solutions for all sorts of problems. I'll bet he's invented something for wasp and bee stings which would stop the itching right away!"

"If it doesn't blow you up first," muttered Nell darkly.

Poppy grinned and had to admit that her friend was right. Bertie—Dr Bertram Noble— lived on the other side of Hollyhock Cottage and was a "mad inventor" come to life. His ideas and creations were amazing... and amazingly dangerous and unpredictable a lot of the time. Once a professor at Oxford University, Bertie was now semi-retired and lived a reclusive life, working on his inventions and occasionally consulting for the British secret service. He was sweet, brilliant, absent-minded, and eccentric—and had a childlike enthusiasm for life that was wonderfully endearing. He was also Nick Forrest's father, although you would never have guessed, since Nick refused to talk to him or even acknowledge him. Poppy had tried several times to find out the reason for their estrangement but when it came to the subject of his father, Nick was even more surly than usual.

Bertie's house seemed unusually quiet when Poppy climbed through the gap in the stone wall which divided their adjoining gardens and stood up on the other side. There were no plumes of smoke coming out of the windows, no explosions or flashing lights, and no ominous smells emanating from the doors. She hadn't taken a few steps up the path, though, when she heard a volley of barking and she smiled to herself as she saw a scruffy black terrier come hurtling around the side of the house to defend his master's property.

"Hello, Einstein!" Poppy bent to pat the little dog who sprang up on his hind legs and danced around, waving his front paws in the air. His furry face was covered in strange bits of green foam and there was more of the stuff on his paws, and Poppy wondered what on earth Bertie had been getting up to.

Einstein whined with delight, then led her eagerly around the side the house. Poppy followed the little terrier through the overgrown back garden to the very rear of the property, where she found Bertie hunched over a large decaying log that was half buried beneath a thicket of weeds and bushes.

"Poppy, my dear—how nice to see you!" cried Bertie, looking up from the log. His eyes were weirdly magnified by a pair of modified swimming goggles and he was wearing a headlamp, like those that coalminers wore, which nearly blinded Poppy with its fierce glare.

"Oops... forgive me, my dear. Let me turn this down..." Bertie twiddled a knob beside the headlamp, turning the light off.

"What are you doing?" Poppy asked.

"I'm mushrooming!" said the old man, beaming at her. "Autumn is the best time for hunting mushrooms. Well, November is the height of the wild mushroom season—you get swarms of Wood Blewits and Birch Milkcaps everywhere—but really, if you know where to look, you can find mushrooms all year round: beautiful Velvet Shanks in winter and delicious St. George's Mushrooms in spring—"

"But... don't you have to be out in the forest to hunt for wild mushrooms?" said Poppy, looking at the overgrown garden around them.

"Oh no! Mushrooms will grow anywhere. You get

a wonderful variety of species growing in gardens and grassy verges and hedgerows... I've even seen some growing on thatched roofs or, yes, even in a bathroom!"

"Ugh! A bathroom?" said Poppy, wrinkling her nose.

"Well, it *was* a particularly damp, dark bathroom, but it's more common than you think. *Peziza domiciliana* is the usual culprit." Bertie grinned. "It's so common that it's also known as 'carpet cup'. You probably have some growing in your cottage."

"No way! With Nell around, no fungal spore would stand a chance." Poppy peered over Bertie's shoulder. "So... have you found any mushrooms?"

"Yes, there's a nice little patch of *Grifola frondosa* growing here. 'Hen of the Woods', it's also called...." Bertie pointed down at the log. "Isn't it a lovely sight?"

"Uh..." Poppy eyed the clump of wavy, tongue-shaped fronds in a sickly grey colour. "*Lovely sight*" were not the first words that sprang to mind.

"It's a great delicacy in Japan, you know," said Bertie, cutting off some of the fungal mass with a mushroom knife and holding it out to her. "They use it in their *Nabemono* hot pot dishes. It's full of antioxidants." He placed the mushroom pieces in a wicker basket, then picked it up and got slowly to his feet. "This will be a great addition to my mushroom tea!"

"Mushroom tea?"

Bertie started back towards the house, beckoning eagerly for her to follow. "Yes, yes! I'm just brewing some at the moment. Come... I'll show you!"

He led the way to the front door, with Einstein trotting at his heels. Poppy followed but stopped short as soon as she entered the house.

"Eeuuww! Bertie—what is that horrendous smell?" she cried, scrunching up her face.

"It's my mushroom tea!" said Bertie, beaming. "I have a nice big pot bubbling in the kitchen. I'm trying a new recipe using the stinkhorn mushroom— *Phallus impudicus*—a most fascinating fungus! Very common around the British Isles, of course, as well as Europe and North America, and instantly recognisable by its phallic shape."

"Er... right." Poppy hoped Bertie wasn't going to suggest showing her a specimen. "Um... are you sure this tea is safe to drink? It smells like rotting meat!" she said, gagging slightly.

"Ah, that is the characteristic odour of the stinkhorn. I was hoping that by brewing the caps with tea leaves, it might reduce the odour. You see, *Phallus impudicus* contains compounds that reduce the incidence of platelet aggregation and this could be marvellously helpful in preventing deep-vein thrombosis. It's one of the varieties I'm testing for a new range of infusions that will actively prevent disease." He looked at Poppy eagerly. "Would you like to try some?"

"Er..." Poppy couldn't think of anything worse

than drinking tea brewed from a stinking, penis-shaped fungus!

"You wait here, my dear, and I'll bring you some," said Bertie, showing Poppy to the sitting room.

"No, wait, Bertie—" Poppy broke off as she heard a strange whirring noise, and the next moment she did a double take as a bizarre machine entered the room after them.

It was almost as tall as her and looked a bit like a mechanical scarecrow, with body parts composed of an odd assortment of everyday items. *It's a robot*, she realised; it had a blocky, rectangular torso covered in compartments and buttons, a single column leg which ended in a pedestal foot mounted on wheels, two metal arms with "hands" that looked like a scrubbing brush and a sponge respectively, and— weirdest of all—a head that was the customer display from a supermarket cash register (except that instead of saying "TOILET PAPER 6pk...£3.50", it was displaying the message "HOUSEHOLD DUSTING MODE").

"Ah! Meet my latest invention: CLARA," said Bertie proudly. "That stands for Cleaning Legacy Adaptive Robot Assistant. She is designed to be a multi-purpose cleaning robot, equipped with sensors to locate even the smallest speck of dirt! I have been testing her all week and she is doing a marvellous job. What do you think?" He swept a hand around the room.

Poppy followed his gaze and had to admit that she

was impressed. Bertie's house normally looked like a hurricane had had a party in a chemical warehouse, with laboratory equipment, books, pieces of electronic hardware, and half-finished plates of food haphazardly stacked on every available surface. Today, however, the sitting room was neat and tidy, with every surface gleaming and the floor freshly vacuumed. Even as she watched, the robot motored past them to the window and began busily dusting the windowsill. Poppy was amazed to see that one of its hands had changed from a sponge to a soft dusting cloth and the other one was carefully wiping the windowpane.

"Wow! That's amazing," she said, staring in wonder.

Bertie beamed. "Thank you, my dear. I am convinced that CLARA will be a revolutionary new step in household cleaning! Her advanced GDS—that's Grime Detection System—means that I can programme her to search for and detect particular items, such as mould spores or sand or charcoal dust. This means she achieves a far superior clean. In fact, she could replace humans altogether! Wouldn't that be wonderful, my dear? Then no one would have to bother with the tiresome chore of cleaning their house any longer."

"That *would* be amazing. Have you shown the robot to anyone else?"

"No, not yet—she is just a prototype and will still need extensive testing. In fact, I am looking for some real-life settings to run some trials... Perhaps your friend, Mrs Hopkins, might like to borrow CLARA to help her clean the house? The poor lady always seems to be scrubbing and scouring all the time."

Somehow, Poppy didn't think Nell would take kindly to a robot muscling in on her cleaning territory, but she kept her thoughts to herself. "I think Nell actually enjoys scrubbing and scouring, believe it or not," she said, chuckling. "But I'll ask her."

Bertie settled her on the sofa, then—despite her protests—left to fetch the mushroom tea. Alone in the room, Poppy watched the robot with a mixture of awe and amusement. It had just finished dusting the windowsill and was now rolling slowly across the room, making for the door that led out into the entrance hallway. As it passed her, however, it paused suddenly and swivelled its strange rectangular display head, for all the world as if peering at her. The words "FOREIGN OBJECT DETECTED" flashed across the display. Its wheels turned and it came closer. Poppy leaned backwards uncertainly.

"Er... um... hello...?" she said with a nervous giggle.

To her shock, a mechanical voice replied: *"Human subject. Foreign origins. Possible contamination from external environment. Commencing scan."*

A probe appeared suddenly from a compartment in the robot's body and extended towards her.

"Er..." Poppy squirmed as the probe began moving over her body, emitting a strange blue light.

It halted above her bare arm and lowered until it was inches from her skin, which was tanned and freckled from the many hours she had been spending outdoors in the sun all summer. A siren sounded suddenly, making Poppy jump.

"SGS Alert! Serious Grime Situation detected!"

One metal arm shot out and began industriously wiping Poppy's skin with a cleaning cloth.

"No, no, you've got it wrong—that's not dirt. Those are my freckles," said Poppy, chuckling.

The robot paused and said: "*Preliminary cleaning unsuccessful. Escalating Response Protocol initiated.*"

The grin faded from Poppy's face as the robot extended its other arm and began scrubbing her skin with a stiff cleaning brush.

"Hey—OW! That hurts! Stop! I'm telling you— that's not dirt! You can't clean it off. Those are my freckles!"

The robot ignored her, scrubbing harder. Poppy was about to push it away when it stopped. But before she could breathe a sigh of relief, another compartment in its body opened and something that looked scarily like a cross between a roll of barbed wire and a giant suppository shot out.

"*Standard cleaning procedures ineffectual,*" the mechanical voice said. "*Progress to Steel Wool Power Grinder.*"

"Wait—what?" Poppy yelped, springing off the

sofa. She backed away from the robot.

"No! Stop! Deactivate, you stupid machine!" she said as the robot rolled determinedly towards her. She gave up and turned for the kitchen. "Bertie— HELP!"

CHAPTER ELEVEN

Feeling slightly traumatised (not to mention partially exfoliated), Poppy finally returned to Hollyhock Cottage to find Joe Fabbri in the rear garden. He was standing at the back of the cottage, surveying the outside of the greenhouse. Poppy was shocked to see that his face was badly swollen, with the skin around one eye bruised and purple, and his lip split at the corner, showing bloodied gums. He also seemed to be holding himself in a ginger fashion and, when he turned towards her, she saw that he was favouring his right leg.

"My God, Joe—what happened?" she cried. "Did you get into a fight?"

"Naw," he said quickly. "No fight. Fall."

"You fell? From where?"

"Ladder."

"Oh." Poppy eyed his injuries doubtfully, wondering how you got a black eye from falling off a ladder. "Um... well, have you been to see a doctor?"

He shrugged, then winced with pain. "Naw. No need."

"What do you mean, no need?" Poppy protested. "Those injuries look nasty... and is there something wrong with your leg? What if you've broken a bone? You need to get checked out. You don't want to get an infection or—"

"No need," said Joe again, his voice firm.

Poppy started to argue, then took a deep breath and swallowed her words. She could see that it was no use pressing him. There was a long pause, then— to fill the awkward silence—she gestured to the greenhouse and said:

"What d'you think? I haven't quite finished, but I've managed to get rid of most of the slime and algae on the glass, and all the dirt and moss embedded in the corners of the frame. I just need to give the floor a good scrub now."

Joe leaned back and gave the greenhouse an assessing look, then he nodded and said: "Aye. Not bad."

Poppy smiled to herself. Coming from Joe, that was high praise. While he had always been a patient and supportive teacher and mentor, he didn't dispense compliments lightly, and she felt inordinately proud every time she got his approval.

"Thanks—I'm glad you think so. I'm going to try

and finish off the last bits today." She sighed. "I don't know what I'm rushing for, though—it's not as if I have anything else to do. All I seem to be doing is 'waiting'! Waiting for spring to come, waiting for my seedlings to grow so I can start selling plants, waiting for the cottage garden to start blooming again so I can produce flower arrangements... but I don't know how I'm going to earn money in the meantime!"

"Clean greenhouse."

Poppy looked at Joe quizzically. "What d'you mean? I *have* cleaned it."

"Others."

"Others? Other greenhouses?"

"People hate doing 'em. Pay good money."

"You mean... people would pay me to clean their greenhouses for them?"

He put his right hand into his overalls pocket, flinched in pain and hurriedly switched to his left hand. After some tugging, he managed to pull out a battered old notebook. He flipped clumsily through some pages, still with his left hand, then held the notebook out for Poppy to see. There was the name "Mrs Walpole" scrawled at the top of the page, followed by an address in the village and the words "Clean greenhouse" underneath.

"Today. Twelve o'clock," said Joe. Then he showed her several more pages with similar notes. It looked like Joe was booked up cleaning greenhouses for the rest of the week!

"Wow..." said Poppy. "I never thought about

earning money that way."

Joe inclined his head. "Odd jobs. Autumn tidy-up. Rake leaves. Clean gutters. Plant bulbs."

"I can do all those things!" said Poppy eagerly.

"Give you some of my jobs," said Joe.

"Really?" said Poppy, delighted. "Oh, that's really kind of you, Joe! I could—"

She was interrupted by Nell bustling out of the house, her arms laden with dressings and bandages.

"This was all I could find so it'll have to do, though I still say you should go and see a doctor. I've got some nursing experience but I'm not a nurse, and that eye looks terrible—I'll bet you didn't ice it immediately, did you? Men! Always trying to play the hero! And what about your right hand? I'm telling you that wrist is badly sprained, if not broken—you should really go to hospital and have it X-rayed... my lordy Lord, what on earth were you doing on that ladder to fall off so badly?"

Joe mumbled something incoherent as Nell fussed over him, examining bruises, applying antiseptic ointment, and tying bandages around dressings. Finally, she stood back with a sigh.

"There! I've done what I can. Don't get any of the dressings wet and make sure you keep applying ointments to those cuts... And I've set your wrist as best I could," she pointed to Joe's right hand, which was in a makeshift splint made up of a wooden spatula bound by strips of torn tea towels. "But if you start to have a fever or any of the wounds start looking red and infected, you're going to the hospital if I have to drive you myself!" Nell glowered at the handyman. "And no work for the next few days! You have to keep that wrist still—and you should rest your leg as well. Besides, I doubt you can see properly out of that eye. Probably end up smashing a hammer into your hand and causing yourself even more injuries! You need to cancel all your jobs."

Joe shook his head urgently. "Job today at twelve o'clock. My other hand—"

"Oh no, you don't!" said Nell, wagging a finger at him. "You're not going anywhere, mister, except home to bed."

"Always turn up to the job."

"Not when you're injured," Nell said, setting her lips.

Joe glowered. "Not your business—"

"*I'll* go," Poppy spoke up. She patted Joe on the arm. "Nell is right—you need to let your injuries heal, otherwise you could be off work for even longer. You said I could help you with some of your jobs, so why don't I start today? I'll go to Mrs Walpole's place and make sure her greenhouse is cleaned. And I'll make sure that you still get paid—"

"Don't care about money. You earn it, you take it," growled Joe. "Forty years. Never let customers down."

"Well, you're not letting Mrs Walpole down—you're sending me," said Poppy, adding with a laugh: "I can't believe I'm volunteering for more greenhouse-cleaning. Maybe I should take CLARA with me."

"Who?" said Nell, looking puzzled.

"Oh, CLARA is Bertie's new invention; she's a cleaning robot."

"*Cleaning robot?*" Nell looked scandalised.

Poppy nodded. "She's amazing! She's got special sensors and multiple cleaning modes and attach—"

"Bah!" Nell sniffed. "No robot could do as good a job as a human." She turned back to Joe. "Now, you wait here: I'm going to make you a cup of ginger tea before you leave. My mother always swore by ginger; cures everything, she said. Hang on, I'll be back in a tic…" She bustled away, her voice getting fainter as she headed back into the cottage.

A moment later, though, Poppy heard Nell's steps returning. She was just about to make a joking comment about how quickly the ginger tea had been brewed, when she saw that her friend was accompanied by two men: one a uniformed police constable and the other a man in plainclothes. Poppy recognised the latter as Detective Sergeant Aidan Lee of Oxfordshire CID. Instantly, she stiffened. She had clashed with Lee several times in the past and disliked his supercilious manner. Now, she watched warily as he approached.

Lee marched up to Joe. "Mr Fabbri?"

Joe nodded without speaking.

"We would like you to accompany us to the station."

"What's going on?" asked Poppy.

Lee ignored her, although when Joe didn't move, he gave an irritable sigh and added: "We'd like to question you in connection with Rick Zova's death." He beckoned to the police constable. "Escort Mr Fabbri out to the car."

"Hang on!" cried Poppy, jumping in front of Joe. "You can't just come here and arrest him without some kind of explanation—"

"I'm not arresting Mr Fabbri—at least, not yet," said Lee, giving her a contemptuous look. "In any case, even if I was, it would be none of your business. I have the authority to do as I see fit in a murder investigation."

"*Murder investigation?*" cried Nell. "But... but wasn't Rick Zova's death an accident?"

"Yes, didn't he die of anaphylactic shock?" asked Poppy.

"We were led to believe that Zova died of anaphylaxis from wasp stings, but when his body was examined, he also had several bruises and abrasions on his face and body, consistent with injuries sustained in an assault." Lee looked at Joe accusingly. "And there was something found under his body when they moved him—something that could have been used as a weapon: a garden trowel." Lee leaned closer to the old handyman. "We've checked it for prints and found a match: yours."

Poppy and Nell stared at the detective sergeant in disbelief.

"You're suggesting that *Joe* might have killed Rick

Zova? That's crazy!" Poppy cried.

Lee ignored her, instead continuing to address Joe: "You were there at Chatswood House last night, weren't you, Mr Fabbri? You were called in to fix something—Mrs Nowak confirmed that. A broken plant trellis. She says that she spoke to you after you finished the job, but then she returned to the party and she cannot be sure that you left the premises. You would have had plenty of opportunity, while everybody was busy inside with the party, to creep up on Zova out in the garden and attack him." He peered at Joe's black eye and the various bandages he was sporting. "Looks like you've been in a fight. Where did you get those injuries from?"

Joe shrugged. "Fell. Ladder."

It was obvious from Lee's expression that he didn't believe the old handyman, and Poppy had to admit that, even to her ears, it sounded dodgy. Hastily, she said:

"Why on earth would Joe want to kill Rick Zova? He'd never met Zova before—he had nothing to do with him, so what motive could he possibly have?"

"Ah, that remains to be determined, doesn't it?" said Lee. Turning to the constable, he said once again: "Escort Mr Fabbri to the car."

Poppy caught Joe's arm as the constable began leading him away and said urgently, "Joe, you need to speak to a lawyer! Don't say anything until you've had legal advice. And if there's anything I can—"

"Mrs Walpole," said Joe.

"Wh-what?" said Poppy, bewildered.

He thrust his notebook into Poppy's hands and said, "Twelve o'clock."

Poppy looked at him in bewilderment. "Joe, it doesn't matter. I'm sure Mrs Walpole will understand. I'll call her, if you like, and explain—"

"No! Always turn up to the job!"

"All right, all right—I'll go," Poppy said soothingly. She wanted to say something else but didn't get a chance as the constable grabbed Joe's arm and pulled him away from her. All she could do was watch helplessly as they led him down the path around the cottage and out of sight.

CHAPTER TWELVE

"Oh my lordy Lord... what an awful thing to happen... poor Joe..." said Nell, twisting a cleaning cloth between her fingers as she leaned against the kitchen sink.

Poppy sat brooding at the wooden table. It had been over two hours since the police had taken Joe away and although she had made a half-hearted attempt to finish cleaning the greenhouse, she couldn't really focus on anything other than what had happened. And judging by the way Nell kept walking distractedly around the kitchen and wiping the already gleaming counter over and over again, her friend felt the same way.

"It's ridiculous what they're suggesting!" Poppy burst out suddenly. "I can't believe they seriously think that Joe could have murdered Rick Zova!

Sergeant Lee is a total plonker; I'm sure he's got things completely wrong—as usual!"

"Maybe once they question Joe, they'll realise their mistake," said Nell.

"No, they won't," said Poppy bitterly. "I know Lee— I've seen the way he works cases before. He loves jumping to conclusions and then bending facts to conveniently fit his theory. If Lee's decided that Joe's guilty, he'll never give him the benefit of the doubt— he'll just twist everything so that it supports his own pet theory." She heaved a sigh of frustration. "I wish I could do something to help Joe—"

"Maybe you could speak to that nice lady inspector you're so friendly with? You know, the one who is Nick's ex-girlfriend. Susan—"

"You mean Suzanne," said Poppy. "Detective Inspector Suzanne Whittaker."

"Yes, she seems far nicer than this sergeant chap and I'm sure she would listen if you spoke on Joe's behalf."

"Mmm, I suppose so..." said Poppy, still preoccupied with her own thoughts. "The thing is, why are they jumping immediately on Joe? I know his fingerprints were on that stupid trowel, but then, they *would* be, wouldn't they? After all, it's a garden tool and he does gardening jobs... What about the other guests at the party? That chap, Geoff—he acted like he hated Rick Zova. Do the police know about him? And what about that crazy woman who was crying all over Zova?"

Nell looked at her in puzzlement. "Who's Geoff? What crazy woman?"

Poppy started to explain, then caught sight of the kitchen clock and sprang up from the chair. "Yikes! Is that the time? I'd better get going if I'm going to do Joe's greenhouse job for him!"

Poppy hurried to collect some cleaning equipment, then carried it out to where her new car sat parked in the lane outside the front gate. After months of relying on the slow and unreliable buses servicing Bunnington, she had finally caved in and purchased a second-hand Fiat. After all, she would need a reliable vehicle to transport plants and flower orders once the nursery business got busy in spring. Still, she'd been nervous as she signed the papers, wondering if she was doing the right thing. The deposit had eaten up most of her remaining savings and the monthly repayments added to the credit card debt she was already struggling to pay off. But now, as she loaded everything into the compact boot, then started the engine and pulled smoothly out of the lane, she felt relieved and pleased that she had made the investment.

Ten minutes later, Poppy stood in front of a row of terraced houses and surveyed the area with interest. It was a new development built on the outskirts of Bunnington, and the streamlined architecture and modern building materials seemed at odds with the older parts of the village. Still, although the street lacked "Olde Worlde charm", it was still pretty in its own way, with most of the front gardens well maintained, filled with neatly clipped shrubs and pots of flowers balanced on steps and windowsills. Mrs Walpole's tiny plot was the most colourful of all and it was obvious that the old lady loved flowers as her front garden was practically overflowing with pansies, violas, and multicoloured primroses, and even some little bushy chrysanthemums with tiny pom-pom blooms.

Poppy pressed the front doorbell, then waited nervously, hoping that Mrs Walpole wouldn't be too surprised to see her there instead of Joe Fabbri. The door opened a moment later and a white-haired lady in a floral apron peered out at her.

"Mrs Walpole? My name is Poppy Lancaster. I'm... er... a friend of Joe Fabbri's. Unfortunately, Joe can't make it today, but I've come in his stead. I'd be happy to clean your greenhouse for you... if you're okay with that?"

"Oh, that would be lovely, dear! I've been meaning to give the greenhouse a good clear-out and proper clean for ages, but I hurt my back a few months ago, you see, and my son, who's a doctor, has forbidden me from doing anything too strenuous... and especially no gardening. Not that I was going to listen to him, of course! I had all those pots to plant up for the front... but they haven't been too bad as I could do them up on a table. It's the bending and squatting and lifting that's difficult... Anyway, I'll be so pleased to get the greenhouse cleaned. I've been worrying about what to do with my tender plants, now that the weather is starting to turn cold..."

As she chattered away, Mrs Walpole led the way through the house and out the back door into a long, narrow, rectangular garden. There was a small section of lawn and several beds planted with perennials, but the bottom section was devoted to a large greenhouse. It was in much better condition than the one at Hollyhock Cottage, but its dusty glass panes still needed a good clean.

"And when you've done that, dear, do you think you could give me a hand with a few other jobs? There are a few plants I need to divide and some that need to be cut back... oh, and there's that dreadful ivy..." She pointed to a thick, tangled mat of ivy that covered the wall on one side of the garden. "It's actually in my neighbour's garden but he doesn't seem to make any effort to control it so it's grown completely wild, all over the wall and down my side. I can't stand looking at it—it has all sorts of spiders and other creepy-crawlies making webs and nests in it..." Mrs Walpole shuddered. "I've tried offering to go next door and trim it for him, but he wouldn't hear of it. In fact, he got so stroppy that I'm a bit afraid to ask him anything now. So I've just been trying my best to keep it controlled by clipping it back on my side."

"Have you got a ladder?" Poppy asked.

"Yes, there's one behind the greenhouse."

"Then don't worry—I'll sort it out for you. I've

recently had to tidy up a really overgrown ivy on a wall in my own garden," said Poppy cheerfully. "So I know exactly what to do."

"Oh, thank you, dear—that would be wonderful! Now, would you like a cuppa before you start?"

Poppy declined politely and—after assuring Mrs Walpole that she also didn't need any stewed prunes, home-made Madeira cake, smoked kippers, or orange jelly—she got to work. The greenhouse didn't take as long as she'd expected, and before long she was fetching the ladder and grabbing her secateurs in preparation for attacking the overgrown ivy. She was standing beside the wall, staring up at the tangled vine and trying to decide which section to start tackling first, when she heard harsh voices coming from the other side of the wall. It sounded like two men had just come out of the adjoining house and into its rear garden—and they were arguing passionately.

Poppy didn't pay much attention at first, until she heard the words: *"...murder... too good... make Zova pay... justice..."*—then she froze. She looked up, straining her ears to hear more, but the voices had settled into an unintelligible rumble. One of them sounded very familiar, though, and she frowned trying to place it. Then she gasped quietly as she realised where she had heard that pleasant baritone before: at Nowak's party last night. In fact, she was sure that the voice belonged to the billionaire businessman himself.

Who is he talking to? And what are they saying about Rick Zova's murder? Gripped by curiosity, Poppy leaned closer to the wall, but no matter how hard she strained her ears, she couldn't make out what they were saying. The wall itself, as well as the dense thatch of ivy, acted as a buffer, muffling the sounds.

Poppy looked up at the top of the wall, then, on an impulse, she grabbed the ladder and leaned it against the ivy mass. Quickly, she climbed the rungs, only slowing as she neared the top and peered carefully over the edge. Through a tangle of ivy leaves, she saw two men below her, on the other side of the wall. They were at the far end of the adjoining garden and although they had their backs to her, she recognised the balding man immediately as David Nowak. The other man also looked familiar and as he turned into profile and she got a better look at his face, Poppy realised that it was the man called Geoff who had been furious when Rick Zova had arrived unexpectedly at the party.

As she watched, Nowak put a restraining hand on his friend's shoulder, but Geoff shook it off angrily. Their voices came over in drifts:

"...*don't patronise me! I'm not some child to be... you know what he did to me—how could you have even let him in? ...stand there chatting with him like that... thought you were on my side!*"

"*I am, Geoff, I am... try to understand... had guests... couldn't make... unpleasant scene—*"

"A true friend wouldn't have cared about that! ...stood up to him for me... knew how he had ruined my life..."

It was frustrating only being able to hear snatches of their conversation. Poppy climbed up higher, swinging both legs over the wall. Thankfully, a laurel tree was growing next to the wall and its dense branches shielded her from view, should either of the men look her way. She leaned further out and strained harder to hear.

"...aww, come on, Geoff, now you're being melodramatic! ...big blow, but it was a long time ago... life doesn't end... successful business now—"

Geoff gave a bitter laugh. *"A piddly hardware shop! Yeah, I'm a real success story... make fun of me—"*

"...not making fun of you... in the local business community... but you need to pull yourself together!" Nowak caught hold of his friend's arm urgently. *"You have to be careful what you say to the police... strong alibi... keep our stories consistent, then you'll be fine... tell them you were down in the wine cellar with me—"*

Poppy gasped as she felt herself suddenly toppling forwards. She hadn't realised how far out she was leaning from the wall and she jerked back, flailing her arms and trying to throw her weight backwards. But it was too late. With a muffled cry, she lost her balance and fell headlong, tumbling off the wall and into the garden next door. Luckily, a large shrub broke her fall and she landed in a tangle of leaves and stems.

The men whirled around and stared at her. Poppy wriggled her fingers and toes experimentally— nothing seemed broken—then she attempted to sit up.

"Who the hell are you?" demanded Geoff, rushing over. He made no move to help her up, just standing and glaring at her.

Nowak, however, quickly bent and put a supportive hand under her elbow. "Are you all right?" he asked. Then his eyes widened as he looked at Poppy properly for the first time and he cried, "Christelle! What are *you* doing here?"

Oh bugger, thought Poppy as she suddenly remembered that she'd never had a chance to confess her real identity to her host the night before. Slowly, she stood up, brushing herself off and searching for the best way to break the news.

"Um... my name isn't actually Christelle," she said, giving Nowak a nervous smile. "It's Poppy. Poppy Lancaster. And I'm not Hubert Leach's girlfriend," she added hurriedly. "I'm his cousin."

"His cousin?" Nowak looked bewildered.

Quickly, she told him about Hubert's request. "I'm really sorry," she added. "I would never have agreed to the whole ridiculous charade if I'd known... I thought I was just helping him out by being his date for a night, so he wouldn't 'lose face', you know, for not having a girlfriend—"

"That still doesn't explain why you're in my garden!" said Geoff suspiciously. "You fell off the wall, didn't you? What were you doing up there?"

Poppy flushed. "I... I was cutting back the overgrown ivy."

Geoff narrowed his eyes. "You're lying! You're a spy, aren't you?"

"What? No!" Poppy cried.

"Yeah, you're a bloody journalist coming here to spy on me!"

"No, no! I'm—"

"Thought you could dig up some dirt on me, did you? So you could write a juicy piece on Rick Zova's death—just like all the others camped out on my doorstep this morning. Well, I'm sick and tired of you people pestering me!" He glared at her. "Fine! You want a comment? You're going to get it: I'm *glad*! Glad that he's dead, all right? The bastard had it coming to him—"

"*Geoff!*" Nowak looked slightly shocked. "Geoff, you know you don't mean that! We're all devastated by Rick's death."

Geoff laughed. "*You* might be—you were always Mr Nice Guy, David—but I'll bet no one else misses that son of a bi—"

"Yes, well, it was still a tragic accident," Nowak cut in hastily. He frowned. "Except that now the police are telling me that it may not have been an accident. They think Rick's death could be suspicious. I couldn't believe it when the forensics team arrived at my house this morning and roped off the entire area around the orangery as a crime scene. I mean, who on earth would want to harm Rick?"

Geoff gave a bark of laughter. "Are you serious, David? After the way he's treated people all these years? I'm surprised there aren't more people lining up to kill him!" He saw Poppy's expression and gave a sneer. "Yes, how about that for a soundbite? And I'll tell you something else: Rick was murdered, all right. I'm just sorry I wasn't the one who did it!"

Turning, he stormed back into the house.

CHAPTER THIRTEEN

There was a long, awkward silence after Geoff had gone into the house. Nowak looked intensely uncomfortable and embarrassed. He cleared his throat and said: "You'll have to excuse Geoff's behaviour. He's... he's under a lot of strain at the moment and... well, he can be quite emotional, you know, and he takes things very personally. It makes it easy to take advantage of him—"

"Like Rick Zova did?" said Poppy

"No... well... that is..." Nowak fumbled for the words. "Well... yes, there *is* some bad blood between them but it's all history, really."

"It didn't seem to be history to Geoff," Poppy pointed out.

"Oh no, you really mustn't take what he says seriously! Geoff can get a bit... er... histrionic, sometimes. But he would never hurt a fly. You have to believe me. I've known him a long time, almost all my life."

Poppy looked at him curiously. "You were friends as children?"

Nowak nodded. "Yeah, we were all local lads. Well, Rick was originally from up north, but his family moved here when he was ten. The three of us met in school and we were really close, always getting into trouble together..." A reminiscent smile lit his face for a moment. "In our late teens, we decided to form a rock band. Actually, it was Rick who was the driving force behind that. He was just plain Rick Barnsby in those days. That was his real name, you know. He changed it to Rick Zova because... well, it sounds a lot cooler as a stage name, doesn't it? We used to meet up for band practice—Rick, Geoff, and me—and muck around, pretending we were performing on stage to thousands of fans..."

Poppy leaned back slightly, trying to imagine the balding, middle-aged businessman in front of her in a rock band and failing. "So you actually performed in a band together?"

"Oh, yes, eventually... after years of practice. We managed to get a few gigs at local pubs and social clubs—nothing major. It was obvious pretty quickly that Rick was the only real performer amongst us. He had the personality, you know; he loved the limelight and he knew how to wow an audience and turn on the charm. Geoff was very keen—he's good with words, see, and he wrote a lot of the song lyrics—but he didn't have the confidence. As for me..." Nowak gave a sheepish laugh. "To be honest with you, I didn't have any ambitions to become a rock star—I just thought it would be a good way to meet girls."

"Is that how you met your wife?" asked Poppy, now trying to imagine the woman she had met at the party in a rock-band scenario and failing even more miserably.

Nowak burst out laughing. "Oh, no, no, no... Lena used to be my accountant. It's probably just as well that I married her, instead of some empty-headed little groupie. Lena's been a wonderful partner in the business. She takes a personal interest in every store—all twenty-seven branches across the country!—and she's in charge of new business development, plus she's got an amazing eye for detail." He chuckled. "I sometimes think that she only married me to get her hands on the business."

"So did you and Geoff leave the band and Rick Zova went on to become famous on his own?"

Nowak shook his head. "The band was long gone by the time Rick shot to fame. We didn't officially split up or anything. We just got busy with other stuff and stopped meeting up. I suppose you could say that we drifted apart, went our separate ways."

"Had you started your garden centre business already?" asked Poppy.

"Not quite, but I was in my early twenties by then, you know—we all were—and I was starting to think about getting a 'real job', a career... I was still bloody surprised, though, when we found out that Rick had secretly gone off and recorded an album on his own! He'd sent it to a music label and they'd given him a record deal." He shook his head in admiration. "His first single hit number one—he became a big star practically overnight."

"But... wasn't that like going behind your back? Weren't you upset?" said Poppy.

Nowak shrugged. "Well, not really. Like I said, I never took the band stuff very seriously and I'd sort of moved on by then. I was working part-time in a nursery and saving up some capital, and I was thinking seriously about starting my own garden business. Even if Rick had tried to involve me, I probably wouldn't have been interested."

"What about Geoff?"

Nowak hesitated. "Geoff took it harder," he admitted. "He did think that Rick had betrayed us and gone behind our backs, when we should have been a team. That's why he's still so angry, you see," he added.

"Really?" Poppy was sceptical. It seemed a lame reason for the other man's bitterness and hatred, especially after so many years. "But... when you were talking at the party—I'm sorry, I couldn't help overhearing—I heard Rick Zova say something about the courts finding him innocent. Was there some kind of court case?"

Nowak looked uncomfortable. "This was all such

a long time ago—water under the bridge really." He gave a forced laugh and deliberately changed the subject. "So you're not Christelle Bellini, huh? And I suppose you're not really a property developer either?"

It was Poppy's turn to look uncomfortable. "No, sorry. I didn't mean to deceive you about that. I'm in your line of work, actually. I inherited a cottage garden and nursery from my maternal grandmother and I'm trying to get it back up and running at the moment."

"Oh?" Nowak looked at her with interest. "Here in Bunnington?"

"Yes, it's called Hollyhock Cottage and Gardens—"

"My goodness, you're Mary Lancaster's granddaughter?" Nowak looked at her with new eyes. "I was acquainted with your grandmother; she was very respected in the nursery trade for her skills as a plantswoman. In fact, I went to see her quite a few times—I was interested in acquiring her nursery and bringing it under the Róża Garden Centres umbrella. It's got so much potential and with my company's network and contacts, we could really develop the site and bring in a greater flow of customers. But she rejected all my offers. Insisted on being independent." He gave a rueful chuckle. "She was a stubborn old goat, if you don't mind me saying so."

"Yes, I've heard that from other people too," said Poppy, laughing as well. "In fact, I've even been accused of following in her footsteps... Well, I wouldn't mind being like her if I could inherit her green fingers too," she added with a wistful sigh.

Nowak eyed her shrewdly. "Are things not going well?"

"Oh, I'm sure it's just teething problems," said Poppy hurriedly. "I knew nothing about plants or gardening, you see, when I first took this on, so it's been a bit of a steep learning curve. But I'm getting there," she added, giving him a determined smile. "I'm sure it's just a case of holding on until spring gets here and I can start selling plants."

"Well, if things get too difficult..." Nowak paused meaningfully. "I'd just like you to know that my interest in your cottage garden nursery still stands. I could make you a very attractive offer."

"Oh." Poppy stared at him, not knowing what to say. "Um... right... thanks."

"Do you have any experience of running your own business?"

"Uh... no."

"Well, I don't mean to put you off," Nowak said gently. "But it can be a tall order for someone like yourself, with no horticultural or entrepreneurial experience, and no professional support network, to take on a struggling nursery business and turn it around. I'm willing to pay very handsomely for the pleasure of continuing your grandmother's legacy. And you could remain involved—you'd have a job within the company and remain in charge of the day-

to-day running of Hollyhock Cottage and Gardens."
He smiled at her. "Think about it."

CHAPTER FOURTEEN

Poppy had never been in a police station before, much less a CID unit, and she looked around with keen interest as she followed an officer into a large open-plan office. But if she had been hoping to see gory evidence of exotic crime-fighting, she was disappointed. The place looked much like any other government office, with desks overflowing with folders and papers, and dusty filing cabinets in the corners—and the most exciting detective work she could see involved officers hunched over keyboards, peering blearily at their computer screens.

She waited, as instructed, by the door, scratching her hand absently. The wasp sting was starting to bother her again. Since Bertie hadn't had any special salve to give her that morning, she had made do once again with the ancient tube of antiseptic ointment at

Hollyhock Cottage before leaving for Mrs Walpole's greenhouse job. But the cream didn't seem to be very effective and now the sting was red and sore, and really itching again.

The officer went across the room to a private office in the corner and, a moment later, a woman in her late thirties with a sleek bob of dark hair came back out with him. Detective Inspector Suzanne Whittaker smiled warmly as she approached and, as always, Poppy admired the other woman's elegant beauty and wished that she possessed the same cool self-assurance.

"Poppy! Great to see you—you're looking well." Suzanne paused and gave Poppy a shrewd look. "I take it this isn't a social call? I hear that you've got yourself mixed up in a murder once again."

"How did you know?" asked Poppy, surprised.

Suzanne smiled and gestured behind her. Poppy looked beyond the other woman's shoulder to see a tall, dark-haired man coming out of Suzanne's office: it was Nick Forrest.

"Nick's been giving me a statement about Nowak's party and he told me about meeting you last night," Suzanne explained. "It was just as well, because we've been going through the guest list from the party, in order to speak to witnesses, and we've been struggling to locate a woman named Christelle Bellini."

Poppy gave an embarrassed laugh and hung her head. "Yeah. That was me," she admitted. "But I wasn't trying to deceive anyone—at least, not on purpose. I was sort of... um... forced to take on a fake identity."

"Yes, Nick said something about you being there as your cousin's fake girlfriend?" Suzanne looked slightly puzzled. "Well, anyway, that clears up one mystery. I'll be sure to pass the information on to Sergeant Lee so he can update the records—or perhaps you already told him when he questioned you?"

"He hasn't questioned me."

"He hasn't? That's odd..." She glanced at Nick. "He hasn't questioned you either, has he?"

Nick shook his head.

Suzanne frowned. "I would have thought that he'd be keen to speak to you both, given that you were the ones who found the body. Perhaps he's been busy with other things and he'll contact you later today..."

More like he couldn't be bothered to question us because he's so convinced that he's got the killer already, thought Poppy sourly.

"Well, I'd better get back to work." Suzanne looked at Poppy expectantly. "Unless there was something else?"

Poppy nodded. "Yes, it's... it's actually about the Rick Zova murder inquiry. I've got some information which could be important to the investigation."

"Lee should be back soon, so if you'd like to wait for him—"

"Can't I tell *you*?" asked Poppy.

"I'm not actually on the case," said Suzanne.

"You're not?" said Poppy in dismay. "But... but Sergeant Lee isn't a detective inspector so how can he —"

"Actually, detective sergeants do often lead investigations, especially in smaller CID units. But in any case, Lee is up for a promotion to Inspector soon. In fact, this case is a deciding factor in assessing his skills and competence, so I'm keen to let him take charge as much as possible. He's reporting to me, of course, but I'm trying to maintain a hands-off position."

Poppy wanted to say something caustic about Lee's "skills and competence" but she bit her tongue. Instead, she said: "I'd really prefer to speak to you, Suzanne. I don't... um... feel so comfortable talking to Sergeant Lee." She paused then blurted, "I think he's got the complete wrong end of the stick!"

Suzanne raised her eyebrows.

"He thinks Joe Fabbri is the murderer but he's wrong!" said Poppy. "I *know* Joe. He wouldn't hurt anyone... and besides, he hasn't got a motive to kill Rick Zova. It's crazy to think that he could be a suspect. I tried to explain this to Sergeant Lee this morning, but he just wouldn't listen to me!"

Suzanne hesitated, then sighed and said, "Come on... we'd better go somewhere quieter."

A few minutes later, the three of them were settled in one of the interview rooms, with Suzanne facing Nick and Poppy across the table.

"I know Lee can be a bit high-handed sometimes, but you have to see it from the police's position, Poppy," Suzanne said gently. "Joe Fabbri's prints are on what could effectively be the murder weapon."

"Have they proven that? Have they confirmed how Zova was killed?"

"I don't believe the full autopsy report has come through yet but from the forensic pathologist's preliminary examination, it seems very likely. They're currently analysing the trowel for any traces of blood."

"Okay, but that doesn't mean that Joe was the one holding it, right?" said Poppy pleadingly. "*Anyone* could have got hold of that trowel. Any of the guests, or even the staff, could have found the trowel after Joe dropped it."

"Joe's prints are the only ones on the handle," Suzanne pointed out.

"What if the murderer wore gloves?" said Poppy. "They wouldn't leave any prints then, would they?"

"No," Suzanne agreed. "There's always that possibility and we *are* taking that into account."

"And the other guests? You have questioned them too, haven't you?" asked Poppy worriedly. "You're not just focusing on Joe without checking anyone else out, are you?"

"Yes, of course the police are questioning several other people," Suzanne reassured her. "In fact, that's been one of the challenges of the case so far. Because it was initially treated as an accident due to the wasps, none of the usual crime scene procedures were followed. If we'd known that it would be escalated to a murder inquiry, we wouldn't have allowed the guests to leave last night without each giving a statement. Now, we're having to go through the slow process of tracking each one down and questioning them."

"There's one man in particular that you really need to speak to," said Poppy earnestly. "His name is Geoff. I don't know his last name. He's an old friend of Rick Zova's who was at the party last night. He's got blue eyes, sandy hair, and a sort of wispy beard..."

Suzanne furrowed her brow, obviously trying to remember the guest list. "Sorry, I'm not as familiar with this case, as Lee is handling all the details and he hasn't reported in to me yet today..." She got up suddenly. "Hang on a moment while I see if I can find the case notes on Lee's desk."

She returned a few moments later carrying a file, which she rifled through as she sat back down. "Ah, here it is: Geoff Healey. Yes, apparently Lee questioned him this morning. I've got his statement here," she said, pulling out a piece of paper. "Lee spoke to him straight after speaking to Nowak, who was also an old friend of Zova's, I believe."

"Yes, the three of them were really close when they were boys; they even formed a band together when they were in their late teens—early twenties," said Poppy.

Suzanne looked at her curiously. "You seem to know a lot about them."

"I happened to... er... bump into Geoff Healey earlier today. I was cleaning a greenhouse for a lady and it turned out that Healey lives next door. He was *really* hostile and bitter when I mentioned Rick Zova's murder. He said that Zova 'had it coming to him', and that he was surprised there wasn't a line of people waiting to kill Zova for treating them badly."

Suzanne shook her head and laughed. "I'm surprised he didn't just come out and confess to the murder."

"Well, he did say that he was sorry he hadn't been the one to do the deed," said Poppy. "But that could be a sort of double bluff, couldn't it? It would be the clever thing to say if he really had done it. Anyway, Nowak seemed really nervous and kept making excuses for Geoff afterwards and telling me not to take anything he said too seriously."

"David Nowak?" Suzanne raised her eyebrows.

"Oh, yes, I forgot to say—he was there too. I think he must have come to visit his friend."

"And what 'excuses' was he making? I thought you said the three were great childhood friends. Why the hostility now?" asked Suzanne.

"I think they fell out because of the band. Nowak said that Geoff was upset with Zova for secretly recording an album and getting a record deal without them; he saw it as a betrayal because they were supposed to be a band together." Poppy frowned.

"The thing is, something didn't quite add up to me... I mean, it seems a bit out of proportion for Geoff to still be so angry about it, so many years later. Seriously, you should have heard him today—and last night at the party too. The way he was talking... the hatred in his eyes... There's so much bitterness there."

"That's because it wasn't about the band," Nick spoke up for the first time. "It's because Zova might have stolen songs that Healey had written and passed them off as his own, without giving his old friend any credit. In fact, his first single—the one that launched his career—was one of the songs supposedly written by Geoff Healey."

He turned to Suzanne. "Poppy and I were discussing Zova in the car on the way home last night and I got curious. I vaguely remembered a scandal involving him, but I couldn't remember the details, only that it had something to do with stolen IP. Anyway, I did some digging when I got home last night and I found some references online. Geoff Healey tried to bring a case against Zova for stolen intellectual property but it was thrown out in court because of insufficient evidence."

"But Nowak told me that Geoff did write all the songs!" said Poppy.

Nick shrugged. "It's all about proof—and Healey didn't have anything concrete to back up his claim. It was a case of he said/she said... or he said/he said, in this instance. It didn't help that cases like that can cost a fortune and Healey didn't have a job then; he was relying on his savings, whereas Zova had the backing of the record company."

"Oh! That's why he kept ranting about Zova ruining his life," Poppy said, sitting up. "I overheard a bit of the conversation between the two men before I fell over the—er, I mean, before I spoke to them, and Geoff was really having a go at Nowak for letting Zova into the party and being nice to him. He accused Nowak of not standing up to Zova, even though he knew what Zova had done. I thought he was being really childish, if it was just because of the band thing... but if it was because of the stolen songs and the court case, then it makes more sense."

"Yes, in the end, Healey lost the case and ended up badly in debt, with nothing to show for it. It's probably taken him years to climb out of that hole. I suppose it could be seen as 'ruining' his life."

"That's motive enough for murder," said Poppy, looking at Suzanne. "Isn't it?"

"It could be," said Suzanne cautiously. "But why now? It's been over thirty years since that case— Healey's done nothing in all this time, so why should he suddenly decide to get revenge now?"

"Maybe Zova taunted him at the party and he snapped?" suggested Poppy. "I mean, Geoff seems to have a really short fuse. Even Mrs Walpole—his neighbour—was telling me how bad-tempered he is."

"Since we're talking about old friends, what about Nowak?" asked Nick, leaning back in his chair.

"Nowak? But you saw how distressed he was!" protested Poppy. "He wanted to rush out and save Rick Zova when he heard about the wasps."

"People can put on an act."

"Maybe," said Poppy sceptically. "But why would he want to kill Zova? What motive could he have?"

Nick shrugged. "Perhaps he felt betrayed too."

"*He* didn't have his songs stolen... and he wasn't really interested in the band. It was just something he did for a laugh," Poppy said. "By the time Zova got the record deal, Nowak had already moved on. He was starting up his garden business and all that."

"Yes, and he's certainly done very well for himself since," said Suzanne. "You could hardly accuse Zova of ruining *his* life."

Nick raised his hands in a defensive gesture. "It's just a thought. Everyone's a potential suspect until proved otherwise."

"Yes, you're right," Suzanne conceded. She glanced back down at the file, flipping through some papers. "And to be fair, it looks like Lee *has* questioned Nowak and done some background checks on him: one of the most successful businessmen in the UK, owner of one of Britain's largest garden centre chains, well-known philanthropist—he's on the board of several charities and has a charitable foundation of his own, an organisation which provides support for those recovering from drug abuse—and it seems he's universally respected and well liked. Even his business rivals haven't got a bad word to say about him. He's active in local politics too; in fact, he's planning to run for MP in the next elections and there's even talk that he might have what it takes to get to the top: become Prime Minister."

"I'm surprised such a paragon of respectability would want to be associated with Rip Zova and his debauched rock-star lifestyle," Nick remarked.

"He *did* look very uncomfortable and embarrassed when Zova showed up," Poppy said. "And it was obvious that he hadn't invited Zova to the party."

"I hope you two are not going to suggest next that Nowak murdered Zova for gatecrashing his party," said Suzanne dryly.

"No, I don't think Nowak killed Zova but... I wonder if he might be involved in a cover-up," said Poppy, suddenly remembering. "It was something I overheard him say to Geoff... something about alibis and keeping stories consistent..."

Suzanne glanced down at the file again. "Hmm... well, it *is* interesting that Healey's alibi comes from Nowak. He says that the two of them were down in the wine cellar together for quite a while— apparently, they were searching for a rare vintage— and they didn't know what had happened until they came up and heard the commotion about the wasp swarm."

"I don't remember seeing them together when we ran back into the orangery... do you?" said Nick, glancing at Poppy.

She shook her head helplessly. "I don't know—I wasn't really paying attention," she confessed. "It was so chaotic with people shouting and screaming... and the wasps outside... I remember seeing Nowak push his way out of the crowd to come and speak to us, but I don't remember seeing Geoff with him."

Suzanne made a note in the file. "I'll ask Lee to speak to both men again and check their alibis."

"What about Rick Zova's crazy fan?" asked Poppy. "Did Sergeant Lee speak to her?"

"Crazy fan?" Suzanne looked surprised. "Lee didn't mention anything about that."

Poppy described the woman she had met. "I think she might have gatecrashed the party too—it sounded like she followed Zova there. She was a real drama queen, actually," said Poppy, making a face. "She threw herself on him and started wailing and making a fuss. Zova got really annoyed and stormed off."

"So you think she might have killed him because... what? She didn't get his autograph?" asked Nick, grinning.

Poppy bristled at his sarcastic tone. "She was obsessed with him. Maybe she was stalking him or something... you know, like Glenn Close in *Fatal Attraction*."

Nick rolled his eyes but Suzanne said hastily:

"We would certainly want to question her. It's just a case of finding her. If she wasn't on the guest list, it may take us a while to track her down. You didn't get her name?"

Poppy scratched the wasp sting on her hand absently. "She called herself 'Bunny', but I don't know if that's her real name."

Suzanne made another note in the file. "And was she a big woman? Tall? Strong?"

"No, she was quite petite, actually. Well, not super-skinny but she was quite short and not particularly muscular. Why?"

"Because whoever killed Rick Zova had to have been strong enough to overpower him. From his injuries, it looks like there was a fight... and then the killer cleverly used the wasps as a cover-up for the murder. If Bunny was a small, slight woman, it's unlikely that she could have been the killer."

Poppy looked at Suzanne pleadingly. "But you have to admit that she could have had a motive, right? And Geoff Healey—he had a motive too. And they both knew Zova. It's a fact that most murders are committed by someone close to the person or known to the person. Joe Fabbri didn't know Rick Zova—he had no connection to him at all."

"Are you *sure* he had no connection to Zova?" asked Suzanne.

"What do you mean?"

"How well do you *really* know Joe Fabbri? You only met him a few months ago."

"I... I've seen a lot of Joe. He's been around to Hollyhock Cottage a lot, doing various repairs and things... and... and he's taught me a lot about gardening," stammered Poppy.

"But that doesn't mean that you really know him. Would you say that he sees you as a close confidante? A friend? Would he talk to you about personal matters?"

Poppy hesitated. "Joe never talks much about anything. That's just his way." She took a deep breath. "I might not know his favourite colour or... or whatever... but I *know* he would never murder anyone."

"You weren't so sure a few months ago when you first met him," Suzanne reminded her. "You suspected him of being involved with Valerie Winkle's murder."

Poppy bit her lip. She hated to admit it, but it was true. "That was different," she argued. "I know him better now."

Suzanne sighed. "I'm sorry, Poppy, but at the moment, Joe has to remain our main suspect. That doesn't mean we won't be investigating other leads, but we cannot exonerate him simply on the basis of your feelings about him. In any case, he's not under arrest yet; he has simply been detained for questioning," she added, seeing Poppy's expression. "He won't be charged with anything until all other suspects have been thoroughly investigated."

CHAPTER FIFTEEN

Poppy walked slowly out of the police station, feeling quite drained after the long discussion. She didn't know how Suzanne and the other detectives could interview witnesses all day. She was exhausted after just one session! She didn't realise that Nick had followed her out until she heard her name being called.

"Poppy... can you do me a favour?" he asked, catching up with her on the street. "I'm catching a train in an hour—my publisher's organised a last-minute book signing and PR jaunt up north—and I'll be gone for a few nights. Do you mind feeding Oren while I'm gone? It's just once in the morning and once in the evenings. I was going to ask Suzanne but seeing as you're next door..."

"Oh, sure," said Poppy. "If you just give me a spare

key—"

"But you *must* stick to Oren's new diet food from the vet, nothing else," Nick warned her. "He'll probably kick up a fuss—he's been knocking his bowl over and chucking the food around in protest—but you've got to be strong and ignore him."

"Okay." Poppy saw Nick looking at her sceptically. "What? You don't think I can?"

"Frankly, you seem to be putty in Oren's paws," said Nick with a teasing grin.

"That's not true!" said Poppy indignantly. "You talk as if I'm a total pushover!"

Nick raised an eyebrow. "You seemed to be going along with Hubert's ridiculous charade last night without putting up much of a fuss."

"That... that was different. He sort of twisted my arm, okay? But it was for a good reason." Poppy recounted the whole story about the favour she owed Hubert for giving Nell a job. "Of course, he never told me that I would actually be impersonating a fake client, not his girlfriend. The rat! If I'd known, I would never have agreed to go."

"Lucky for Joe Fabbri that you did. He's got a personal cheerleader in you."

Poppy looked at Nick sharply. "You don't seriously believe that he could be the murderer?"

"It doesn't matter what I believe. What matters is the evidence."

"Well, the evidence points at other people too! Like Geoff Healey. He was there, he had a strong motive, *and* he looks like the kind of man who could just snap and lose it."

"If that was the case, wouldn't you expect him to just punch Zova in the face? It's a bit of a stretch for him to use a garden trowel as the murder weapon." Nick shook his head. "Why go to all that trouble? There must have been a dozen other things he could have picked up—like a knife or a hammer—that would probably have done the job better."

"It's obvious: Geoff wanted to frame Joe and make him a scapegoat."

"Then that means there *was* planning and premeditation—and that doesn't fit with your profile of Geoff lashing out in a temper," Nick pointed out.

Poppy gritted her teeth, annoyed that Nick seemed to have a reasonable counter-argument for everything she said.

"In fact, thinking about it," Nick mused, "using the wasps to make it look like an accident is a clever ploy for covering up the murder. That would have required some serious thinking and planning beforehand."

"But that just points the finger to Geoff even more!" Poppy said earnestly. "It means that the murderer had to be someone who knew about Zova's anaphylaxis issue. It's the kind of thing only close friends and family would know. It was the first thing Nowak mentioned when he heard about the wasp swarm last night, and I'm sure Geoff would have known about it too."

"Not necessarily. Zova could have been wearing one of those medical ID bracelets, in which case anyone—"

"But he wasn't," Poppy protested. "I saw him at the party; his arms were bare and there was nothing around his wrists, except one of those braided leather bracelets that some men wear..." She gestured at her own wrist, then moved her fingers to scratch the wasp sting again.

"You shouldn't do that," said Nick, watching her. "You'll break the skin open and get it infected."

Poppy looked down guiltily and was dismayed to see that the sting site was even more swollen and red, with the skin around it looking ragged and tender now.

"Have you put anything on it?" asked Nick.

"Yeah, there was a tube of antiseptic cream in the kitchen drawer at the cottage—"

"Did you check the expiry date? I wouldn't put it past your grandmother to have kept that tube from the last world war," said Nick dryly. "It's probably long lost all effectiveness."

"I'll stop off in the pharmacy in the village on the way home," Poppy promised.

Half an hour later, she made her way down Bunnington high street to the village pharmacy situated at the end of the road, beside the churchyard. It was a large, rambling shop with low ceilings and shelves that looked like they hadn't been dusted since the 1950s. Still, it did seem to be surprisingly well stocked, selling everything from anti-ageing collagen masks to men's sweatproof socks, and Poppy was pleased to see a shelf marked "First Aid" brimming with pharmaceutical offerings.

She grabbed some bandages, antiseptic wipes, a salve for insect bites, and a tube of anti-histamine cream to help relieve the itching, then took the items to the counter at the back of the store to pay. It was mid-afternoon and half the village residents seemed to be in the pharmacy, exclaiming over new products and exchanging gossip. Poppy joined the queue for the cash register, only half listening to the conversation around her which all seemed to be speculation about Nowak's cocktail party and the murder.

Poppy noticed the woman in the queue, right in front of her, who seemed to be listening too and looking very uncomfortable. Curious, Poppy leaned sideways, trying to catch a surreptitious glimpse of the woman's face. She felt a flash of recognition. It was Dawn, the woman who had wanted to talk to Nowak so urgently at the party. Was she a resident in the village?

The queue moved forwards and Dawn stepped up to the counter. She mumbled something to the pharmacist, who replied: "I'll see if there's any out the back", then disappeared through a door behind the counter. Dawn fidgeted, shifting her weight from foot to foot. Poppy hesitated, then, on an impulse, reached out and tapped the other woman on the shoulder.

"Hello!" she said brightly as Dawn turned around. "It's Dawn, isn't it?"

The woman eyed her warily. "I'm sorry—do I know you?"

"We met at the party last night. Well, not 'met' really..." Poppy gave a forced giggle. "...but you came over while I was chatting with Mr Nowak and I bumped into you again later—"

"Oh... oh yes," said the woman, obviously recalling the encounters and looking none too pleased with the memory.

"Isn't it awful what happened?" Poppy continued in a chatty tone. "That wasp swarm was like something out of a nightmare! I mean, I don't even know where they came from. It was like they appeared magically from the tree—"

"No, actually, their nest was in the crack in the trunk," said the woman. Then she pressed her lips together, looking annoyed with herself for speaking up.

"Oh! I didn't realise... do you live at Chatswood House as well?"

The woman flushed. "I am... I mean, I *was* David Nowak's PA."

Poppy noted the "was" and recalled Nowak's reluctance to speak to the woman. He'd mentioned something about lawyers and an employment tribunal—had there been a dispute about Dawn's dismissal? It seemed odd that she had wanted to come to her employer's party after she'd been fired. Some of her thoughts must have shown on her face because Dawn added, in a defensive tone:

"The party was the last thing I'd organised and I'd put a lot of effort into it, so I wanted to check that everything had gone as planned."

"Oh, you did a great job," Poppy gushed. "I think it was the best party I've ever been to!"

The woman relaxed slightly and a faint smile touched her lips. "Thank you. That's kind of you to say. Especially as you must have had a very traumatic experience. I remember now: you're the girl who came running in from the wasps, aren't you?"

Poppy grimaced. "Yes, and I got stung too—that's why I'm here." She raised her hand and indicated the swollen bump. At that moment, the pharmacist returned and handed something over the counter.

"You're in luck. I found the last bottle at the back. But are you sure you only want calamine lotion? It's quite an old-fashioned remedy and isn't always very effective. Some hydrocortisone cream would work better to treat those wasp stings and relieve the itching."

Wasp stings! Poppy turned to look sharply at Dawn.

The other woman shifted under her scrutiny and deliberately avoided Poppy's eyes, keeping her gaze on the pharmacist.

"Er... no, that's fine," she said as she handed

some money across the counter.

"Did you get stung last night too?" asked Poppy. "I didn't see you out on the terrace when we were running from the wasps." She noticed for the first time that there were two large welts just peeking out from beneath the sleeve on the other woman's right arm

Dawn saw her looking and tried to tug her sleeve down. "Me? Oh no, I didn't go outside last night," she said quickly. "These stings are from the day before. I was outside the orangery, overseeing final preparations for the party, and I disturbed a wasp that was flying around."

"Oh. They look really 'fresh'. I would have thought the redness and swelling would have gone down by now," said Poppy, eyeing the other woman's arm.

"I... I believe you can get a delayed reaction to wasp stings and it can take days for the itching and redness to settle down. But don't worry, I'm sure yours will heal sooner," said Dawn hurriedly. She grabbed the bottle of calamine lotion and, with a hasty nod of goodbye, pushed her way out of the shop.

Poppy shoved her own things across the counter and paid for them as fast as she could, then raced out of the store in Dawn's wake. She was dying to ask the woman more questions. But when she stepped out of the pharmacy, she could see no sign of Dawn on the street.

"Bugger!" she muttered, turning and scanning the

area.

Then her attention was caught by something a few metres down the road, at the entrance to the churchyard. At first she thought that it was a pile of rubbish, but as she got closer she realised that it was a small heap of flower bouquets, hand-written cards, photos, newspaper clippings, bandanas, and more.

It's a shrine, she realised as she saw the faded poster of Rick Zova that had been pinned to the side of the churchyard gate. It showed him as a much younger man, at the height of his fame, in a costume similar to the bandana-and-leather-waistcoat outfit that he had worn to Nowak's party, and with a half-smoked cigar jutting from the corner of his lips. Someone had scrawled: "We love you, Rick!" and "Zova Forever!" on the sides of the poster, and she could see similar messages on the cards heaped below. It was not a large tribute—Zova had been an ageing rock star whose fame had already begun to wane several years ago and who was probably largely unknown to the younger generation—but it showed that there were still some who remembered and mourned the dead man. Bunnington might not have been where he was born, but he had spent most of his childhood and formative years in the local area, and the village was probably a natural place for fans to set up an impromptu memorial.

Footsteps sounded behind her and Poppy turned to see that there was someone else approaching the makeshift shrine. She stood aside for a woman to bend and lay down a bouquet of red roses. The woman was crying audibly and, despite the dark glasses she wore, Poppy could see tears running down her face, collecting in rivulets and dripping off her chin. She stumbled slightly as she straightened and stepped back, and Poppy put out a hand to support her.

"Th-thank you," the woman mumbled, then pulled her coat tighter and hurried away down the street.

Poppy stood for a moment, watching her go. It had been hard to see the woman's face behind the enormous black shades and she'd had a headscarf wrapped around her hair, Grace Kelly style, but there had been something familiar about her... Poppy turned back to look at the bouquet of red roses left by the woman. There was a note tucked amongst the blooms. She bent to get a better look and her heart skipped a beat as she read the scrawled words:

"I will never stop loving you, Rick.
My heart will cry forever.
Bunny
XXX"

CHAPTER SIXTEEN

Poppy jerked upright and whirled to look down the street again. She caught a glimpse of the woman turning a corner in the distance. Cursing herself for not realising sooner, she took off, running as fast as she could. When she reached the corner, she was relieved to see that the woman was still visible further up the road. Poppy put on a burst of speed and caught up with Bunny just as she was nearing a bus stop.

"Bunny?" she called hesitantly.

The woman turned around and looked at her in surprise.

"Hi..." Poppy went up to her and gave her a friendly smile. "I don't know if you remember me, but we met at Nowak's cocktail party?"

The black shades looked at her blankly for a

moment, then recognition flickered in Bunny's expression and she said: "Oh... You're the girl who was talking to Rick."

"Yes, that's right. Um..." Poppy glanced around and saw that the village tearoom was two doors away. "I'd really like to talk to you. Do you have time for a cup of coffee?"

Bunny hesitated. She gestured vaguely towards the sign above the bus stop and said, "I've got to catch a bus in half an hour."

"We'll just have a quick cuppa," said Poppy brightly, taking the woman's elbow before she could change her mind.

A few minutes later, they were settled at a cosy table in the window nook of the tearoom. Bunny had taken off her shades and her scarf and coat, and Poppy could see now that her eyes were red and puffy, her blonde hair tangled, and her clothes rumpled. She looked like she hadn't slept, and Poppy wondered if she had kept an all-night vigil for the dead rock star.

"I'm... I'm really sorry about Rick Zova," she said. "I know he meant a lot to you."

Bunny's eyes filled with tears again and her face crumpled. "I saw it on the news this morning," she said, pressing a soggy tissue to her mouth. "I wanted to die too!" She sobbed into the tissue, making it even soggier.

Poppy watched helplessly, unsure what to do. She had acted on an impulse, but now she was beginning to feel bad for making the woman talk to her. She was relieved when the waitress arrived at that point, bringing their order. By the time the pot of tea and accompanying cups and oat biscuits had been placed on the table, Bunny had regained some of her composure.

"I'm sorry. I didn't mean to upset you," said Poppy.

"It's... it's all right..." Bunny gulped back a sob. "Rick had been a part of my life for so long... I just can't believe that he's gone."

"Had you been a fan for long?" asked Poppy.

"Forever," said Bunny in a forlorn voice. Then she sat up a little straighter and pushed her hair back. Her face was flushed and mottled from crying and her eyes were so puffy, she looked as if she had been punched in the face, but she seemed to be slightly calmer.

"I remember the first time I saw Rick," she said in a pensive voice. "It was at a concert. I knew instantly that he was the most amazing man I'd ever met. Well, not that I'd really met him yet, of course, but I knew I just had to be patient. I made sure that I went to every one of his concerts... I was always in the front row... and then—" Her mouth curved into a smile. "— then one day, I managed to get backstage and get his autograph! There were so many other girls there, hanging all over Rick—it was disgusting!—but I knew he could see that I was different. I told him that I was his biggest fan ever—I was a *super*fan!"

Poppy's ears pricked up at the mention of "lots of

girls". Suddenly forgetting the mystery, she wondered if *Bunny* might be able to help her with information about her mother's past, now that Zova was gone.

"What do you mean 'lots of girls' backstage? Do you mean like groupies?" she asked eagerly.

But Bunny didn't answer. She seemed to still be lost in her memories. She gazed dreamily out of the window, saying: "...and then I started writing to Rick. I would leave him letters and gifts after every concert." She gave a coy smile. "And of course, there was that time I threw him my red lace knickers!"

"These other girls backstage," Poppy tried again. "I don't suppose you remember any of their names? Were you friends with any of them?"

"No." Bunny scowled. "Why should I be friends with them? They just wanted to take Rick for themselves!"

"Oh... well... I just thought... well, I thought groupies were often friends—"

"I wasn't a groupie," Bunny snapped. "I was a superfan! I was different, do you hear me? I was nothing like those other girls!"

Poppy sat back, startled by the woman's sudden aggression. "Yes, of course," she said in a soothing voice. "But I just wondered if you might have got chatting with any of them some time? For instance, do you remember a blonde girl called Holly? Holly Lancaster?"

Bunny shrugged. "I don't know. I don't remember.

I never paid much attention to the other girls...
Sluts," she added viciously.

Poppy felt a flash of anger on her mother's behalf
and started to snap something back, then forced
herself to hold her tongue. She realised that she had
been very naïve. Somehow, when she had imagined
speaking to Bunny, she had thought that the other
woman would blithely tell her everything she needed
to know about her mother's teenage years. But
Bunny was too wrapped up in herself to notice
anything not relating directly to her own concerns.

Sighing, Poppy sat back and said: "Well, thanks
for chatting with me. Will you give me your number
or some other way to contact you? The police would
like to speak to you too—"

"The police?" Bunny looked at her wide-eyed.

"Yes, they're trying to find out who murdered Rick
Zova—"

Bunny gasped. "No! No, it wasn't murder. It was
the wasps. Rick is allergic, you see. He went into
anaphylaxis and—"

"I know the news said that, but the police are
actually treating the death as suspicious."

"No, no, no, it was an accident!" cried the woman.
"No one would want to murder Rick! He was amazing!
He was the most wonderful man who ever lived! How
could you think that anyone would want to kill him?"

"Bunny, the police found evidence—"

"The police are wrong! It was an accident," the
woman whimpered.

"Okay, but they'd still like to talk to you," said Poppy in a soothing voice. "Can you give me your number? Or tell me where you're staying?"

"It's... it's a pub... I can't remember the address... oh, wait, I think I have a card in my bag..." Bunny reached for her handbag but her hand missed the strap and it fell to the ground, spilling its contents everywhere.

Not again! thought Poppy with an inward groan. *Why doesn't she zip up her handbag when she's not using it?* Sighing, she bent over to help the other woman pick up all the things scattered on the floor around their table. It looked like Bunny was carrying even more junk than on the night of the party. Alongside the usual assortment of lipstick, keys, crumpled receipts, hairbrush, and chewing gum, there were also healing crystals, playing dice, broken earrings, nail polish, a Christmas bauble, and—

Poppy paused, then picked up a small plastic tube. It had a tapered orange end and a bright yellow label with "EpiPen" printed on the side. She caught her breath and looked quickly at the woman sitting opposite her.

"Bunny, why do you have an EpiPen?" she asked, holding up the injection device. "Are you allergic to bee and wasp stings too?"

The other woman's eyes widened and she snatched the autoinjector out of Poppy's hands. "N-no... I mean, yes... Maybe... I don't know," she mumbled.

Poppy frowned. "What do you mean? Surely you'd know if you're carrying a life-saving adrenaline injection around?"

Bunny looked evasive. "I just wanted to do everything that Rick was doing. Like twinsies, you know?"

"You mean you're *pretending* to have the same allergy?" said Poppy in exasperated disbelief.

"It made me feel closer to him," said Bunny in a defensive voice. "Like we shared something together." She shoved something towards Poppy. "Anyway, here's the card. You can have it, if you like. I can get another one from the reception when I get back."

Poppy took the business card, which displayed the details of a local pub that also offered bed and breakfast accommodation, but she was still thinking about the EpiPen. She started to question Bunny further about it, but the other woman suddenly let out a cry as she picked up something else that had fallen out of her handbag. Poppy leaned over and saw that it was a promotional badge with a picture of Rick Zova strumming a guitar printed on the surface.

"I... I got this at the very first concert that I went to..." Bunny said, her voice wobbling. "Oh my God— I will never forget that night! Rick was so... so magical! So wonderful! Oh... ohhh... I can't believe that he's dead!"

Her face crumpled and she dissolved into tears again. Poppy shifted uneasily, watching her cry. Even though Bunny was silly and immature, her grief was still dreadful to witness. Poppy felt even more guilty now about badgering the other woman for information, and decided to abandon any more questions.

"Um… Would you like anything else, Bunny?" she asked awkwardly. "A glass of water? Or another cup of tea?"

Bunny sobbed into her tissue and made an incoherent sound which sounded like "No" or "Go".

Poppy hesitated, then said, rising slowly from her seat: "Okay, well, I'm going to go now. The… um… the police will be in touch soon… I'm really sorry for your loss."

With one last troubled look at the crying woman, Poppy quietly left the tearoom.

CHAPTER SEVENTEEN

Nell was out when Poppy finally returned to Hollyhock Cottage. She washed her hands, then rummaged through the bag of things she'd bought at the pharmacy and, after disinfecting the area, applied the soothing creams to the wasp sting. Then she made herself a cup of tea and, carrying it with her, wandered into the greenhouse to check on her gardenia. With the flurry of things that had happened in the past two days, she had hardly had time to think about the plant and she was hopeful that it would have perked up since she last saw it. As she approached the pot, however, she was dismayed to see that there were even more yellow leaves now, plus several more fallen buds littering the soil.

"Why? Why? Why?" she muttered, looking at the gardenia in puzzled despair.

Poppy checked the soil moisture, then adjusted the position of the pot, but she couldn't think of anything else that she could do. Finally, with a sigh, she picked up her now-cold cup of tea and left the greenhouse. She wandered into the small sitting room at the front of the cottage and flopped onto the sagging sofa. *Whew!* Poppy heaved a sigh and massaged her neck. Then she glanced idly at the pile of mail waiting unopened on the coffee table next to her. A feeling of unease filled her as she saw a couple of envelopes with windows—the kind normally used by businesses to send bills and invoices. Money was tight and she was still paying off a hefty credit card debt, not to mention the new car repayments, so the last thing she needed right now was another invoice.

She tore the envelopes open, then relaxed as she scanned their contents. One *was* a bill, but only a small one for milk delivery. The other was a renewal notice for a personal alarm monitoring plan— obviously something her grandmother had used but which she, thankfully, wouldn't need. Poppy tossed the bills aside and picked up the remaining mail. Her eyes lit up as she spotted a catalogue showing brightly coloured flowers. Eagerly, she ripped off the plastic wrapping and flipped through the pages. It was a catalogue from a wholesale bulb supplier and Poppy stared in delight at the pictures in front of her: tulips blooming in bright candy hues, daffodils scattered through verdant lawns, and bluebells lighting up shady corners. There were fragrant hyacinths and dainty white snowdrops, pretty anemones and classic "Grandma's" freesias, elegant Dutch irises, and fat crocuses glowing like amethyst gems... Poppy felt overcome with plant lust as she pored over the pages.

Oooh... these would all look so gorgeous in the garden, she thought, her mind filling with visions of blooms in a rainbow of colours. After her disappointment with the gardenia, the thought of growing all these beautiful flowers filled her with hope and confidence once again. Before she realised what she was doing, Poppy had grabbed her laptop and hopped onto the supplier's website. It all looked so easy: a few clicks and she could have a big order of bulbs delivered to her door. And she could get great savings from bulk buying too—it would mean forking out an even bigger sum of money initially, of course, but it was far better value in the long run...

Poppy hesitated. *It's not an extravagance; it's an investment in the business,* she told herself. *After all, if the cottage garden looks gorgeous, then customers are more likely to come and visit and buy plants, aren't they? And I could sell some as fresh-cut flowers or make arrangements with them too. Besides, don't they say bulbs multiply? So in a couple of years, I'll have double or triple the number of plants!*

She looked excitedly again at the images on the website, then began scrolling and clicking, rapidly adding items to her cart. When she finished and proceeded to the checkout, however, she reeled back in horror as she saw the total at the bottom of the page.

Yikes! Okay, so maybe I don't need ninety daffodil bulbs—fifty will do, she thought. *And forty corms of freesias are probably enough—I don't need to order eighty... Those Parrot tulips look a bit weird—I suppose I could leave them out. And the Dutch iris collections are nice, but it would be cheaper to just get one variety. Ooh, but I have to get some of those gorgeous Italian ranunculi—I know they're expensive but they'll be worth it...*

After going through her list and regretfully deleting or reducing quantities, Poppy looked at the total cost again. It was better but still an uncomfortably large bill. She stared at the screen, thinking rapidly. She had a small amount of money set aside which would be just enough to fund the purchase. She'd been intending to save it to pay any bills that came in or even some more of her credit card debt... But surely the credit card could wait another month? And as for utility bills, she doubted they'd be very much—after all, it wasn't as if she was a fully functioning nursery yet. Besides, if she could start doing some gardening odd jobs, like Joe had suggested, she would start bringing in a regular income again.

Smiling to herself, Poppy clicked "Order" and went through the payment details, then leaned back on the sofa and stared dreamily into space, imagining how beautiful the cottage garden was going to look in spring. A loud, demanding cry interrupted her daydream; it seemed to be coming from outside the front door, and when Poppy opened it, she found a large ginger tomcat standing on the threshold.

"*N-oww? N-OWW?*" said Oren, lashing his tail

Poppy glanced at the clock on the wall and realised guiltily that it was much later than she'd thought. No wonder Oren was looking peeved. It was well past his dinnertime! He marched into the cottage and began heading for the kitchen, but Poppy hurriedly scooped him up.

"Sorry, Oren, no tuna fish on the menu tonight. You're only allowed your new diet food."

"*No-o-o-ow!*" protested Oren, squirming in her arms.

He was a big boy, with a thick, muscular body, and Poppy had to wrestle to keep hold of him. Somehow, she managed to carry him out of the cottage, through the garden, and into the property next door. Once inside Nick's house, she set the orange tomcat down in the kitchen and leaned against the counter to catch her breath.

Nick's kitchen was modern and open-plan, with a large central island and a dining area overlooking the rear garden. It was unexpectedly neat and tidy— Poppy had half expected to find congealed plates of food and forgotten mugs of cold coffee lying around— but the kitchen island was empty except for what looked like a home-made doll's house. As she examined it closer, Poppy realised that it wasn't so much a child's doll's house as a small-scale model of an apartment, made from bits of cardboard, masking tape, and other random materials. It had been meticulously decorated on the inside, with miniature paper curtains, cardboard cut-out sofas, tiny vases of paper flowers, and even miniscule plates and utensils on the dining table. In what was supposed to be the living room, someone had drawn a classic "dead body" in outline on the crepe-paper rug—in the kind of sprawled pose often seen on TV crime shows.

Poppy marvelled at the meticulous work and attention to detail that must have gone into creating the model, and wondered if Nick had made it. Then she caught sight of a note stuck to the outside of one of the "walls".

"To my favourite author... Love your books! Here's a model I made of the eerie apartment from your first book, 'Kill the Night'. I hope you like it! Your biggest fan, Nikki"

Wow, thought Poppy, eyeing the paper model again. *That's fan dedication.* It must have taken days or even weeks to recreate the setting of Nick's novel with just home-made items. This sort of fan art must be priceless!

She walked carefully around it and made her way to the kitchen cupboards lining the opposite wall. She began to open them, searching for the cat food, as Oren weaved between her legs, complaining loudly. From the first time she'd met him, Poppy had always thought that the ginger tom sounded uncannily like he was saying "Now!" and that illusion was now stronger than ever as he demanded his dinner.

"*N-ow! N-owww!*"

"All right, all right, it's coming…" muttered Poppy, opening cupboards and scanning shelves.

She found the diet food at last, with its severe, clinical packaging, and used the kitchen scales to measure out the designated amount, then tipped it into a cat bowl and put it down in front of Oren.

The ginger tom stared disbelievingly at the modest pile of dry biscuits in front of him, then looked up at her, as if to say: *"Are you serious?"*

"Be a good boy. Eat your dinner," said Poppy.

"*N-ow?*"

"Yes, now."

He walked over to the fridge and stood in front of the door, looking over his shoulder at her. "*N-ow?*" he said hopefully.

Poppy pointed to the bowl. "No, Oren. That's your dinner."

"*No-o-o-ow!*" He growled, lashing his tail. "*No-o-no-o-no-o-ow!*"

Poppy crossed her arms. "There's no use having a tantrum. I've got strict instructions and you're not getting anything else."

"*N-O-OWWW!*" yowled Oren. "*N-O-O-O-OWWWW!*"

He stalked back over to the bowl and batted it with

his paw, sending some of the dried biscuits flying.

"Hey! Oren, stop that," said Poppy.

The tomcat ignored her and batted the bowl again, sending more cat biscuits skidding across the floor.

"Oren!"

"*N-OW!*" he said, glaring at her. Then he smacked the bowl with his paw, flipping it over completely and scattering the rest of the cat food across the kitchen floor.

"Oren!" cried Poppy, annoyed. "What are you doing?"

She got down on her hands and knees to pick up the dried cat food and return it to the bowl. Oren sat nearby, twitching his tail and watching her with a basilisk stare.

"There," said Poppy, pushing the refilled bowl towards him again. "Come on, Oren! Don't be difficult... You have to eat this, whether you like it or not."

"*No-o-ow...!*" Oren got up and stalked over to his water bowl, turning his back to her as he bent to drink.

Poppy lifted the bowl of cat food and carried it over, setting it down next to him. He paused in his drinking to shoot her a defiant look, then smacked his paw against his water bowl, flipping that over and sloshing the water all over the biscuits.

"Aw... *Oren!*" Poppy groaned as she looked at the soggy mess. The biscuits in the bowl were inedible now.

Still, refusing to be bested, she took a deep breath and emptied the bowl into the bin. Then she washed and dried it, and took it back to the kitchen island, where the original box of cat food was still standing open. She picked it up and shook it at Oren, making the biscuits inside rattle.

"You're not going to get out of eating this," she said to the ginger tomcat.

Poppy started to tip more biscuits out of the box, then remembered that she was supposed to measure the exact amount. She turned to retrieve the scales from the kitchen counter but, when she turned back, she was horrified to see that Oren had jumped up on the counter and was eyeing the box of cat food with an evil gleam in his eye.

"Oren—no!" cried Poppy, lunging forwards.

But it was too late. The ginger tom raised a paw and smacked it hard against the side of the box, sending it flying across the island. It hit the side of the paper model and exploded, scattering cat food everywhere.

"Noooo! Oren!" gasped Poppy.

The delicate structure of the paper model had caved in, with the walls collapsing inwards and ripping away the tape that held the support sections. Poppy looked at the mess in dismay. Nick's beautiful fan art had been destroyed.

CHAPTER EIGHTEEN

"Oh, Oren, what have you done?" Poppy cried.

"*N-ow?*" the ginger tom said innocently, then began languidly washing his ears. Poppy gave him a dirty look—she was beginning to see why Nick often wanted to kill Oren!—then she turned back to the broken model again.

Gingerly, she lifted up the sections which had collapsed inwards and tried to prop them upright. To her relief, she realised that the damage wasn't as bad as it initially looked. Although the apartment was very fragile and precariously built, it was also fairly easy to restore most of the parts with a bit of pushing and prodding. She found some masking tape in the kitchen drawers and restuck several sections that had come undone, and used a bread knife to carefully push folds and creases back into their original positions.

Finally, she stood back, satisfied. She had managed to repair most of the damage, except for a few items that needed gluing—in particular, a beautiful replica cuckoo clock hanging on one of the house walls. It had been fashioned with miniature sections of wood and its tiny pendulum had snapped from the impact. Poppy was just looking through the kitchen drawers again for superglue when her phone rang shrilly.

It was Suzanne Whittaker:

"Poppy—you left a message asking me to call you back?"

"Yes, that's right. Oh Suzanne, I found her! Bunny, I mean. You know, Rick Zova's crazy stalker fan," Poppy said breathlessly. "It was a fantastic stroke of luck. I happened to see her when she was in the village. She came to leave flowers at Zova's shrine-thingy in the street and I had a chat with her."

"Great! Did you get her contact details?"

"Yes, but... you know, I don't think Bunny's the killer, after all. You should have seen her: she's absolutely devastated by Zova's death and she also seems much too hysterical to plan a cold-blooded murder. And besides, I've been thinking about what you said—you know, about Zova's killer having to be fairly strong to overpower him. Well, Bunny is a fairly petite woman so it's unlikely to be her, since the murderer had to be a man or a big woman—"

"Actually, that's not necessarily true anymore,"

Suzanne cut in.

"What do you mean?"

"I just got the autopsy report. It looks like Zova didn't die of his injuries, after all. In fact, on closer examination, they weren't that severe—Zova wouldn't even have been admitted to hospital."

"Oh. So you mean, it wasn't the assault that killed him? But then... how was Zova killed?"

"The forensic pathologist found evidence of..." Suzanne paused, then her voice changed, sounding as if she was reading from a paper: "...mucous plugging, hyper-inflated lungs and laryngeal oedema. These are usually typical signs of asthma— but Zova didn't suffer from asthma. They also found elevated levels of mast cell tryptase—mast cells play a role in inflammatory processes."

"I don't understand," said Poppy.

"Basically, it looks like Zova suffered a massive, fatal allergic reaction."

"You mean... the *wasps* killed him?"

"Yes. And it means that whoever murdered Rick Zova didn't need to be strong enough to overpower him. They simply had to disturb the wasp nest... and the wasps did the rest."

Poppy drew a sharp breath. "So the wasp attack wasn't an accident used to cover up a murder—it *was* the murder."

"I've spoken to the pest control company who removed the nest. They said a section of the nest looked damaged, like something hard had smacked into it. If the killer had thrown a stone or something into the nest, it would have been a sure-fire way to disturb the wasps and send them out in a frenzy. And if Zova had been standing nearby, he wouldn't have stood a chance."

"Wow… it's a pretty elaborate way to kill someone," said Poppy. "I mean, why not just hit him over the head or something?"

"Actually, I think it's ingenious," said Suzanne. "Especially if the murderer knew that Zova was severely allergic to bee and wasp venom. A single sting could have killed him and it could have all been passed off as a tragic accident. After all, people die of bee stings every year. It was the perfect way to murder Zova without actually touching him, and the killer had a high chance of getting away with it."

"It's a horrible way to die, though, isn't it?"

"Well, in a way—the tissues swell up and you usually die of asphyxiation, if you don't die of shock and heart failure first—but in Zova's case, it probably all happened fairly quickly."

"But it seems really *personal*," Poppy said.

"Murder usually is personal," said Suzanne, sounding amused.

"No, I mean, it's as if the murderer wanted Zova to suffer… like to pay for something he'd done…"

"You're thinking of Geoff Healey again?"

"Well, he *is* very bitter," Poppy pointed out. "And he would know all about Zova's allergy to bee and wasp stings."

"So would Nowak," Suzanne pointed out.

"Yes, but do you know who *wouldn't* have known?" asked Poppy excitedly. "Joe Fabbri! If Zova really was killed by the wasps, then it proves that Joe couldn't have done it!"

Suzanne's voice was cautious. "Not necessarily. Joe could have thrown a stone into the wasp nest. Even if he didn't know about Zova's allergy, he could have just done it with malicious intent. People can die from being attacked by a wasp swarm even if they don't have an allergy—so much venom, all at once, just overwhelms your system."

"Joe would never do anything so nasty!" protested Poppy.

Suzanne gave an impatient sigh. "Poppy, I know you're friendly with Joe and you have a lot of faith in him. But you have to remember that you only met this man a few months ago, and you said yourself that he doesn't talk much, that he isn't easy to get close to... So how can you be so sure that you really know what Joe Fabbri would or would not do?"

Poppy started to argue, then stopped herself. They'd been over this before. And in any case, while she hated to admit it, she knew in her heart that Suzanne was right.

"I just don't want Joe to be unfairly blamed because he was in the wrong place at the wrong time. Please, Suzanne, don't let Sergeant Lee use Joe as an easy scapegoat."

"I won't," said Suzanne crisply. "I'm keeping an

open mind and I will make sure that Lee follows all avenues in this investigation. But *you* need to keep an open mind about Joe too and remember the weight of evidence against him."

"Okay," said Poppy in a chastened voice. "But aside from the trowel, there isn't really that much evidence against him, is there?"

"Well, for one thing, Joe has no alibi. He says he left the party and drove home, but there are no witnesses to corroborate that. He lives alone, and nobody remembers seeing his pick-up truck at the relevant times."

"But what about the other suspects? David Nowak could be covering up for Geoff Healey and giving him a false alibi. He could have been lying when he said Geoff went down to the cellar with him."

"Perhaps, but Nowak's executive secretary—Stuart Southall—certainly confirmed seeing them go down to the cellar together."

"Okay, well, what about Bunny?" asked Poppy. "We don't know what her alibi is. And if you're saying whoever murdered Rick Zova just had to disturb the wasp nest, so they didn't need to be strong enough to overpower him... well, that means Bunny could definitely be in the frame. And she knew about Zova's allergy! She told me about it herself. In fact, she even has this crazy idea of pretending she has the same allergy, just so she could share something with him."

"What do you mean?" Suzanne sounded puzzled.

"I got her to have a cup of tea with me in the village

tearoom when I saw her earlier today and she dropped her handbag again—she did it at the party too—and everything spilled everywhere. I helped her pick things up and I noticed that she was carrying an EpiPen. I asked her about it and that's what she told me. She said she wanted to be 'twinsies' with Zova." Poppy rolled her eyes. "I can't believe the things these crazy fans do."

"We need to question Bunny. If you give me her contact details, we can speak to her first thing in the morning."

"She's staying at a local pub. I've got the business card, actually. Hang on a sec..." Poppy found the card that Bunny had given her and read the address out loud over the phone.

"And Bunny seemed happy to give her details? She didn't sound worried about being questioned by the police?"

"No, she didn't act guilty or worried at all." Poppy sighed. "I have to admit, I really can't see her as the killer. She seems like such an emotional mess... I just can't see how someone like that could be cool-headed enough to plan a murder. Oh, what about Nowak's PA?" asked Poppy, suddenly remembering. "Does she have an alibi?"

"You mean Stuart Southall?"

"No, that's his executive secretary. I mean his PA—personal assistant. Well, ex-PA, actually. It was a woman called Dawn; I don't know her surname."

"Hmm..." There came the sound of papers

rustling. "Ah yes... Dawn McLaren. According to this, she was dismissed the day before so she was no longer in Nowak's employ at the time of the party—"

"No, but she was there. I saw her myself—she turned up when I was chatting with him and she seemed very tense. She kept asking to speak to him privately, and Nowak looked really uncomfortable," Poppy said.

"In what way?"

"Sort of like furtive and embarrassed... Nowak mentioned a 'tribunal'. I wondered if it had something to do with her dismissal and he was afraid she was going to make a scene."

"Hmm... I'll ask Lee to speak to her again."

"Yes, tell him that I happened to bump into her in the village pharmacy today and I noticed that she had wasp stings on her forearm."

"Wasp stings? Are you sure?" Suzanne's voice had sharpened with interest.

"Yes, she was buying calamine lotion for the itching. When I asked her about the stings, she said she'd got stung by a random wasp on the day *before* the party. Her stings looked really red and swollen, though, like... like they were 'fresh'. I asked her about that and she said you can get a delayed reaction from wasp stings—"

"Which is true," Suzanne conceded. "But this certainly bears following up. Thanks for letting me know. I'll have Lee check her alibi and movements on the night of the party." She hesitated, then added,

"I'm probably going against protocol, but since you've been so helpful and I know I can trust you, I'll make sure to keep you updated after we speak to Bunny and Dawn."

"Oh! Thank you! I'd really appreciate that," said Poppy, smiling.

She hung up to find Oren looking expectantly at her. Taking a deep breath, Poppy rolled up her sleeves and said, with a determined look at the ginger tom:

"All right, Oren... Round Two!"

CHAPTER NINETEEN

Poppy had a better night's sleep and awoke feeling refreshed and in much better spirits. She washed and dressed quickly, then wandered into the kitchen, which was already warm with the smell of fresh baking. Nell had gone out but she had left a note propped up against a loaf of freshly baked bread. Poppy cut a couple of slices, toasted them lightly, then slathered them with jam and butter. She was just enjoying her last bite and licking her fingers clean when she heard a knock at the front door of the cottage.

"Oh, hello, Bertie! My goodness, you're very smartly dressed," said Poppy in surprise as she opened the door and found the old inventor on her doorstep.

He was wearing a tweed jacket and brown

corduroy trousers, and even sported a red spotted bow tie. Looking down, Poppy half expected to see his feet encased in flippers or something equally ridiculous, but to her surprise, Bertie was actually wearing a pair of ordinary shoes. Granted, one was brown and one was black, but considering the sort of outlandish outfits that she'd seen him wearing in the past, this was the height of "normal" for the old inventor. There was not a fishing wader, inner tube, or gladiator helmet in sight.

"Oh, I need to look my best, as I am on my way to an important business meeting, my dear," said Bertie, beaming. "But I wanted to pop by and give you this. You were asking for something to put on your wasp stings yesterday. Well, I felt bad that I didn't have anything for you, so I stayed up last night developing something." He handed her a flat metal tin. "Here... put some of this salve on your stings. It should help with healing tremendously."

"Oh, Bertie—that's so sweet of you," cried Poppy, touched, as she slowly unscrewed the tin. "I did pick up some things from the village pharmacy but I'm sure your salve will be much more—*eeuugghh!*" She gagged at the putrid smell coming from the open tin. "Oh my God, Bertie, what's *in* this thing?"

"Stinkhorn mushroom salve," said Bertie proudly. "I realised that in addition to making a wonderful tea, *Phallus impudicus* can also be reduced to gelatine form and then combined with wax to create a marvellous medicinal salve! There hasn't been any published research, but I posit that it has similar wound-healing properties to that of *Agaricus bisporus* and other better-studied mushroom species. I am convinced that my stinkhorn salve will promote increased skin regeneration and reduced scarring." He grasped Poppy's hands excitedly. "In fact, you are to be my first guinea pig, my dear!"

"Oh. Er... thanks for the honour," said Poppy dubiously. She caught another whiff of the stench from the tin and reeled back. Trying to breathe through her mouth, she said, "Er... Bertie, wasn't there any way to make this salve without including the stinkhorn's... um... odour properties?"

"Ah, you mean the smell? Yes, it is slightly overpowering, my dear," conceded Bertie.

"Slightly?" Poppy coughed. "It's like the most revolting combination of rotting meat and sweaty feet and sewage! Honestly, Bertie, you could probably bring corpses back to life with one whiff of this thing."

"AHHH!" Bertie stared at her, his eyes wide with delight. "What a marvellous idea!"

"I was joking," said Poppy hastily.

But Bertie wasn't listening. He was rubbing his chin and murmuring excitedly to himself, "Yes... yes... olfactory stimulants are already used in athletic competitions... boxers knocked unconscious... and the Second World War, the British Red Cross... of course, the active compound is normally ammonium carbonate, but that could be easily substituted with the hydrogen sulphide, phenylacetaldehyde, and dimethyl trisulfide compounds found in the mushrooms..."

Poppy screwed the lid back on and shoved the tin into her jeans pocket. Keen to change the subject, she asked, "So who are you going to meet today, Bertie?"

"Mrs Lena Nowak of Róża Garden Centres."

Poppy stared at him. "You mean... David Nowak's wife?"

Bertie nodded. "Yes, indeed. Mrs Nowak contacted me a few months ago, you see, because she heard about my work on robotic systems for cleaning and sanitation. She'd noticed how popular robot vacuums and robot lawnmowers had become, so she was wondering about the possibility of creating a machine which could clean vertical surfaces—such as the glass in greenhouses. She thinks that there could be great demand for such a machine—"

"Oh God, yes," said Poppy with a groan, thinking of the many hours she had spent cleaning the greenhouse. "Lena Nowak is a clever woman. I'll bet lots of people would snap up a machine like that!" She looked at Bertie curiously. "So, are you developing something for Róża Garden Centres?"

"Mrs Nowak wants an exclusive product line." Bertie lifted the faded leather briefcase he always carried and held it up to show Poppy. "I have done some preliminary designs and I am going over to Chatswood House now to show them to her. Wouldn't it be wonderful, my dear, if Róża Garden Centres decide to invest in one of my inventions?"

On an impulse, Poppy said: "Listen, Bertie—would you like a lift over to Chatswood House?"

"Why, that would be marvellous, my dear! I was just wondering how I would transport CLARA. My Quadracycle needs a replacement wheel, you see, and square wheels are so difficult to source. In any case, there isn't really enough space to strap her to the back—"

"Wait—why do you need to take CLARA?"

"Oh, I want to show her to Mrs Nowak! Naturally, the model that I will develop for the garden centres will be much simpler, but CLARA demonstrates what my inventions are capable of."

In more ways than one, thought Poppy wryly, but she kept her thoughts to herself. When she got out to the car, however, she found yet another passenger waiting by her Fiat: Einstein the terrier.

"Bertie, you can't bring Einstein as well," she protested.

Bertie looked bewildered. "But he goes everywhere with me."

"*Ruff-ruff!*" agreed Einstein, wagging his tail.

"Yes, but this is a private property. Maybe Mrs Nowak doesn't like dogs."

"Oh, not to worry. Einstein can always wait for me outside the house," said Bertie cheerfully.

Poppy sighed and gave up. After all, the Nowaks had a large estate and she was sure they wouldn't mind a small terrier waiting outside in the grounds somewhere. She loaded inventor, dog, and robot into the car and they started for Chatswood House. When they arrived, however, instead of just dropping them off, Poppy found herself offering to accompany Bertie inside.

Why am I doing this? she wondered as she followed Bertie up the steps to the front door. Well, if she was honest with herself, she knew why: she wanted another look at the "crime scene". *It's not as if I'm interfering with the investigation. And I know the forensics team have been over the grounds, but it is possible that they could have missed something...*

They were greeted at the door by a self-important young man whom Poppy recognised from the party: Stuart Southall, the executive secretary. He looked startled at the sight of the robot standing next to Bertie and he frowned at Einstein, sniffing around his ankles, but he didn't object to them all trooping in. Once inside, he led them through the manor house to a large hall at the rear, which had been converted into a sort of gallery. There were paintings hanging on the walls, as well as display cases housing various ornaments placed strategically beneath large spotlights. The centre of the room was dominated by an enormous *chaise longue*, with a gilt frame and upholstery so sumptuous that Poppy was afraid to sit on it.

Stuart paused beside the *chaise longue* and indicated the long seat. "If you could wait here, Mrs Nowak will be along in a minute. The police forensics team finally packed up and left this morning, and she is just supervising the clean-up of the area."

Bertie took no notice of Stuart's words and wandered off to peruse some paintings, with Einstein at his heels and CLARA rolling quietly behind him, like a mechanical lady companion. Poppy watched them out of the corner of her eye. Going out with Bertie was a bit like going out with a toddler: you never knew what he might get into next. Still, the old inventor looked happily preoccupied at the moment, admiring the artwork on the walls, and Poppy relaxed slightly. She perched carefully on the edge of the *chaise longue*, then stole a glance at Stuart, who remained standing stiffly beside her. She wished he would either leave them alone or—if he was going to remain there—make some attempt at conversation. The silence stretched on awkwardly between them until finally Poppy said at random:

"Um... is Mr Nowak here today?"

"No, he has gone up to the police station in Oxford. They wanted to ask him some more questions. I really don't know why they're bothering Mr Nowak again, though—I thought they already had a suspect in custody?" said Stuart, pursing his lips. "And naturally, the media are having a field day! There were TV crews and journalists camped at the front of the estate all day yesterday, you know. They've only dispersed now because most of them have followed Mr Nowak up to Oxford. I shudder to think what they'll say when they hear that he is being questioned again. He's only helping the police with the investigation out of civic duty—I stressed that in the press release—but the media love to sensationalise everything. Really, it's ridiculous the amount of fuss that's being made. It's extremely embarrassing for a man in Mr Nowak's position, you know," he added, looking like he took the embarrassment as a personal affront.

"Well, a man *has* been murdered," Poppy pointed out. "That is quite a big thing."

Stuart sniffed. "This whole unpleasant episode could have been avoided if Dawn had done her job properly."

Poppy looked at him in surprise. "What do you mean?"

"It was her responsibility to check everything for the party—which should have included making sure that the wasp nest was removed, but it seems even that simple task was too much for her... Well, what do you expect from an ex-drug addict?" said Stuart contemptuously.

"Dawn was a drug addict?" said Poppy in surprise.

"Didn't you know? She's one of Mr Nowak's charity cases. He met her through his own Beneficium Foundation; she was in the recovery programme where they help ex-addicts find a job and reintegrate into society. I don't know what happened but all of a sudden, one day, Mr Nowak told me that Dawn would be taking over as his PA. His previous PA had just gone on maternity leave and instead of hiring someone via the usual recruitment agencies, Mr Nowak just decided to give Dawn the job."

"Well... surely that was very nice of him?"

Stuart made an exasperated sound. "Yes, fine! I feel sorry for them too and it's commendable of Mr Nowak to want to help, but the woman doesn't even have any proper qualifications or training for the job!" He rolled his eyes. "Not that you needed much training to get *this* done. It was such a simple thing— all she had to do was call the pest control company and organise for them to come and take the nest away, and kill any remaining wasps. I'm sure she forgot. She's always so scatterbrained and forgetful— it's probably the drugs. They say extended drug use causes permanent brain damage, you know, and can affect things like memory," he said with fastidious disdain. "I *told* Mr Nowak to give her a job as an office clerk or a receptionist or even a maid in the house or something... not hire her as his personal assistant! And letting her organise this party was a big mistake. But Mr Nowak just wouldn't listen. He's too generous and forgiving; that's his problem. I advised him to hire a proper event organiser but he said he wanted to give Dawn the opportunity. Really, though, she doesn't have the skills or the experience to handle such a project. If *I* had been the one overseeing things, such an oversight would never have occurred."

Poppy was starting to find the young man's smug superiority very irritating. "Maybe Dawn was busy with other stuff. If you knew about the wasp nest, couldn't *you* have called the pest company—?"

"Me?" Stuart gave her an incredulous look. He drew himself up to his full height. "I'm Mr Nowak's executive secretary! I take care of his business affairs and his manoeuvres in the political arena. I liaise with the team who is coordinating Mr Nowak's election campaign, oversee agendas and meetings, prepare reports for him, conduct research... *I* can't be expected to deal with mundane domestic matters—that's what his PA is for! I'm far too busy."

Poppy started to say something sarcastic, then stopped herself as she suddenly realised that she could use the man's pompous self-importance to her advantage. Giving him a wide-eyed, admiring look, she said: "I heard that the police needed *your* assistance in determining what happened on the night of the party?"

"Yes, I gave them a detailed statement—probably the most comprehensive one they received," said Stuart loftily.

"And you were the one who confirmed Mr Nowak's alibi, isn't that right?"

Stuart puffed his chest out. "That's right. The police had some doubts, but I was happy to put them straight—I personally witnessed Mr Nowak leaving the orangery in the company of his friend, Mr Healey. They were on their way down to the cellar beneath the main house."

"Did you see them actually go down into the cellar

together?"

"Well, no, but I saw them head into the corridor connecting the orangery to here..." Stuart pointed across the room to the opposite corner where Poppy could see an open doorway leading off from the gallery. It was obviously the start of the long corridor which connected the main house to the orangery.

"See those doors at the start of the corridor?" said Stuart, gesturing. "One is for the guest toilet, one is for Mr Nowak's study, and the third leads down to the cellar."

But what if the two men hadn't remained together once they entered the corridor? thought Poppy. *What if they had parted company once they were out of sight?*

She thought back to what she had overheard yesterday, when she had been eavesdropping on Nowak and Healey in the latter's garden. Nowak had said something like: *'tell them you were down in the wine cellar with me'*... Now, why would he say that unless Geoff Healey *hadn't* been with him? Stuart had been in the orangery himself, so he would only have seen them go behind the Chinese screen and enter the corridor together. But Nowak could have continued down by himself and gone to the cellar alone. In the meantime, Geoff Healey could have doubled back once he was sure that no one was watching. He could have slipped outside unseen through a side door and gone down the steps at the side of the terrace to the walled garden, where Rick

Zova was standing unawares, smoking his cigar beside the tree...

She looked back up at Stuart and asked, "How long were Mr Nowak and Mr Healey down in the cellar?"

Stuart shrugged. "I don't know... about ten minutes? I didn't see Mr Nowak again until the commotion about the wasps. He must have just come back up from the cellar because he was holding the bottle of wine he'd gone down to get."

"Was Mr Healey with him?"

Stuart thought for a moment. "I don't recall seeing him. Of course, things were very chaotic then. We were more concerned with finding out what had occurred."

"And what about—"

CRASH!

Poppy spun around. Her heart sank as she realised that Bertie was nowhere to be seen. She should have been keeping an eye on him, but she had become so engrossed in talking to Stuart that she had completely forgotten about the old inventor.

What had he done?

CHAPTER TWENTY

There was another crash. Stuart rushed across the gallery to the corridor with Poppy following at his heels. The sound seemed to have come from Nowak's study and they burst into the room, then faltered to a stop at the scene in front of them.

Bertie was grappling wildly with CLARA in front of the fireplace, in a tangle of spinning wheels and burgeoning brushes and bristles. The robot had somehow climbed into the chimney and was now industriously sweeping one arm across the floor of the hearth. An enormous suction nozzle was attached to the end of the arm and it was sucking up all dirt and ashes in the fireplace. The only problem was, the suction was so strong that everything else in the room was getting caught up in the air flow as well: Post-It notes, documents, paperclips, rubber bands, shredded paper, mailing labels, and postage stamps were whirling around the room in a miniature tornado, twisting and spinning towards the robot... Poppy even felt her hair lifting from her head and being tugged towards CLARA.

She rushed across to Bertie and shouted above the roar of the vacuum, "Bertie! What have you done?"

"Oh, not to worry. Not to worry, my dear," said the old inventor, pushing buttons and twiddling knobs on the robot's torso. "Just needs a slight adjustment..."

"Turn her off, Bertie—turn her off!"

To her relief, the robot suddenly ceased and the vacuum suction died. The sudden silence in the room was deafening. Poppy turned around to see Stuart standing by the door, open-mouthed. His hair was standing on end and his tie had been whipped up and over his shoulders. Bits of paper floated down around them.

"What on earth...?" A woman appeared suddenly in the doorway behind Stuart.

Poppy recognised her as the glamorous woman she had seen chasing Joe Fabbri on the night of the party, except that Lena Nowak looked very different now. Instead of a luxe velvet cocktail dress and flamboyant jewellery, she wore an elegant cream trouser suit and designer heels. She stepped into the room, arms akimbo, and surveyed the mess. Where Nowak was all diffidence and affability, with such a low-key manner that no one would have expected him to be one of the most powerful and successful men in Britain, his wife was the complete opposite. She radiated a nervous energy and looked like a power executive on the warpath, ready to give any hapless employee a tongue-lashing.

"What's going on here?" she demanded.

Bertie rushed towards her and grabbed her hand, pumping it up and down. "Ah! Mrs Nowak, I presume? I am Dr Bertram Noble."

"Oh. Right. Er... how do you do," said Lena Nowak, peeling off a Post-It note which had floated down and stuck on her forehead.

"I'm delighted that you are interested in my inventions," continued Bertie. "I have brought several designs to show you, but I have also brought CLARA, who is my finest creation! She will be able to show you the full extent of her functions and capabilities."

Lena Nowak eyed the silent figure beside the fireplace warily. "Right... ah... CLARA is a cleaning robot?"

"Oh, CLARA is so much more than that!" said Bertie. "She can be programmed to detect anything: dust, soil, hair, mould—vomit might be a bit tricky, but I'm sure I could do it with some calibration—and she will then target that type of particle only. This means that she can be incredibly specific in the type of task that she can perform."

"Are the sensors really that powerful?" said Lena,

looking impressed.

"Oh yes! Come... come here." Bertie beckoned eagerly.

Lena Nowak hesitated, then went across to the fireplace, signalling Stuart to follow her. The executive secretary looked alarmed, but he swallowed in a manly fashion and complied.

Bertie pointed at the hearth, which was now completely clean, with not a speck of ash in sight. "I was just testing her sensors with a sample of ash from your fireplace. As you can see, CLARA has removed all traces of powdered carbon residue," he said proudly.

She nearly removed half the room as well, thought Poppy, gazing around the study, which looked like a hurricane had torn it apart.

"And I am adding more types of particles to CLARA's database every day," Bertie continued. "I have just started including a variety of human tissue in her memory bank, so that she can perform some grooming tasks as well."

"*Grooming* tasks?" said Lena, looking puzzled.

"Ah yes! You see, I realised that many personal grooming activities are really just a form of cleaning. So it seemed logical to expand CLARA's functions to include expunging human orifices too."

Stuart looked alarmed. "O-orifices?"

"I will show you." Bertie looked Stuart up and down. "Aha... young man, you are the perfect specimen!" He grabbed the secretary and hauled him over next to the robot.

"What...? Wait—Now, look here... what the...!" spluttered Stuart, struggling to free himself.

But before he could wriggle away, one of CLARA's arms shot out. The end had converted from a scrubbing brush into a sort of metallic claw which lowered over Stuart's head and clamped around his forehead.

"Aaaggghh!" cried Stuart. "What is it doing? Let me go!"

"Don't worry, CLARA is just making sure that you are comfortable," said Bertie. "It's important that your head is kept very still, otherwise the blades might cut too deeply."

"*Blades?*" squeaked Stuart. "What blades?"

As if in answer, a buzzing noise started up and CLARA raised her other arm. Its end had converted from the vacuum nozzle into a sort of rotating clipper. Stuart yelped and tried to jerk away but the clamp around his head held him fast. His eyes were terrified as he watched the robot raise the buzzing arm and bring it towards his face.

"*Giant nose hair detected. Extreme growth. Trimming required,*" came the mechanical voice.

"*Arrghh...uunngg...gaarrr...aargghh...*" blubbered Stuart, twitching and squirming as CLARA went to work.

Poppy stared in horror, not knowing whether to laugh or cry. A few minutes later, it was all over and the robot released Stuart, who stumbled backwards, a hand clamped over his nose.

"She's done a marvellous job, hasn't she?" said Bertie proudly. "So much more precise than if you did it yourself. The vortex motor means that it can cope with nose hairs which tend to be thicker and bushier—like yours."

Stuart's face was beetroot-red and he looked as if he was struggling to speak.

"Oh, there's no need to be embarrassed," said Bertie heartily, patting him on the shoulder. "It's actually an advantage to have vigorous nose hair, you know. Researchers at Hacettepe University School of Medicine have found that people with sparse nose hair are nearly three times more likely to suffer from asthma than those with shaggy nostrils."

Stuart made an incoherent noise, then bolted from the room. Bertie turned back to Lena Nowak who was standing dumbstruck, and said:

"CLARA is also extremely proficient at removing earwax. Would you like a personal demonstration?"

***

Poppy had half expected Bertie to be shown the door after CLARA's "cleaning demonstration", but to her surprise, Lena Nowak hadn't been put off by the fiasco (or the threat to her earwax) and she spent the next hour closeted in the study with Bertie, going over his designs in depth and discussing the logistics of producing and testing his machines. Poppy was left with the job of babysitting one over-zealous robot and one scruffy black terrier. Thankfully, CLARA seemed to finally be running low on battery and had subsided into an electrical coma in the corner, so Poppy only had to worry about Einstein.

Deciding that it would be easier to keep the lively terrier occupied outdoors, Poppy took the dog down the corridor, through the orangery—now eerily empty and silent—and out onto the terrace. It was a typical blustery autumn day, with the skies grey and promising rain later. Poppy walked slowly to the edge of the terrace, retracing her route from the night of the party, and paused at the top of the steps leading down to the walled garden. A small area around the base of the yew tree, which had held the wasp nest, was still cordoned off by crime scene tape, but otherwise the rest of the garden was free to enter.

Einstein tugged at the end of his leash, whining to be let loose.

"No, sorry, boy—I can't let you off," said Poppy, keeping a tighter hold on his leash but allowing him to pull her down the steps.

They walked down the path and approached the yew tree. There were no wasps in sight and there was only a gaping hole in the trunk where the nest had once been, but nevertheless, Poppy gave the area a wide berth. *Once stung, twice shy*, she thought grimly as she hustled Einstein past the tree.

A bit beyond the tree, she was delighted to stumble upon a pretty, sheltered area around the corner, where the plants grew up against the side of the main house in such a way as to mimic a woodland grotto. Bushy stands of rowan and hawthorn showed glossy berries against their dark leaves and a thicket of dog roses sprawled between them. A few hellebores peeped through the undergrowth, not blooming yet but pretty nonetheless, and clumps of *Cyclamen hederifolium* provided splashes of magenta-pink in the green gloom.

Poppy paused to admire the secluded area. It was so pretty and peaceful, out of sight of the main house and the orangery, almost like a secret garden. A series of flat pavers—almost like stepping stones— led from the main path to a garden bench tucked against one of the trees. It looked inviting and Einstein strained eagerly on his leash, but Poppy held back. Somehow, it seemed wrong to step into the little grotto and ruin the peaceful ambience.

"Come on, Einstein... this way," she said, tugging gently to lead the dog away.

He resisted at first, then suddenly his head went up, his nose quivering as he stared at something further up the path. The next moment, he charged past her, barking at the top of his voice.

"Einstein!" gasped Poppy as the leash was torn from her unsuspecting fingers.

The little black terrier scampered off into the distance, chasing a squirrel with great delight, his leash trailing after him.

"Einstein!" Poppy shouted, scrambling to her feet and racing after the terrier. "Einstein, come back here!"

CHAPTER TWENTY-ONE

Poppy's phone started ringing as she took off after the dog and she was forced to slow her steps as she answered it.

"Ye...yes?" she gasped.

"Hi, Poppy... Suzanne here. I've decided to take a personal look at the Zova case and I wanted to go over a few things. Do you have a moment to talk?"

Poppy cast an agonised look at Einstein's tufted tail disappearing into the distance, then sighed and stopped running. "Uh... yes... sure."

"Yesterday, when we were talking, you mentioned seeing an EpiPen in Bunny's handbag when you met her in the village. And you said that she also dropped her handbag at Nowak's party and you helped her pick things up then too... Do you remember if you saw the EpiPen in her handbag on the night of the

190

party?"

Poppy thought for a moment. "Mmm... I don't remember seeing it, but that doesn't mean it wasn't there. I mean, Bunny had so much junk in her bag and she picked up things too, so it's possible that *she* picked up the EpiPen herself that time at the party and that's why I missed seeing it that night. Why are you asking?"

"It's just a thought I had. It might be significant if she didn't have an EpiPen when you saw her at the party—which was before Rick Zova's murder—but she had one two days later."

"You mean... she could have stolen the EpiPen from Rick Zova?" Poppy said excitedly. "Oh my God, Bunny could be the murderer! She set the wasps on Zova and she took the only means he had to save himself!"

"Well, we mustn't jump to conclusions, but it's certainly something to consider," Suzanne cautioned. "Of course, it could also be the reason she gave you: that it was simply a way for her to feel closer to him. It does seem far-fetched, but then fan behaviour can often be illogical and bizarre."

"What did she say when you questioned her? Did she stick to the same story she told me?"

"We haven't questioned her. We haven't been able to find her."

"*What?* What do you mean? Wasn't she at the address I gave you?"

"No, apparently she'd checked out quite suddenly.

She was gone by the time Lee went to talk to her this morning."

"You mean—she's gone on the run?" cried Poppy, aghast.

"Not necessarily. We're trying to track her at the moment. We have her booking details at the pub and we know her name—her real name, that is. It's Ruth Hollis. She's an itinerant with no close family. She's been through a series of casual jobs: waitressing, temporary shop girl, babysitting, but never stays in anything for long."

"Do you think she just followed Zova to the party?" asked Poppy.

"Yes, it looks like it. Her name wasn't on the guest list and she's been known to follow him around before. She calls herself a 'superfan' but there are some who would label her behaviour as verging on stalker territory. In fact, Zova himself reported her to the authorities twice, although he never took out a restraining order against her. It seems that he saw her as more of a nuisance than a serious threat."

Poppy wondered if Rick Zova ended up regretting that. "Does this mean that Joe is off the hook?" she asked hopefully. "I mean, with her history with Zova, Bunny has to be far more of a serious suspect than him."

"No, Joe Fabbri is still under investigation," Suzanne said evenly. "The fact that he has no alibi and that his trowel was found under Zova's body hasn't changed."

"Oh. So you're still holding him?" asked Poppy.

"No, he was released this morning. He has to remain in Bunnington, though, and we may bring him in for questioning again." Suzanne's voice remained pleasant but there was a steely quality in her tone which reminded Poppy that although she and Suzanne had become friends, the latter was still very much a detective first and foremost.

She hung up in a sober mood and was about to look for Einstein again when she heard a voice calling her name and turned around to see Lena Nowak walking down the path to join her.

"Ah... here you are," said the older woman. "I was wondering where you'd got to."

"Sorry. I thought I'd bring Dr Noble's dog out for a walk in the garden. I hope that's okay?"

"As long as you don't let him loose," said Lena Nowak, pursing her lips.

Uh-oh. Poppy looked surreptitiously around, hoping against hope that Einstein might actually be nearby and she could somehow snatch up the end of his leash, but there was no sign of the little terrier.

"Um... well, actually... he... um... he's gone off for a little run by himself. But he's very well trained. He won't dig or destroy anything," Poppy added hastily, crossing her fingers behind her back.

"Hmm..." said Lena Nowak, compressing her lips. "I've never liked dogs. Yappy, smelly, dirty little beasts! David loves them and is always suggesting that we get one, but really, who would have time to look after it? He's forever at various meetings and I'm far too busy with the company—I'm in charge of New Business Development, you know, and I have a team which is continually looking into new product lines, expansions, and diversification for the company." She made a clucking sound with her tongue. "Not that I can really leave them to it—they need so much supervision and direction! David keeps telling me that I should delegate more, but how can I when I can see that they aren't doing their jobs properly? You won't believe the number of times I've found issues when I've stepped in to check, or processes that weren't being followed to the letter."

She paused at last for a breath and Poppy felt a rush of pity for her employees. Lena Nowak must have been the worst micro-managing boss on the planet! Once again, she wondered how Nowak could be married to her—they seemed such opposites. The businessman's calm temperament and unassuming manners made him such easy company, whereas his wife's critical demeanour was incredibly off-putting.

"Um... this walled garden is lovely," said Poppy, trying to change the subject. "I love the way it's been laid out and the choice of planting. You must have spent a lot of time and effort designing it."

Lena glanced around with distaste. "Oh, this is all David's doing. I don't have much interest in gardening, to tell you the truth."

Poppy blinked in surprise and couldn't stop herself blurting, "But... but you own a chain of garden centres! You said you're in charge of product development and new business—"

Lena Nowak gave her a tight smile. "Oh, I certainly know enough about plants and gardening—everything that's necessary to run the business. I'm just not interested in mucking in myself and getting my hands dirty. Unlike David," she added, rolling her eyes. "He's never happier than when he's out in the garden, covered in soil. We have a full-time gardener who is more than capable, as well as a team from the garden centre that comes in regularly to do the heavier maintenance, but David always insists on doing as much as possible himself." She gave an impatient sigh. "And he's so fussy about not using pesticides in the garden. He is obsessed with maintaining the 'natural balance', as he calls it. He says all insects have a role to play, even the ones that we see as pests... like those dreadful wasps." She shuddered.

"Yes, I heard that you knew about the nest in the tree before the party—"

"Who told you that?"

"Dawn... I mean, Mr Nowak's PA... er... I mean, ex-PA."

Lena Nowak's face took on a sour expression. "That woman! Faffing around with bits of paper all the time and never getting anything done. We even paid for her to attend workshops and training courses, you know, but she was still hopeless. Of course, David kept saying we had to be patient and give her more chances... That is his greatest weakness, you know—always being too generous! Even with people who don't deserve it, like that silly woman. I would have dismissed her without pay, but David gave in and offered her a redundancy package.

"Anyway, I'm pleased she's gone now. And hopefully we can get rid of her ridiculous desk too; it takes up half the study! I told David it's ridiculous that the PA should have a bigger desk than the boss—image is everything, you know—but David never seems to understand that. He insisted that he preferred to sit at the smaller desk by the window." Lena Nowak gave an irritable sigh. "Well, at least it's only his study at home. I've made sure that his office at our headquarters has a proper big executive desk, suitable for the CEO of the company."

There was a pause, then Lena Nowak gave Poppy a sidelong look and said, "I suppose Dawn was gushing about David as usual?"

"Sorry? I don't know what you mean," said Poppy in surprise.

Lena snorted. "Didn't you know? Dawn has a pathetic crush on David. She was always mooning over him when she was working as his PA. I used to come home and find her in his study, on some lame pretext or other... It was cringe-worthy to watch! And of course, David was much too nice to do anything about it, even though he found it deeply embarrassing. I had to put my foot down in the end. I'm glad he finally listened to reason and dismissed her." Her gaze sharpened. "How did you meet Dawn, anyway? She wasn't at the party, was she? She was dismissed the day before."

"Oh... er..." Poppy hesitated, remembering the furtive way Nowak had looked around when Dawn had suddenly appeared and asked to speak to him. She realised now that he must have been worried about his wife seeing the PA and the last thing she wanted to do was to make life difficult for the businessman. "No, no, I just happened to bump into Dawn in the village pharmacy yesterday. She... she must have heard about what happened through the local grapevine."

"Hmm..." Lena Nowak pursed her lips. "Well, I hope she doesn't go around spreading gossip. As I say, image is everything these days and damaging PR could be very bad for the company." She turned back towards the orangery and said briskly, "Well, Dr Noble is ready to leave now so... I assume you can call your dog back?"

"Oh! Er, yes... of course."

Poppy cleared her throat and called Einstein's name, aware of Lena Nowak's critical gaze on her, and was relieved when the little terrier's head popped up from behind some shrubs in the distance. She called him again, beckoning him to come. Einstein stared back at her without moving.

"Einstein! Good boy, come on!" Poppy called. "Here he comes!" she said brightly to Lena as the terrier started moving.

Einstein took a few steps, but instead of heading towards her, he went over to a nearby olive tree and cocked his leg.

Grrrr. Poppy gritted her teeth.

"EINSTEIN!" she shouted. "Come here! Good dog... COME!"

Einstein looked at her and wagged his tail, then he turned and trotted off, disappearing into the shrubbery.

Aaarrrgghh! Poppy wanted to shake the little scamp.

"Um... I'll just go and fetch him," she said breezily to Lena. "We'll be back in a flash!"

After some hunting around, Poppy found the mischievous little terrier back in the secluded grotto they had discovered earlier. He was next to the bench, busily sniffing around a small, square, wooden platform that was embedded in the ground. From the look of its weathered, soil-stained surface, it had been here a long time and had probably once been a base for a statue or maybe even a flat area to place a small table and two chairs.

Poppy approached slowly, hoping to grab the dog's leash before he noticed her. She tiptoed across the stepping stones that led from the path to the bench and bent down, reaching towards the end of the leash, which had fallen into the space between two of the pavers. It was tangled in several clumps of tiny pink and white daisies which had self-seeded and grown in the space between the pavers.

Erigeron daisies! Poppy thought suddenly, smiling to herself. She was still enough of a novice at gardening to feel a thrill of delight every time she managed to recognise a plant or flower. Crouching down, she ran her hands through the clump, pulling the leash out while marvelling at how the tiny flowers were still blooming so profusely this late in October, when most other plants were fading.

Something aside from the leash caught in her fingers and when she pulled her hand out of the mound of hairy, grey-green leaves, she stared at the object in her palm. It looked like a small wine stopper, with a carved wooden head and a pointy stainless steel shank to fit in the neck of a bottle. It looked fairly new and Poppy wondered if it had been dropped recently. Gripping the leash firmly, she rose to her feet. She was just turning the wine stopper over curiously in her hands once more when she heard Lena Nowak's voice calling her name. Shoving the stopper into her pocket, she gave the leash a gentle tug.

"Come on, Einstein!"

Dragging the reluctant terrier behind her, Poppy turned and hurried back up the path towards the orangery.

CHAPTER TWENTY-TWO

Early the next morning, Poppy unlocked the front door to Nick's house and hurried into the kitchen. She looked eagerly at the cat bowl in the corner, then her face fell as she saw that it was still heaped high with dry cat food.

"Oh, Oren!" she groaned, huffing in frustration.

"*N-owww?*" The big ginger tomcat sauntered into the kitchen and regarded her with an expectant gleam in his yellow eyes.

Poppy sighed. This was the second morning in a row that she had come in and found the bowl untouched. Last night, after she had returned from Chatswood House and dropped Bertie, Einstein, and CLARA off, she had come over to give Oren his dinner and had been dismayed to see that he had not eaten any of the food she had set out the previous morning.

She had hardened her heart and ignored his demands for treats from the fridge, and instead refilled his bowl with fresh prescription cat food. She had set it down in the hope that the ginger tom would be motivated enough by hunger to at least eat a bit... but now she could see that it had been a vain hope.

Poppy bit her lip, wondering what to do. Unless he was managing to catch mice or something, Oren had now missed three meals since Nick left on his trip yesterday and hadn't eaten anything. Surely she couldn't let him continue to go hungry?

"*N-ow?*" said Oren, as if reading her mind. He walked over to the fridge and looked at the door meaningfully. "*N-ow? N-oww?*"

"Ohhh... all right!" said Poppy, caving in. She opened the fridge and examined the contents. There was an unopened packet of sliced honey-roast chicken. She hesitated, then took this out and emptied it into a bowl, then placed it on the floor.

Oren was on it in a flash. His purring filled the entire kitchen, sounding like a jumbo jet revving up to take off. In spite of herself, Poppy smiled. There was nothing as lovely as the sound of a cat purring in contentment. The ginger tom polished off the whole lot of roast chicken in under a minute, then looked at her expectantly, licking his lips.

"*N-orrr?*" he said hopefully.

Poppy shook her head. "Uh-uh, Oren, I can't give you more. I shouldn't even have given you that, as it is! Anyway, you be a good boy now and eat your diet food, okay?" She looked at him pleadingly.

The tomcat made a chirruping sound and rubbed himself against her leg as she threw out the uneaten biscuits and refilled the bowl from the box in the cupboard. She set it back down and Oren walked over to look at the dry cat food. Then he flicked his tail contemptuously and stalked out of the kitchen without a backward glance.

Great. Poppy sighed. *Well, maybe he'll come back later and eat his diet food once he gets hungry again.* She gave the kitchen a quick tidy up and was just about to leave when her eyes fell on the paper model on the kitchen island. Grimacing, she remembered that there were still a few broken items left to fix. She hadn't been able to find any superglue in the house and she was keen to repair things before Nick returned home.

I'll pop up to the village now, Poppy thought. She was sure that she'd be able to buy superglue at the post office shop. Locking up, she headed up the lane towards the village high street. She hadn't gone a few hundred yards, however, when she met Nell coming from the opposite direction. Her old friend was carrying a canvas tote bulging with fresh groceries.

"Hi, Nell! I thought you'd left for work already," said Poppy.

"My cleaning jobs start later today. I'll be leaving in an hour," said Nell. She indicated the overflowing tote. "The village grocer told me yesterday that they were getting a delivery from the local farms this morning, so I wanted to make sure that I had first dibs! Look at these!" She fished a couple of plump, rosy apples out of the tote. "Aren't they beautiful? The first of the autumn harvest. And I got some fresh eggs too—laid this morning—and a wonderful slab of goat's cheese. I bought two, actually; I'm going to give the other one to Abby when I see her at church on Sunday. Poor thing, she could do with some cheering up."

"Abby? Who's Abby?"

"She's Joe's niece. I saw her in the village yesterday. She had just been to pick him up from the police station and drop him home. She's so upset about Joe being a suspect in the murder investigation, you know. They're very close, you see; Abby's mother is Joe's younger sister and her father left them when she was just a little girl, so Joe's really been like a father to her. Lovely girl, Abby. Such a shame that she's all alone; she says she just hasn't found the right man, but between you and me, I think it's because her leg puts people off."

"Her leg?" Poppy was really confused now.

Nell nodded. "She was in a dreadful hit-and-run accident when she was younger: fractured pelvis and broken leg, and then there was infection afterwards... She's ended up with terrible scarring and hip deformity. It means she walks with a limp, poor thing, and is often in a lot of pain... And she's only in her thirties, you know. She's desperate to meet someone, settle down, and start a family, but as I said, a lot of chaps are put off by her limp, I think. Men can be so shallow, you know..." Nell clucked her tongue disapprovingly, then she brightened. "Of course, I told her romance can happen anywhere, anytime, so she mustn't give up hope! Have you finished that copy of *Love's Hidden Fire*? I told Abby I'd lend it to her—it's such a wonderful story and I'm sure it would cheer her up! It's about this lovely girl who loves horses and has a terrible riding accident which means she ends up with a limp... then she meets a handsome billionaire who falls in love with her, but he can't tell her because he's already engaged to someone else... although, of course, *she* thinks it's because he's repulsed by her limp, so she runs away..."

And this is supposed to cheer Abby up? thought Poppy with a wry smile. But she wisely held her tongue and, after a few more minutes of chatting with her friend, she continued on her way. When she got to the village post office shop, however, she was disappointed to find that, for once, the store that usually had everything didn't stock what she needed.

"No, sorry, we're out of superglue. We only have white craft glue and kids' glue sticks," said the lady behind the counter. "You could try the hardware shop."

"There's a hardware shop?" said Poppy, scrunching her face as she tried to remember the layout of the village.

"Yes, it's down at the other end of the high street.

It's easy to miss because it's quite small and poky. Really, if Geoff Healey could make the effort to put up a better window display, I'm sure he'd get more business. The shop itself is well stocked with things. I reckon it's just as good as some of the big hardware stores you get in Wallingford or Didcot."

Geoff Healey! Poppy's ears perked up. Now that she thought about it, she vaguely recalled hearing Healey mention a hardware shop when she had eavesdropped on him and Nowak. Her interest piqued, she followed the directions and, a few minutes later, found herself stepping into a small, gloomy shop crammed floor-to-ceiling with hand tools, cleaning products, plumbing supplies and building materials, paint, electrical supplies, and various other housewares.

Geoff Healey looked up from behind the counter. "Yes... can I help you?" he asked. Then his face changed as he recognised Poppy and he snarled: "What d'you want? Come to spy on me again?"

Poppy was taken aback by his hostility. "No, Mr Healey. Actually, I came here because I needed some glue and I assumed that I would receive decent customer service in your shop. I guess I was wrong."

He looked slightly shamefaced at this and said grudgingly, "What kind of glue are you after?"

"Superglue, I think. I need to stick some pieces of wood together."

"You mean like furniture?"

"No, it's for a model—sort of like a doll house,"

Poppy explained.

"I've got superglue but you're probably better off with proper wood glue. If you wait a moment, I'll have a look," he said before slouching off to the rear of the shop to rummage through some shelves.

Poppy leaned against the counter to wait, scanning the shelves behind it with idle interest. They were filled with a hotchpotch of items: from tin openers to drawer knobs, from nails and buttons to hairpins, candles and duct tape... Then something on the bottom shelf caught her eye. She leaned further across the counter to get a closer look. It was a box of wine stoppers, each with a carved wooden head and a stainless-steel shank.

Poppy felt her pulse quicken. They looked exactly like the wine stopper that she had picked up in the Nowak's walled garden yesterday! *Was it just a coincidence?* She groped around in her pockets, glad that she was wearing her favourite jeans again. On the right side, she found the small, round, flat tin that Bertie had given her, and remembering that it contained the stinkhorn salve, she hastily shoved it back into her pocket. She had better luck with her left pocket and pulled out the wine stopper that she had picked up. Throwing a glance at the back of the shop to check that Geoff Healey wasn't returning, Poppy darted behind the counter and held her stopper up to compare it against the others in the box.

They were identical.

Footsteps sounded behind her. "I've got a bottle of Gorilla glue. It's not specifically for wood but it should—*hey, what are you doing?*"

Poppy whirled to find Geoff Healey standing on the other side of the counter, holding a bottle of glue and staring at her with hard, suspicious eyes.

"You are snooping!" he cried angrily. "You just used the glue as an excuse to distract me so you could sneak behind the counter and look through my private—"

"No, no! I wasn't... I wasn't snooping! I just... er... happened to see these wine stoppers and I was intrigued," said Poppy, gesturing to the box. "They're... um... really beautiful. Are they locally made?"

Geoff Healey looked slightly mollified. "Yeah, you could say that. I made them."

"Really?" said Poppy, putting on an expression of exaggerated admiration. "Wow, you must be really talented. The craftmanship is superb!"

Healey thawed even more. "Well, I've always been pretty good at woodwork," he said, his gruff tone unable to hide his pride.

"Do you sell a lot of these?" Poppy asked. "I imagine they must be really unique. After all, they're handmade by you and no one else, right?"

"Yes, they're one-of-a-kind. As for whether they're popular, well, I'm hoping that they will be. I don't know yet as this is a new item I'm trialling. I only put them out in the shop yesterday. Up until then, I'd only been giving them to a few friends."

"Did you take any with you to David Nowak's party three nights ago?"

He furrowed his brow. "David's party? Yes, I might have taken a couple to give David... why do you ask?"

"Oh... I just wondered if you might have dropped one that night," said Poppy, watching him carefully. "There was one found in the walled garden, beside the orangery, quite near to where Rick Zova's body was found."

Geoff Healey's face suddenly darkened. "Hang on a minute... is this something to do with the murder? It *is*, isn't it? You little witch—you *are* here to spy on me!"

Poppy took a step back, intimidated by his aggression. "No, I—"

Healey grabbed her wrist, wrenching her arm up to look at the wine stopper clutched in her hand. "What are you trying to do? Frame me by planting evidence?"

"No, of course not!" Poppy said indignantly, yanking her wrist out of his grasp. Her fear was turning to anger. "I *found* this out in the walled garden. It's obviously one of yours and it's strange that it should be out there, but I wasn't jumping to any conclusions until *you* got so defensive!" she shot back.

"I...I'm not defensive," Healey blustered. "I'm just protecting myself. I've had the bloody media hounding me ever since David's party, and I'm sick and tired of it! Everyone just wants a sensationalist story—I wouldn't put it past any journalist to concoct a bunch of lies, just to get a scoop!"

"Well, I'm not a journalist," snapped Poppy. "I don't need to *concoct* a story—I can just go by what I saw with my own eyes. I don't see why you should be so defensive unless you *are* guilty." She held up the wine stopper she had found. "You dropped this, didn't you? It probably fell out of your pocket as you ran away... *after* you set the wasps on Rick Zova."

"*What?*" Healey exclaimed.

"It was the perfect murder: using the wasps to trigger his anaphylaxis and kill him, without you having to actually do the deed."

"That's... that's preposterous!" spluttered Healey. "You think I would have come up with a crazy idea like that?"

"Why not? It's not that crazy. As one of Zova's oldest friends, you'd know about his allergy, and you had a strong motive: you wanted revenge for what he did to you all those years ago. You said yourself that he deserved what he got and that you're glad he's dead!"

"Well, I... that was just... I was angry and I—"

"How did you do it? Did you sneak up behind Zova and shove him against the nest? Or did you stay a safe distance away and just throw a rock into the nest? And how did you steal the trowel from Joe?"

"I... I don't know what you're going on about," cried Healey. "I never went out to the garden that night. I was down in the wine cellar with David—"

"Aww, come on! That's a lie and you know it. I heard you and Nowak talking in your garden—yes, I admit it, I was eavesdropping—and I heard you talking about sticking to the fake alibi—"

"It wasn't fake! It was true! I *was* down in the wine cellar. Just ask David!" cried Healey.

"Why? I know he's lying to protect you—"

"What? Him protecting me? Bollocks! I'm the one who's lying for *him*!" snarled Healey.

Poppy faltered. "What do you mean?" she asked.

Geoff Healey gave her an impatient look. "David told the police that we were both down in the wine cellar but in actual fact, it was only me. We went down together but David left soon after."

"Where did he go?"

Healey shrugged. "Dunno. Out into the walled garden, I suppose. He went up the stairs."

"What stairs?"

"There's a second set of stairs in the cellar which lead up to a trapdoor that opens out into the walled garden. It's not normally used anymore, because everyone uses the stairs in the house now."

Poppy stared at him. "Are you telling me that Nowak went out into the garden via a secret route?"

Healey rolled his eyes and gave an exaggerated sigh. "It's not a 'secret route'. Most of the staff probably know about it. It's just not used very much anymore because they carry the wine down now using the stairs in the house."

"So why did Nowak use it?"

He shrugged again. "Dunno. He said he had to pop out to meet someone in the garden. I suppose it was quicker than going back up into the house and then out again."

It also meant that no one else saw him, Poppy thought. She shook her head with exasperation. "He was out in the garden at around the time that Rick Zova was attacked. Didn't you think that was relevant to the investigation? Why didn't you tell the police?"

Healey scowled. "Because they were already after me as a murder suspect! If I told them that I was alone in the wine cellar—without David there to corroborate the fact—then it basically meant that I had no alibi. So when David suggested that we lie and keep our stories the same, I went along with that." He raised his chin defiantly. "Besides, I knew David couldn't be the murderer, so it wasn't like I was withholding important information."

"How can you be so sure?" asked Poppy in frustration. "You don't know who he went to meet or what he was doing out in the garden."

"I don't need to—I know David! I've known him for nearly forty years now; the man's too soft. He was always making excuses for Rick, even back when we were lads," said Geoff Healey bitterly. "He was always telling me to forgive Rick, always trying to smooth things over after that selfish bastard made yet another big cock-up..." He paused, then added with a humourless laugh: "Besides, David wouldn't dare say boo to a goose without checking with his wife first." He shook his head. "You'd think someone who's head of a huge company, with all those billions, wouldn't be so terrified of the missus."

"You need to tell this to the police," Poppy insisted.

Geoff glared at her. "Don't try to boss me around, young lady. If you go to the police, I'll deny everything—and I'm sure David will back me up." He shoved the bottle of glue at her. "Now, if you don't mind, I'd like to get back to work."

CHAPTER TWENTY-THREE

Poppy found a handsome, ginger-haired male waiting for her by the front gate when she returned to Hollyhock Cottage.

"*N-ow? N-ow?*" said Oren hopefully.

Poppy chuckled. "No, you can't have your dinner now, Oren. It's barely midday!"

The cat gave her a disgruntled look and stalked ahead of her, up the path and to the front gate of the cottage. Once inside, he settled in his favourite spot—the only armchair in the sitting room—and began to sulkily wash his face. Poppy took off her coat and paused to examine the new pile of mail waiting for her on the coffee table. There were a few brochures and leaflets, and three more business envelopes. She opened the first of these absent-mindedly as she walked through to the kitchen. Then she stopped short, her heart lurching as she unfolded the single sheet of paper.

It was a water bill and Poppy's eyes widened at the amount. How could she have used so much water? Okay, it *had* been very hot over the summer months and she *had* watered the garden a fair bit, but surely it couldn't have been *that* much? With some trepidation, she opened the second envelope and her heart sank even further as she saw that it, too, was a bill—for council tax. This was something she hadn't even thought of, never having owned a house before. But now she stared at the piece of paper with "*South Oxfordshire District Council*" emblazoned across the top and the horribly huge number with the pound sign at the bottom.

Her stomach started feeling queasy. Where was she going to find the money? Poppy thought of the small amount that she had saved "for a rainy day"— which was now gone, blithely spent on an extravagant order of flower bulbs—and she felt even sicker. What was she going to do? She couldn't pay the water bill with freesia corms and tulip bulbs!

Before she could think further, Poppy heard a knock at the front door. Hastily, she put the bills down on the table and went back to the front of the cottage. She was surprised to find Nowak standing on the threshold.

"Miss Lancaster? I hope it's not a bad moment?"

"Uh... no, not at all," murmured Poppy. "Please come in."

She stepped back to let him in, then led him to the sitting room. "Um... would you like to sit down?"

"Thanks, that would be great." Nowak started to lower himself into the armchair, then bolted upright again as a loud yowl sounded beneath his bum.

"*N-O-O-O-OW!*"

"What the—" Nowak jerked around and stared at the enormous ginger tomcat glaring back at him from the depths of the armchair.

"Oh... sorry, that's Oren and he tends to think of that chair as his," said Poppy with an apologetic smile. "I can force him off if you'd really like to sit there, but if you don't mind sitting on the sofa instead...?"

"Oh, sure—no problem," said Nowak, giving Oren a wary look and moving hastily across the room. He sat down, carefully arranging his trousers and suit jacket, then regarded Poppy with a smile and said: "I was passing through the village and thought I'd pop in. This is a lovely little place."

Poppy laughed. "It hardly compares with Chatswood House, but thank you. It's very small and quite basic."

"Oh, on the contrary, I think it's charming. Very snug and cosy," said Nowak, looking around the room. "I remember coming in briefly when I came to see your grandmother before, but it seems a lot brighter and more spacious now. Have you done any redecorating?"

"No, not really. Just a few small changes here and

there, rearranged the furniture..."

"Well, I like what you've done, Miss Lancaster. And I have to say, much as I hate to admit it, I have to thank your cousin Hubert in a way, because if it wasn't for him, we would never have met. I do hope that you enjoyed the party, in spite of the sad circumstances?"

"Oh yes, just seeing the orangery was treat enough—it's absolutely gorgeous!" said Poppy with genuine enthusiasm. "I just wish I could be as successful with my gardenia as you are with yours," she added with a sigh. "I don't know what I'm doing wrong, but mine seems to be getting worse and worse. Almost all the flower buds have fallen off now and more and more leaves are turning yellow. Maybe it's just not warm enough in my greenhouse? It's not heated, like your orangery. I suppose that really limits what you can grow?"

"Oh, you might be surprised. When I had my first house, many years ago—it was much more modest than Chatswood House." Nowak gave a self-deprecating laugh. "And I had a small, unheated greenhouse then, but I still managed to grow and overwinter a lot of tender plants. As long as the greenhouse keeps plants frost free—which they usually do, even unheated—then that's the main thing. Also, keeping them dry," he added. "It's the damp that kills them, you know, because a wet plant is more likely to freeze than a dry one. That's the lethal combination. So as long as they get plenty of light, because natural light levels are a lot lower in winter, then many plants manage fine in an unheated greenhouse.

"As for your gardenia, I don't think it's anything specific that you've done wrong," Nowak continued kindly. "I think the cold nights we've been having might be the problem. A sudden drop in temperature could easily cause gardenias to drop their flower buds and the leaves to turn yellow too. If you're worried that the greenhouse isn't warm enough, you could always bring it into the house for the winter. A nice bright windowsill in the kitchen might be a good temporary home until the weather warms up in spring," he said with a smile.

Poppy stared at the amiable man in front of her and thought of what Geoff Healey had told her. If he could be believed, it meant that David Nowak had lied about his whereabouts on the night of the party and couldn't be trusted either. But... Poppy looked again at the billionaire businessman. Could Nowak really be the murderer? He certainly knew about Zova's fatal allergy, but what motive could he have? It seemed as ludicrous to suspect him as it was to suspect Joe. And yet it couldn't be denied that Nowak had been outside in the garden at around the time that Zova was murdered. If he was innocent, then what had he been doing out there and why hadn't he told the police about it?

"Miss Lancaster...?"

Poppy jumped. She realised belatedly that she

had been staring blindly at Nowak's face, without really seeing him or listening to what he had been saying.

She flushed. "Sorry... I didn't mean to be rude—"

"You looked like you were deep in thought. Is something bothering you?"

Poppy hesitated. A part of her just wanted to blurt out: *Why did you lie about your alibi at the party? What were you doing outside that night?* But it was one thing to confront the aggressive, dislikeable Geoff Healey and quite another to accuse the benevolent, courteous David Nowak of involvement in Rick Zova's murder.

She cleared her throat. "I... um... I was just wondering how things were going with the murder case. I suppose it must have been very hard, having the police crawling all over your property?"

Nowak gave a small sigh. "Oh, I'm keen to help the police in any way I can—anything to help find Rick's killer." He ran a hand over his face. "I still can't really believe he's dead, you know. He was always so... so much larger than life! D'you know what I mean?"

Poppy nodded sympathetically. "Yes, he seemed like quite a character. I suppose you remained close through the years?"

"Well... to be honest, not really. I hadn't seen much of Rick at all, actually, in the last ten years. He lived in the US and our lifestyles... well, our paths just didn't cross that much." Nowak gave a sad smile. "But he was still one of my oldest friends and... well, the friends you make in childhood or in youth are different to the ones in later life, aren't they?"

"I'm afraid I wouldn't know," said Poppy. "My mother and I moved around so much as I was growing up that I never really stayed in one place long enough to make proper friends."

"Oh. That must have been hard for you," said Nowak, looking at her with compassion.

Poppy gave an embarrassed shrug. "It wasn't always easy, but I suppose you get used to it." She gave him a bright smile. "It's good in a murder case, though, if the victim had long-time friends from childhood—they can give the police important background information, like whether the victim might have had any enemies." She looked at Nowak enquiringly. "Did he? Can you think of anyone who might have wanted to harm Rick Zova?"

"The police asked me that." Nowak rubbed his jaw. "And I hate to say it, but Rick probably *did* have some enemies. He could be quite outspoken and he was also..." He sighed. "Look, I loved him, in spite of his faults, but I wasn't blind to them. Rick was very good at 'looking out for number one', as they say. He was ruthless about taking care of his own interests and he wasn't shy about grabbing things with both hands—even if it meant hurting others in the process."

"Like his old friend Geoff?" said Poppy. "I know what really happened and why Geoff is so bitter. It had nothing to do with being left out of a rock band—

it was to do with Rick Zova stealing songs that Geoff had written."

Nowak looked uncomfortable. "Nothing was proven. It was really Geoff's word against Rick's and, in the end, the courts decided that there wasn't enough evidence to support the case."

"But it would certainly give Geoff motive, wouldn't it?" Poppy paused, then added casually: "And he doesn't have an alibi either."

"What do you mean? Of course he has an alibi," Nowak protested. "He was down in the wine cellar with me."

"No, he wasn't. Or, at least, he wasn't with you," said Poppy, looking Nowak straight in the eye. "I spoke to Geoff this afternoon and he admitted that you both lied to the police. You weren't in the cellar together. Oh, you certainly went down together, but Geoff told me that you left soon after. In fact..." Poppy paused, watching the man in front of her carefully. "In fact, he told me that you left via a second set of stairs, which lead out into the walled garden. You were outside, just at the time that Rick Zova was probably attacked and the wasps set on him."

Nowak stiffened. "I... I had a good reason for going outside. But it was nothing to do with Rick."

"Then why did you lie to the police?"

Nowak shifted uncomfortably. "I didn't do it to lie... I just... I didn't want it to come out that I—" He broke off.

"That you what?"

"That I was meeting someone, all right? But you have to believe me: it wasn't Rick."

"If it wasn't him, then why didn't you tell the police? Why couldn't they know?"

"It's not them!" Nowak burst out. "It's my wife."

Poppy frowned. "Your wife?"

Nowak sighed. "If I'd told the police where I was—who I was meeting—then my wife would have found out too."

Poppy stared at him. She thought of her meeting with Lena Nowak yesterday, of the woman's hostile attitude towards her husband's ex-PA... and then it hit her. She didn't know why she hadn't thought of it before.

"It was Dawn, wasn't it?" she asked softly. "You went out to meet her."

CHAPTER TWENTY-FOUR

Nowak looked for a moment as if he was going to deny it, then his shoulders slumped and he said with a defeated voice, "Yes. I went out to meet Dawn."

Poppy remembered how she had been chatting with Nowak at the party when his ex-PA had approached; Dawn had asked to speak to him and Nowak had tried to brush her off. In fact, now that Poppy thought about it, she recalled the businessman looking furtive and anxiously scanning the room as he tried to dismiss Dawn's request. They had still been arguing when Rick Zova's unexpected arrival had interrupted everything. She guessed that once calm and order had been restored, Dawn had repeated her request and Nowak had finally capitulated.

As if echoing her thoughts, Nowak said, "Dawn just wouldn't take no for an answer! She threatened to go and tell my wife everything if I didn't speak to her."

"You were having an affair?" asked Poppy delicately.

Nowak sighed and nodded. "For about six months. Lena never found out, although she did start commenting on how often she found Dawn in my study when she came home. I don't know if she was suspicious—she never accused me of anything—but she was always finding fault with Dawn and treating her quite rudely." Nowak took a deep breath, then let it out slowly: "In the end, she insisted that I dismiss Dawn. By then, I'd also realised that the affair was a mistake. I... I tried to break it to Dawn as gently as I could, but she didn't take it very well. We had a terrible row and she stormed off the day before the party. I didn't think I'd see her again—it was a bit of a shock seeing her turn up at the party like that."

"I'm surprised you agreed to meet her. Weren't you worried that your wife might see you?"

"Well, the grotto in the far corner of the walled garden is very private and it's out of sight of the house, which is why I suggested that we meet there. I told Dawn to go out first, via the side door, and then I would follow as soon as I could. There's a second set of stairs in the wine cellar, which lead up to a trapdoor that opens into the grotto—"

"Oh! That wooden platform thing beside the bench!" cried Poppy, remembering Einstein's interest in the ground there.

"Yes, that's right. I think in the old days, when the walled garden was used as a *potager*—that is, a kitchen garden, growing fruit and vegetables—it was useful having a trapdoor which led down directly into the cellar. Maybe it was easier to transport and store the jars of jellied fruits, pickles, home-made cordials, and wines that were made... Anyway, I suggested to Geoff that I'd show him a new bottle of vintage *Château Poujeaux*. Geoff's a bit of a wine buff, you see. It gave me the perfect excuse to leave the party with him and go down to the cellar. Then I left him searching for the bottle and went up the steps and out the trapdoor. Dawn was waiting to meet me in the grotto."

Poppy thought back to the night of the party and remembered that just before she and Nick had gone to the terrace to search for Rick Zova, she had bumped into Dawn, nearly knocking the other woman over. Dawn had been breathless, as if she had been running, and her hands, Poppy recalled, had been inexplicably cold. Well, if she had been outside with Nowak, that explained it.

"Did you and Dawn see Zova?" she asked.

"I saw him in the distance, through the bushes— he was standing under the big yew, smoking a cigar. I don't think Dawn saw him. She was facing me, in the opposite direction."

"And did you see anyone with Zova?"

Nowak hesitated. "Actually, I did... yes," he admitted. "I... I've been agonising over this. I know I should really tell the police, but to do that would also mean that I'd have to admit to being out in the garden, and then my wife would find out about—"

"Who did you see?" asked Poppy, ignoring his other words.

"That handyman chap that the police were questioning. Joe Something-or-other... Faber? Fabio?"

"Joe Fabbri?" Poppy recoiled. "No! You can't have seen him!"

Nowak looked at her in surprise. "Why not?"

"I...I mean, it can't have been him. He'd left your property already."

"I know what I saw. It was the same handyman I'd seen with Lena earlier—very tanned, grey ponytail, paint-splattered overalls—"

"No," said Poppy faintly. "No, it can't be him."

Nowak looked at her in puzzlement. "But why not? I thought the police have him down as a main suspect. His trowel was found under Rick's body, wasn't it?"

"Yes, but... it can't be Joe," Poppy insisted weakly. "He has no reason to kill Rick Zova. He has no motive—Joe didn't even know him!"

"Well, he certainly looked like he knew Zova when I saw them talking," said Nowak.

"What do you mean?"

"I was too far away to hear what they were saying but your handyman chap was shoving his face into Rick's very aggressively and waving a fist about... he looked as if he was ready to kill Rick."

"No... it can't have been him..." Poppy repeated in a weak voice. Then she realised how strangely Nowak was looking at her and made an attempt to pull herself together. "Maybe... maybe Joe had forgotten something... like his trowel or... or gloves or something. I mean, maybe he dropped his trowel in the garden when he was working earlier and he went back to look for it." Even as she said it, Poppy knew that it sounded lame. If Joe had simply gone back to pick up a tool he had dropped, why would he have been behaving aggressively towards Rick Zova?

Nowak had been looking at Poppy speculatively and now he said: "Listen... if you're so sure that this Joe is unlikely to be involved in Rick's murder, then surely there's no need for the police to know about my meeting with Dawn?" He cleared his throat, then added, not meeting her eyes: "If we keep this between us, the police will just accept my current alibi."

Poppy stared at him, not knowing how to answer. She felt horribly torn. She knew that the right thing to do was to pick up the phone to Suzanne right now and tell her that Nowak had lied about his alibi and needed to be questioned again. But if she did that, there was no way to stop the police from finding out about Joe. Not only had he been in the estate grounds during the time he said that he'd left, but he had even been observed acting aggressively to the murder victim! Added to all the other things already against him, the police were sure to arrest the old handyman.

What should I do? thought Poppy, her thoughts in turmoil.

"Why don't we leave it until tomorrow?" Nowak suggested gently. "We don't have to rush to make a decision now—we can sleep on it and see."

"Yes," said Poppy quickly, grateful for the temporary respite. "Yes, let's not rush into anything." She looked around, keen to change the subject, and spotted the catalogues on the coffee table. "I've... er... I've been looking at some bulb catalogues."

"Ah, it's that time of year, isn't it?" said Nowak, his face lighting up. "I have to say, I love the process of putting bulbs in the ground and then in the spring, when you see all the tulips and daffodils coming up, it's just such a lovely feeling! Of course, I could get my estate gardeners to plant them, but I love doing it myself if I can." He gave a rueful smile. "I don't always get the time, what with the company commitments and all, but when I can, there's nothing I like better than spending a day in the garden, mucking around in the dirt."

"Yes, your wife was telling me that when I was over at Chatswood House yesterday—"

"Oh, I didn't realise you'd visited?" Nowak looked at her curiously.

"It wasn't really a social visit. I gave my neighbour Bertie—Dr Bertram Noble—a lift over there. Dr Noble is an inventor, you see, and your wife was interested in investing in some of his designs, so Dr Noble took

227

his latest invention over to show her. Cleaning robots for Róża Garden Centres," Poppy explained, seeing Nowak's look of puzzlement.

"Ah, yes, Lena is in charge of new product development. Cleaning robots, you say? You mean like a robot vacuum cleaner?"

"Oh, CLARA is much more advanced than that," said Poppy with a laugh. "She's like a superpowered cleaning machine!"

Nowak still looked sceptical. "Really? Well, I suppose Lena will tell me all about it when I get home later. I had business meetings in London all day yesterday and stayed overnight in the capital, so I haven't been back home yet. I was actually on my way home but thought I'd pop in here first. To be honest with you, I was curious to see your cottage garden again. I remember it being spectacular when I came to see your grandmother a few years ago."

Poppy flushed. "Oh... well, it's not looking so good now, I'm afraid—"

Nowak waved a hand. "Oh, that's only to be expected. We're heading into winter now and if there's one downside to cottage gardens, it's that they're very much focused on colour and flowers, which means that they look spectacular in the spring and summer but can often look a bit bare and bleak in winter. But you can fix that with a few good evergreen perennials and shrubs for structure... Listen, I'll tell you what: my head gardener will be doing some autumn cuttings soon. If you like, I can ask him to set some aside for you?"

"Oh... thank you! That's really kind," said Poppy, surprised and delighted. "Actually, if he doesn't mind, do you think I could spend some time with him, watching how he does it? I'd love to learn how to take cuttings properly. I'm still a beginner, really, when it comes to gardening, and there's so much I don't know."

Nowak looked at her quizzically. "But... I thought you said you've taken over your grandmother's garden nursery?"

Poppy ducked her head, giving an embarrassed laugh. "Yes, I know... I suppose it was a bit ambitious, given my lack of experience."

"Well, I could help you with that," said Nowak quickly. "If Hollyhock Cottage and Gardens was under the Róża Garden Centres umbrella, you would have access to our team of experienced horticulturalists, botanists, garden designers, and growers, and you'd also get support on a range of business aspects, from marketing to bookkeeping to occupational health and safety... And plus, of course, as a salaried employee of one of the largest corporations in the United Kingdom, you'd be assured of regular income and job security." He looked at her earnestly. "I really hope you will consider my offer seriously, Miss Lancaster. I'm sure you'd like to see your grandmother's nursery thrive, and a buyout would be a fantastic way to ensure that, as well as giving you stable, regular income and the chance for professional development."

Poppy swallowed. It would be so easy to say "yes". It would be the answer to all her worries. She thought of the unpaid bills waiting on the coffee table, of the uncertainty of the long winter months ahead with possibly no income... and even once spring arrived, how could she be sure that she'd be able to grow and nurture enough plants to a good enough standard to sell? How could she be sure that she'd be able to maintain enough customer business to bring in a steady income?

She opened her mouth but before she could say anything, the front door of the cottage burst open and Bertie rushed into the room. He was followed by Einstein. As soon as the terrier saw Oren, he went into full combat mode: his hackles rose, his eyes bulged, and he rushed at the armchair, barking at the top of his voice. Oren exploded into a ball of orange fur twice his normal size, his ears flattened and his eyes narrowed to slits. He hissed and spat at Einstein, then leapt out of the armchair and onto the sofa, landing in Nowak's startled lap.

"*Oren!*"

"Einstein, no! Bad dog!"

"Aaaahhh!"

"Oh, God, I'm so sorry, Mr Nowak—"

"Einstein! Down, boy!"

"*N-O-O-O-O-W-W-W-W-W!*"

The sitting room turned into a bedlam of yelling humans, barking dog, and hissing, spitting cat. At last, Bertie managed to get hold of Einstein's collar and drag the little terrier aside, whilst Poppy unhooked Oren's claws from Nowak's suit and picked up the tomcat in her arms. He yowled in protest and started fighting to be free, raking his claws across her hands.

"*Ow!* Stop it, Oren... *OUCH!*" Poppy gasped, struggling to hold on to him.

She rushed to the front door and flung it open, then set the hissing tomcat on the front porch. He shook himself and gave her a reproachful look before stalking off into the garden. Poppy went back in, closing the front door behind her and leaning against it for a moment. She looked ruefully down at her hands. In addition to the wasp sting, she now had several bloody scratches across her skin. She winced and returned to the sitting room, to find that Bertie had managed to calm Einstein down and was apologising to David Nowak.

"Oh dear, I *am* sorry about that," he was saying as Poppy rejoined them. "I didn't realise the cat would be in here... I was just so excited to share my discovery! I have been conducting ongoing research into the flammability of various materials, you see; in particular, different kinds of paper—there can be such variation! Old-fashioned newsprint burns marvellously, of course—it's made primarily of groundwood pulp with very little fillers—but many of the modern papers perform very poorly. The kind used by tabloid newspapers, for example, has a coating applied to the groundwood to make it smoother, and that coating is mostly clay, which doesn't burn at all. The worst is magazine paper, of course—the glossy, coloured kind—which is full of fillers and coated to make it opaque and shiny. It simply chars without burning at all!"

"Er... right," said Nowak, his eyes glazing over. "How... er... how fascinating."

"Oh, it is! And it is marvellous that in the course of her cleaning, CLARA will be able to collect real-life samples to analyse," said Bertie excitedly. "After all, she can be programmed to target specific types of particles or materials, as well as record the relative mass and density, so in this case, she could collect samples of burnt paper for me to analyse and—"

"Uh... yes, that's great, Bertie," Poppy interrupted, coming to the businessman's rescue. "I don't think Mr Nowak needs to know all the details."

"Yes, I really should be going anyway," said Nowak hastily, springing to his feet and edging away from Bertie.

"Oh, but wouldn't you like to see CLARA?" asked the old inventor, looking disappointed. "I can bring her over and give you a demonstration—"

"No, no, that's quite all right," said Nowak with a look of alarm. "I... um... I will ask my wife to tell me all about your robot. Now, if you'll excuse me..."

With a hasty nod of goodbye, the businessman bolted for the front door.

Poppy hurried to see him out. "I'm sorry about

Bertie—I mean, Dr Noble. I know he's a bit eccentric but he's really very—"

"Oh, that's all right. I really should be getting home anyway," said Nowak, giving her a smile. Then he paused on the threshold, his expression turning serious. "I meant what I said, Miss Lancaster. I hope you will consider my offer. It would give me the greatest pleasure to welcome you into the Róża Garden Centres family."

CHAPTER TWENTY-FIVE

Poppy had a difficult time going to sleep that night. It had been a day full of unpleasant surprises and revelations, from the confrontation with Geoff Healey to the shock of his false alibi and Nowak's deceit in order to cover up his affair with Dawn. But perhaps the most disturbing thing of all was Nowak's account of seeing Joe Fabbri with Rick Zova. Poppy was still convinced that there had to have been a mistake or a misunderstanding somewhere. She simply couldn't believe that Joe could be involved in the murder.

But it wasn't just the mystery of the rock star's death that occupied her mind. Nowak's offer to buy out Hollyhock Cottage and Gardens kept intruding on her thoughts as well. It would be the simplest solution, the easiest way out of all her troubles. She wouldn't have to "go it alone" anymore, feeling anxious and out of her depth. She wouldn't have to figure out alternative ways of earning an income over the next few months. She wouldn't have to worry about sudden bills or that looming credit card debt.

But... Poppy couldn't shake off the sickening feeling that she was "selling out". She would be giving up everything she had dreamt of building; she would be handing over her family's legacy and watching a giant, faceless corporation swallow it. She would have no say if they decided to change Hollyhock Cottage and the gardens entirely—perhaps raze it to the ground and rebuild a modern garden centre in its place...

Her agonised thoughts meant that Poppy tossed and turned for a long time after she switched off the lights. It didn't help that a storm seemed to be building, with the wind whistling outside the windows and rain pattering on the roof. After a week of relatively mild weather, it seemed that the autumn gales were finally starting. Poppy pulled the blankets up to her ears and turned over, burrowing her face deeper into the pillow and trying to blank out both the sounds outside and the thoughts in her head.

"*N-owww?*" came a sleepy voice.

Poppy glanced down at the foot of her bed, where Oren was stretched out luxuriously in a nest of blankets. The orange tomcat had turned up on the cottage doorstep just before bedtime and she had let him in, feeling doubly guilty for throwing him out earlier after the Nowak/Bertie/Einstein fiasco, and also for not being able to give him his favourite tuna fish dinner. So when he had followed her into her bedroom and made himself comfortable on her bed, she hadn't had the heart to say anything. In any case, she had never had the experience of sleeping with a warm, furry body in the bed before and she'd found it lovely and cosy, listening to Oren's rhythmic purring in the background.

Poppy lay back and stared at the ceiling for another few minutes, then finally gave up. Sighing, she sat up in bed. *Maybe if I read something for a bit?* She switched on her bedside lamp and looked without much enthusiasm at *Love's Hidden Fire*, the romance novel that Nell had insisted she should read. Her hand reached over to pick it up, then paused and hovered instead over a slim notebook lying next to the novel on her bedside table.

It was her mother's teenage journal, which she'd recently found in a keepsake box hidden away in a hole in the stone wall surrounding the cottage garden. Poppy had been so excited with the discovery at first—she had been sure that she would find clues to the mystery of her parentage in her mother's jottings. But unfortunately, the young Holly Lancaster hadn't kept a diary like most people. Instead of a litany of daily activities, she had simply used her journal as a place to record random thoughts and feelings, amateur attempts at poetry, and pretty sketches of the flowers in the cottage garden. There was no logical sequence to the entries either—the entries at the back of the notebook were not necessarily written later than the ones at the front. And there were no clear references to specific dates or places, or any mentions by name of a man who might have fathered her child.

Poppy had tried several times to decipher her mother's notes, but usually ended up flinging the journal aside in frustration. Now, though, she picked it up once more and flipped to a random page in the middle. From the sections that she had read so far, she *had* noticed several instances of someone mentioned as "He" or "Him"—often with a capital "H"—and she was sure that this man was important, someone that Holly Lancaster had marked as special. Could he be her father?

Poppy squinted in the weak light cast by the bedside lamp and tried to read the squiggly writing at the top of the page:

Natalie keeps saying He just wants a quick shag, but I don't believe her. I told her to take a chill pill and she was really narked. She doesn't know that I'm seeing Him again tonight. I'm going to find out His birthday—I think He's a Taurus! The summer horoscope guide in Bliss *said Cancer, Scorpio, and Pisces are the best signs for a love match with Taurus.*

Poppy skimmed past a few more pages and came across another reference:

I tried that new hair mascara. Looks really fab. Sharon said I reminded her of Cameron Diaz, but I think she was just saying that. I hope He noticed. I saw Him looking at me twice today.

Poppy smiled to herself. It was strange reading these little titbits, like going back in time and catching glimpses of the girl that her mother had been. She flicked though the pages again, then paused to read a small entry at the bottom of a page filled with flower doodles:

Guess what? He showed me His new tattoo today. It's totally wicked! I thought it was a big black feather at first, but He told me it's actually a leaf from a fern. It's called a ponga, *He said. That's Maori for 'silver fern'. It was really embarrassing though—I reached out to touch it without thinking and then I realised it looked like I was feeling His bicep! Natalie says boys are always gagging for it, but I think He's different. He's so amazing. If He asked me... I'd say yes.*

Poppy stared down at the girlish handwriting, her thoughts whirling. In her mind's eye, she suddenly saw Rick Zova's body again, lying slumped under the yew tree, on the night she had found him. She vividly remembered the way the lights from the orangery had played across his body, highlighting the tattoos on his bare arms—in particular, a tattoo of a large black feather encircling his bicep.

She stared down at her mother's journal again, her eyes focusing on the words: "...*I thought it was a big black feather at first... actually a leaf from a fern... I reached out to touch it... looked like I was feeling his bicep...*"

Poppy sucked her breath in sharply.

What if the tattoo she had seen on Rick Zova's upper arm hadn't been a feather? What if it had been a leaf from a silver fern, a leaf renowned for looking like a feather?

Poppy could feel her heart pounding uncomfortably as the startling new possibility hit her: had Rick Zova's relationship with her mother been more intimate than he'd let on? Was he the special man mentioned in Holly Lancaster's old journal? Could the murdered rock star have been her father?

CHAPTER TWENTY-SIX

After that bombshell, Poppy gave up any more attempt to read and instead switched off her bedside lamp and tried to go to sleep. But she tossed and turned for another hour, her thoughts in turmoil. She should have been happy that she might have found her father at last, that her long search could be coming to an end... but instead, all she could feel was dismay at the thought that Rick Zova could be her father.

It was true that when she had first met the ageing rock star, she'd had a moment of excitement wondering if he could be "the one". But that hope had quickly died when she'd found no sign of any resemblance between them, and even more when she had been taken aback by his callous, dismissive attitude towards the groupies who had worshipped him. Then as the murder investigation had progressed and she'd found out more about Zova, she had been even more repulsed by the real man beneath that charming rock-star exterior. Now, the thought that he could be her father filled her with confusion and unease.

Poppy hadn't expected to be able to sleep for the rest of the night, but she drifted off eventually. She was woken by a loud *BANG* and jerked upright in bed, blinking in bewilderment. Oren had started up from his nest at the bottom of the bed too and was now standing stiffly, his yellow eyes wide and his fur on end.

Poppy gazed at the windows. From the weak grey light seeping in through the curtains, it looked like it was barely dawn. There was a shrieking sound outside—which she realised was the wind—and she could also hear rain pounding against the windows. She got out of bed, dragging on her old dressing gown against the chill, and hurried to the window. Pulling back the curtain, she gasped as she looked out. The world outside had been turned into a deluge of grey, with rain pouring down in sheets, and shrubs and tree branches swaying wildly in the wind. Another loud *bang* sounded above her head and Poppy looked up worriedly. It sounded like it had come from the roof. She hoped that nothing had come loose. She had been meaning to ask Joe to climb up and check the roof for broken tiles and anything else that might need repairing, but she hadn't got around to it yet and now she berated herself for being slack.

There was another *bang* and a loud, creaking, wailing sound—followed by a *CRASH* that shook the entire cottage. Poppy flinched as a framed photo of her mother toppled off her bedside table and crashed to the floor.

"Poppy? Poppy! Are you all right?" came Nell's worried voice.

"Yes, I'm fine!" Poppy called, hurrying out of her bedroom and down the small hallway. "Are *you* okay?"

"Oh my lordy Lord—what was that crash?" said Nell, bustling out of her room just as Poppy reached it. Nell's grey hair was in curlers and she was hastily tying the belt of her dressing gown around her waist, but her eyes were bright and alert. "It sounded like it came from the back of the cottage."

Tentatively, Poppy made her way to the kitchen at the rear of the house. Several items had fallen off the counters and some of the kitchen cupboards had shaken open in the impact, but nothing major was broken. Then she remembered the greenhouse.

"No..." breathed Poppy, her heart beginning to beat unsteadily.

She hurried to the rear door which led from the kitchen into the greenhouse attachment built onto the back of the cottage. Her heart lurched as she opened the door to be met by a gust of wind and rain. She stared in horror. Where the high glass ceilings and open space of the greenhouse had once stood, there was now a huge tangle of broken branches, shattered glass, and cracked wood. The beech tree which had been growing on one side of the greenhouse had fallen over, onto the glass roof, and crushed everything beneath it.

"NOOO!" cried Poppy. She staggered forwards, unable to believe what she was seeing.

Her precious seedlings and recently purchased young plant stock, all carefully laid out in trays along the long workbench, had been crushed; the glass roof was smashed, and many of the side windows were too; shattered terracotta pots lay in broken pieces everywhere; even the wooden frame of the greenhouse had cracked and lay in splintered sections amongst the tangle of tree branches. The greenhouse had been completely demolished and with it, all her seedlings, her equipment, her stock, and her hopes for the nursery.

Then she remembered the gardenia. She had meant to bring it into the kitchen last night, following David Nowak's advice, but had been so tired and distracted that she had forgotten. Now she gazed in horror at the corner where the pot had been placed. The glass panes there had completely caved in under the weight of the fallen tree and there was nothing to see except a mound of broken branches and fallen leaves. If the gardenia was underneath that, it was surely crushed. Poppy put a hand to her mouth, fighting back tears as she stared at the mess.

"*Poppy!*"

Nell appeared suddenly in the doorway behind her, staring in horror at the destruction in front of them. Then the older woman reached out and grabbed Poppy, hauling her back into the kitchen and slamming the door shut behind them.

"Poppy, dear—you're soaked!" she cried, hurrying to grab a towel and wrap it around the girl's shoulders.

Poppy clutched the towel gratefully. She hadn't realised until now that her face was wet with rain, her hair windblown and tangled, and her pyjamas drenched and clinging to her body. She shivered, pulling the towel tighter around herself, and did not resist when Nell pushed her down into one of the kitchen chairs. She watched numbly as her friend hurried to light a fire at the stove and get a kettle boiling. A few minutes later, she obediently took the cup of tea that Nell handed to her and clasped her hands around its warmth, trying to stop her teeth from chattering.

"Maybe you're getting hypothermia," said Nell, looking at her worriedly. "Maybe I should run you a hot bath? You should go straight back to bed, except that you need to get out of those wet clothes and dry your hair—"

"I-I-I'm f-fine, Nell... honestly," said Poppy. "It's... I'm n-not cold... it's th-the adrenaline... it's j-just the reaction s-setting in." She took a few gulps of the hot, sweet tea, letting the liquid flow down her throat and into her stomach, warming her. Then she looked at her friend with despairing eyes. "Nell, th-the greenhouse—did you see? The beech has fallen on it... It's completely d-destroyed!"

"Yes, I saw," said Nell with a sigh.

"I've lost everything! All m-my seedlings, all the plug plants I bought, my supply of pots... And... and m-my gardenia..." Poppy's voice wobbled. "Everything's destroyed! What am I g-going to do? How am I going to grow anything over w-winter to be ready to sell in s-spring?"

"You can replace them," said Nell soothingly. "You can plant new seeds and buy more plug plants—"

"But that needs more money! And where am I g-going to put them now that the greenhouse is destroyed? It will need a lot of repairs... Oh, Nell... where am I going to find the money?"

"Didn't you say that you'd put some aside 'for a rainy day'? Well, this is as rainy as you're going to get!" said Nell, with a weak attempt at lightening the mood.

Poppy shrank into herself. She looked down, unable to meet her friend's eyes. "I... I did have some money but... I spent it," she mumbled. "A couple of days ago, I put in a big order of bulbs and—" She broke off, flushing with guilt and misery.

Nell was silent for a moment, then she patted Poppy's shoulder and said: "Well, that's a shame... Don't worry. I expect we'll find a way."

Somehow, the fact that Nell hadn't scolded her made her feel even worse. Poppy wanted to kick herself for her own carelessness and extravagance. Seeing her face, Nell added:

"Anyway, I doubt if the amount you had saved would have made much of a dent if the greenhouse needs serious repairs so... don't feel bad, Poppy. What's done is done. We all make mistakes. As long as you remember for the future... Come on, the important thing now is to get you warm and dry. You can't do anything if you catch pneumonia," she said briskly.

Poppy submitted to Nell's ministrations, quietly changing into dry clothes and towelling her hair. Then she sat in the kitchen with her old friend, wrapped up in a blanket and listening miserably to the rain hammer against the roof and the wind howling outside.

At long last, the storm began to lessen. Poppy ran to the front of the cottage and looked hopefully out of the window. The rain was slowing and the wind dying down. The garden was a quagmire of boggy mud and sodden plants, snapped stems and flattened leaves, but at least no other trees had come down. Throwing on a raincoat, she opened the front door and stepped out. Carefully, she took the path which curved around the cottage, leading from the front garden to the larger garden at the back of the property.

When she rounded the corner and saw the rear of the cottage—with the tree uprooted and the mountain of shattered glass, cracked wood, and wrecked supplies and equipment where the greenhouse had once stood—Poppy stopped in horror. From this angle, the damage was even worse than she had imagined. It wasn't just a few repairs; the greenhouse needed to be completely rebuilt! It would cost hundreds, thousands, much more than she could ever afford...

Despair overwhelmed her. *What am I going to do? What am I going to do?*

Poppy bit down hard on her lip as hot tears came to her eyes. A part of her wanted to just sit down on the ground and bawl her eyes out, but she fought the urge. Instead, she took several deep, shuddering breaths. She blinked rapidly, forcing the tears back. *No. No, I'm not going to cry. I'm not going to let this beat me.*

"Poppy?"

Nell came down the path and paused beside her, her eyes widening as she surveyed the damage.

"Oh my lordy Lord..." she said faintly. "You need to call the emergency services, Poppy. Call the fire brigade. We need help lifting that tree off and clearing all the debris."

"Okay, I'll go and do that now. Maybe... maybe it won't be as bad as we think once they clear things away a bit," Poppy said with forced cheerfulness.

She started to turn away, then froze and whirled back. Something in the debris had caught her eye. Ignoring Nell's calls to be careful, she picked her way over fallen tree branches and shards of broken glass to a small pile of rubble which had once been the front corner of the greenhouse. Her heart skipped a beat as she bent down and lifted a broken branch. She had been right: the glimpse of blue porcelain that had caught her eye was the pot which held her gardenia. She could see it now, lying on its side, but amazingly it was still in one piece and, what's more, the gardenia was still intact! Some of the soil in the pot had fallen out, exposing some of the plant's roots, and several leaves had been torn off, but other than that, it seemed to be undamaged.

Poppy stretched a hand in between the debris and attempted to grab hold of the porcelain pot and pull it out. But it wouldn't budge.

"Poppy!" came Nell's voice. "What are you doing? Be careful—you don't know how stable everything is. You might get hurt!"

Poppy turned a shining face to her old friend. "Nell! My gardenia—it's here! I don't know how, but it hasn't been crushed. I just need to pull it out. It's wedged tight—"

"You're not doing anything else, young lady," said Nell firmly. "If you want to get that pot out, you need to call Joe and get him to help you."

"Oh, yes! Yes! Joe—I must call Joe!" cried Poppy, retreating and backing away from the mound of rubble. She picked her way back to where Nell was standing. "I'll call him as soon as I've called the fire brigade."

Ten minutes later, Poppy set off across the village. She had tried calling Joe several times, but the old handyman hadn't answered. She knew, though, that he often didn't have his mobile with him, or had it muted to "silent" when he was outside working. She was relieved to see Joe's pick-up truck parked outside his small cottage situated on the outskirts of the village, and even more delighted to find the old handyman out in his garden.

"Joe!" she cried. "Oh, Joe—I'm so glad to see you're here!"

He looked up in surprise as she rushed up to him and began telling him what had happened.

"Can you come now? Please?" Poppy asked breathlessly as she finished. "The fire brigade is on the way. They said the emergency services were inundated with calls this morning... everyone's had storm damage... They're coming as soon as they can, but it's going to be a long wait. Nell's waiting for them but I thought we could try to get the gardenia out first... I tried your phone first but there was no answer—you can help, can't you? You have a saw, don't you? And what about tree loppers? And also maybe some rope to tie around things! Maybe we can—"

"Calm water."

"I—*what*?" Poppy stopped and stared at Joe quizzically.

"Calm water," he said again. "All ships go well in calm water."

She digested his words. "Oh..." She gave him a shamefaced smile, then took a deep breath and said in a calmer voice: "Yes, yes you're right."

Joe indicated the shed behind her. "Rope."

Poppy hurried to do as directed and emerged from the shed a few moments later carrying several coils of rope. Joe was already waiting for her, carrying a toolbox, a large crowbar and electric saw, a safety helmet, and a bundle of canvas fabric. He loaded these into the bed of his pick-up truck, where a ladder was already waiting, and held out a hand for the rope. Poppy handed the coils to him and felt a surge of gratitude. Somehow, his calm, matter-of-fact manner was more effective than all the soothing words in the world, and for the first time since waking up that morning, she felt hopeful and encouraged.

Things are going to be all right. Joe's here. I'm not alone, she thought.

She smiled at him as he held open the front passenger door of the pick-up truck, but before she could climb in, a car roared up behind them. She turned in surprise as doors slammed and a grim-faced police constable marched forwards, followed by Sergeant Lee.

"Joe Fabbri?"

The detective sergeant stopped in front of the old handyman and put a restraining hand on his arm as he said:

"I'm arresting you for the murder of Rick Zova. You do not have to say anything. But it may harm your defence if you do not mention when questioned something which you later rely on in court. Anything you do say may be given in evidence."

Lee gave Joe's arm a sharp tug. "Come with me."

CHAPTER TWENTY-SEVEN

"Wait! Sergeant Lee—wait!" cried Poppy, running to the police car, where they were already putting Joe into the back seat.

The detective sergeant shut the car door and turned around with an exaggerated sigh. "Yes?"

"You can't arrest Joe! I mean—" Poppy checked herself as she saw Lee's face harden. "Of course, you *can*, but you'd be making a terrible mistake. Joe didn't kill Rick Zova. I know there's some circumstantial evidence against him, but the fact is, he had no motive!"

"Ah, that's what you think," said Lee, looking smug. "But in fact, he had the perfect reason to want to kill Zova."

"What do you mean?"

Lee glanced through the car window at Joe, sitting

impassively in the rear passenger seat, then turned back to Poppy and said: "He wanted revenge."

Poppy looked at him disbelievingly. "Revenge? Revenge for what?"

"Yes, revenge—one of the oldest motives in the book. Joe Fabbri killed Zova to get vengeance for his niece."

"His niece?" Poppy frowned. Then she suddenly recalled Nell telling her about Joe's niece, "Abby", who had been injured in a terrible hit-and-run accident.

As if echoing her thoughts, Lee leaned forwards and said with a superior smile, "Yes, Fabbri's niece, Abby Colman, who was hit by a motorbike when she was a teenager fifteen years ago. It was a hit-and-run, and we never caught the biker—"

"Why not?"

Lee scowled. "There weren't enough leads, okay? There were no witnesses other than Abby herself, and she was in a coma for days. By the time she came around and the police could question her, the trail had gone cold. Anyway, she couldn't remember much about it—not even the number plate on the bike, just some vague descriptions about what the bike looked like... it was pretty useless. So the rider was never caught. But meanwhile, Miss Colman ended up in hospital for several months and was left with permanent leg and hip damage. She had been enrolled at the Royal Academy of Dance—she had dreams of a career in ballet—but she had to give all that up."

"What does all this have to do with Joe and Rick Zova?" asked Poppy nervously.

Lee raised his eyebrows. "Isn't it obvious? Fine, I'll spell it out. We've been asking around and it seems that Fabbri is very close to his niece. Sees her almost like a daughter—very protective of her. And he's been very angry and bitter that the biker was never caught. In fact, I remember speaking to him about it myself a couple of years ago. He kept turning up at the station, saying he had new information about the bike that hit his niece. He kept hassling us to trace it."

"Did you? Did you find out who owned the bike?"

"Are you serious? The accident was fifteen years ago! Whatever little extra detail that Abby remembered about the bike was hardly worth much. Besides, I had other cases—homicide, robbery, assault. I didn't have time to start digging up an ancient hit-and-run!" Lee said impatiently.

Then he gave a self-satisfied smile. "However... when this murder happened and Fabbri was brought in for questioning, I suddenly remembered his visits and I went back to his statement. I followed up on the additional information he gave us at the time— he says Abby remembered seeing a fancy cover on the bike's exhaust pipe: a metal shield engraved with Zs—and I checked it against Zova's Harley Davidson... *Bingo!*" Lee looked at her triumphantly. "Zova's bike has a custom heat shield exactly like that."

"I still don't see how that shows Joe is guilty," argued Poppy.

"Aww, come on! I would have thought it would be obvious, especially to a little wannabe detective like you."

Poppy flushed angrily. "So you're saying Abby's hit-and-run driver—I mean, biker—could have been Rick Zova. So what? That doesn't prove that Joe killed him!"

"No, but it gives him the perfect motive," said Lee. "Here's what happened: Fabbri goes over to Chatswood House for some repairs, right? And as he's preparing to leave, he sees a biker arrive. Rick Zova came late and gatecrashed the party, didn't he? So Zova goes in and leaves his Harley-Davidson parked outside. Fabbri sees it, notices the custom heat shield, and remembers what his niece told him. He realizes that he's found the man responsible for destroying his niece's life, so he storms back into the grounds and finds Zova out in the garden, smoking a cigar. Fabbri confronts him, maybe assaults him, then he chucks a stone or something into the wasp nest and scarpers." Lee leaned back and crossed his arms, a smug smile on his face. "Case solved."

Poppy wanted to protest, to argue, to say something, anything, but her tongue felt stuck in its place. She didn't want to admit it, but a part of her knew that Lee might have been right, that it really could have happened like that. She glanced sideways through the car window into the rear passenger seat, where Joe was still sitting, staring stoically ahead. The thought that she could be wrong about him, that he could have been the killer, was like a huge, suffocating weight pressing down on her chest.

Silently, Poppy stood back and watched as the police car drove away. Then she walked slowly back to Hollyhock Cottage, feeling numb with shock. She arrived to find that the fire brigade and other emergency council services were already there; they were in the process of cleaning up the damage.

"Poppy! You were gone so long, I was beginning to get worried," said Nell. She smiled and lifted something from the ground beside her. "Look! It's your gardenia. I asked one of the firemen to help get it out first. It's a miracle how it hasn't been damaged."

Poppy stared wordlessly at her friend. Her shock at Joe's arrest robbed her of any joy at seeing the gardenia rescued and she could barely dredge up a smile as Nell handed her the potted plant.

Nell looked at her in concern. "What's wrong, dear?"

"Joe's been arrested," said Poppy.

Nell's mouth dropped open. "What?"

"The police came for him while I was there. They've arrested him for Rick Zova's murder."

"But… but it must be some kind of mistake!" Nell cried. "Joe can't be the murderer. The police must have got things wrong! Poppy, you have to call your friend, that nice lady detective inspector... Yes, you must speak to her and explain that there's been a mistake—"

"Nell, what if... what if there *hasn't* been a mistake?" said Poppy, looking at her friend with haunted eyes.

Nell faltered to a stop. "What do you mean? Of course there's been a mistake! Joe isn't a murderer!"

"But Nell, the evidence—"

"I don't care what they say about him! I don't care what evidence they dig up! It's just not true." She glared at Poppy. "Surely you don't believe it?"

"I... I don't know what to believe," said Poppy, dropping her gaze. "I mean, it's true that we've only known Joe a short time and there's a lot we don't know about him—his personal life, his background, his family..."

"We don't need to know all that to know what kind of man he is," said Nell firmly. "A tree is known by its fruit; a man by his deeds."

Poppy looked at her friend quizzically. "Who said that?"

"Saint Basil." Nell waved a hand. "It's not important who said it—the point is, we've known Joe long enough to know how he acts, what he does... and we know he is a good man. A kind man. A man who would never kill someone else."

Poppy sighed. She wished she had Nell's blind conviction. She wanted desperately to believe that Joe was innocent, but she also couldn't deny the weight of evidence that was piling up against him. She had been hanging on to the fact that he had no motive for the murder… but if what Sergeant Lee said was true, then her last hope there was gone. There was no one else she could pin the crime on instead. Neither Healey nor Nowak were likely suspects now, and there was no one else except…

Poppy gasped. She'd forgotten all about Bunny! Surely a crazy stalker fan was as strong a suspect as Joe? Especially if she'd gone on the run. She couldn't let Sergeant Lee arrest Joe when there was still a chance that Bunny could be the killer.

"I'm going to call Suzanne," she said to Nell, hurrying back into the cottage.

She got through after three attempts and launched straight into a passionate appeal for Joe's innocence:

"…must be some kind of mistake! I mean, that was just Sergeant Lee's theory but he could be wrong! He's just imagining what *could* have happened, but that doesn't mean that it really did happen like that! Maybe Joe never saw Zova's bike or maybe—"

"Poppy… *Poppy!*" Suzanne cut her off. "Joe has confessed—"

"*To the murder?*"

"No, not to the murder. But he admits that he did see Zova's motorcycle and noticed the engraved heat shield, and yes, he did go back to look for Zova, just as Lee suspected. Joe found Zova in the walled garden and confronted him about the hit-and-run."

"And did he assault Zova?" whispered Poppy.

"No, Joe admits that things got a bit heated but he says he never laid a finger on Zova. He says he simply said his piece and left. I suppose he must have dropped his trowel without realising during the confrontation." Suzanne's voice hardened. "But just because he didn't admit to killing Zova doesn't mean that he didn't do it. It's quite common for criminals to confess to a lesser crime, in the hopes that they will get a more lenient sentence. Nobody wants to be charged with murder."

"Joe isn't a criminal!"

"That's up to the courts to decide."

"What about the other suspects?" asked Poppy desperately. "What about Bunny?"

"Well, Healey and Nowak have an alibi, and so does Bunny."

"Wait, we don't know that! Until you question her—"

"We have. We found her. Sergeant Lee tracked her down to another country pub, The Red Lion—just outside Bunnington actually—and he questioned her. She says she left the party straight after she spoke to you. She got a minicab and went back to her room."

"But how do you know that's true? She could be lying—"

"The minicab driver who picked her up from Chatswood House confirmed her story and the times.

Based on his account—and cross-referencing it against the witness statements of those who saw Zova at the party—she was definitely no longer on the property when he was murdered."

"But what about all that stuff about the EpiPen? You know, what you said about Bunny maybe stealing it from Rick Zova."

"No, I think she was telling the truth—she was carrying a pen around just to pretend she had the allergy. You obviously just missed seeing it in her handbag on the night of the party, but it was there all along. In any case, the fact that she has a solid alibi removes her as a suspect."

Poppy slumped back in her chair. She felt completely defeated. She couldn't think of anything else to say to defend Joe; she couldn't think of an alternative angle to investigate.

As if she could sense Poppy's distress, Suzanne said gently: "I know this is difficult for you, Poppy, but I'm afraid that at this point, all the evidence points to Joe Fabbri as the murderer." She hesitated, then added, "Is there anything—any other information, anything else you can remember from the party—which might be relevant to the investigation? I'm willing to consider all other leads before we charge Joe."

Poppy thought furiously. Suzanne still didn't know about David Nowak's fake alibi and his affair with Dawn... but if Poppy told her about that, it would do nothing to help Joe. In fact, it would make his situation worse, because if the police questioned Nowak again, there would be an additional witness account of Joe behaving aggressively towards Zova, which would just strengthen the case against him.

"Poppy?"

"I... no, there's nothing, really. I've told you everything I know," Poppy said, swallowing hard.

Suzanne sighed. "Well, in that case... I'd better go. I've got a press conference in half an hour."

"Oh, wait—actually, there *is* something else," said Poppy on an impulse.

"Yes?"

"It's... it's not directly related to the murder case." Poppy took a deep breath. "In Rick Zova's autopsy report, was there any mention of the tattoos on his body?"

"Well, yes, there was a thorough description of every identifying mark. Why?"

"Do you remember if there was a tattoo on his right bicep which looked like a feather... or a leaf?"

"I don't know about a leaf, but there was definitely one which the forensic pathologist described as a black feather. Poppy, why are you asking all this? Is this related to the case?"

"No, not really." Poppy swallowed, then said, "Um... would the pathologist have done DNA tests too?"

"Yes, of course. They've taken swabs from both Zova and Joe, and will be checking for the presence of DNA material from both men on each other. The results haven't come back yet, but I must warn you, there's a high likelihood that Joe's—"

"I wasn't thinking about Joe," Poppy interrupted quickly.

"Oh? I don't understand."

"I... I was wondering if it would be possible to compare Zova's DNA with a sample from someone else."

"Someone else?" Suzanne sounded puzzled. "Whose DNA do you want to compare it to?"

"Mine," said Poppy in a small voice.

"Yours? But we know that you were in the garden that night—"

"No, I don't mean... I wasn't thinking of the murder investigation. It's... it's a personal thing."

There was a long silence on the other end of the line, then Suzanne said, understanding dawning in her voice: "Are you thinking that you might be related to Rick Zova?"

"I don't know! I... it's very far-fetched and... and I'm probably being... I don't know... I'm sure it's unlikely but... but that feather tattoo on Zova's bicep... you see, my mother's diary mentioned a man with a tattoo similar to that... in exactly the same place..." Poppy trailed off, then she said in a rush: "I... I think... I think there's a chance—a small chance—that Rick Zova could be my father."

Suzanne was silent again for a moment, then she spoke in a carefully neutral voice:

"Well, under the Human Tissue Act, anybody who

wants to do a DNA test in the UK needs to get permission first before they can collect a sample, otherwise they're liable to prosecution." She paused. "However... in this situation, since the DNA samples have already been collected as part of an ongoing murder inquiry and it could be argued that your relationship to Zova could be relevant to the investigation..." She paused again, as if thinking, then said, "I'll speak to Forensics and see what I can do. I can't promise anything, though. In fact, it might be easier if you could obtain a sample yourself."

"Myself?"

"Yes, you could try obtaining a DNA sample from another source, like perhaps some of Zova's hair? It would have to be hair that includes the follicles, though—so hair that's pulled out from the roots."

"Oh," said Poppy, wondering where on earth she was supposed to get something like that. "Um... okay."

"Well, if there's nothing else, I've got to dash—"

"What about Joe?" asked Poppy quickly. "What's going to happen to him now?"

"I'll be interviewing him again this afternoon," said Suzanne. "I promise I will be as fair to him as I can." She paused, then added in a grim tone: "But I also need to do my job—and my job is to ensure that Rick Zova's killer is put behind bars."

CHAPTER TWENTY-EIGHT

"...don't you think, dear?"

Poppy started and looked up from the cup of cold tea that she had been staring into. The fallen tree had been removed, the emergency services had left, and she should have been making an attempt to sift through the remaining debris for anything she could salvage. But the shock of the storm damage, followed by Joe's arrest, had completely overwhelmed her. She felt incapable of doing anything other than sit in the kitchen, filled with a deep lethargy, a feeling of despair and helplessness that she couldn't shake off.

She sat up straighter, making an attempt to focus, and gave Nell a guilty smile. "Sorry, I missed the last bit—what did you say?"

Nell pointed at the open magazine in front of her. "Look at this! Isn't it scary?"

Poppy leaned forwards without much interest to see what Nell was pointing at. It was an article about a stalker who had been arrested for attempting to abduct a young female pop star. When his home had been raided, they'd found all sorts of things he'd collected, from remnants of her meals, extracted from her kitchen rubbish, to some of her mail, intercepted from the postman.

"He even broke into her home and stole items from her bedroom and bathroom! Not just jewellery and clothes, but personal things, like used tissues and bits of hair that had been caught in her hairbrush." Nell shuddered. "Ugh! Disgusting!"

"Wait—what did you say?" Poppy grabbed the magazine from Nell and scanned the article herself, then she looked up excitedly. "Suzanne said that Bunny seemed to show stalker tendencies towards Rick Zova, although he never saw her as a serious threat."

"But I thought you said the police had verified her alibi, dear?"

"Yes, they have; she can't be the murderer... but I was thinking of something else: if Bunny was so obsessed, she might have stolen things from Rick Zova too, to keep as souvenirs. Like... like one of those bandanas he always wears! And there might be some hair caught on that!"

"Hair? What are you talking about?" said Nell, looking thoroughly confused.

Poppy jumped up from the table, suddenly

energised again. "I'll tell you later, Nell," she promised. "I've got to catch Bunny before she packs up and leaves again!"

Ten minutes later, Poppy was standing in the car park of The Red Lion and gazing up at the old country pub. Its exterior was covered almost entirely by ivy, the leaves showing vivid red and gold against the grey stone wall and lending the pub a romantic air. Inside, the pub was warm and cosy, with dark wood panelling and heavy oak furniture. It seemed to be doing a roaring trade: most of the tables were already filled with people tucking into hearty pub lunches of home-made cottage pies, beer-battered cod and chips, and creamy cauliflower soup accompanied by crusty bread. The enticing aromas made Poppy's stomach rumble and she realised that in all the excitement of the morning, she had completely forgotten to eat breakfast.

There were more people standing around the tables, clustered in groups, talking and laughing and swigging pints of beer. Poppy had to jostle her way to the bar and, when she got there, she was forced to wait for several minutes before she could catch the landlord's eye.

"What can I get you, miss?" he asked, busily wiping the counter.

"Er... well, actually, I was looking for someone who might be staying here," she said, raising her voice to be heard above the din of talk and laughter. She described Bunny, then said: "Do you have any guests at the moment who match that description? She might be using the name 'Ruth Hollis'."

"You'd best ask the missus," said the landlord. "She deals with the room and board side of things. Hang on... I'll get her."

He disappeared through a door behind the bar counter and returned a minute later with a harassed-looking, middle-aged woman who was wiping her hands on her apron. Poppy repeated her question and her description, and the publican's wife eyed her suspiciously.

"Why d'you want to know?"

"Oh... I want to return something of hers," said Poppy, thinking quickly. "We met at a party and she dropped a... an earring. I found it and wanted to return it to her."

The landlord's wife considered Poppy for a moment longer, then her face softened. "Yeah, she's staying here. I just took some tea up to her, actually."

Poppy glanced through the doorway next to the bar, where she could see a flight of steps leading upwards. "Her room's upstairs?"

"Yes, I'll ring up and—"

"That's okay. I'll just pop upstairs myself and knock on her door," said Poppy quickly with a disarming smile.

The landlord's wife hesitated, eyeing Poppy up and down again, then said: "Well, all right. It's the first door on the right of the landing."

Poppy found the room with no problem and

knocked eagerly. There was no response for so long that she began to wonder if Bunny was in, after all. She was just about to turn around and head back downstairs when the handle turned and the door swung open to reveal the blonde woman. Bunny looked as if she had just got out of bed: her hair was an uncombed mess, her eyes hollow, her cheeks sagging, and she wore a long shift dress which could have been a nightgown. Poppy felt a pang of pity for her.

"Hi, Bunny—remember me?" she said. "I just wanted a quick word with you. Can I come in, please?"

Without waiting for the woman to answer, Poppy stepped into the room. It was comfortably furnished, with an old four-poster bed and a pretty window seat overflowing with cushions. In fact, it seemed slightly incongruous with the more rustic feel of the pub downstairs, but it was obvious that The Red Lion had wanted to fully capitalise on the new trend of "boutique luxury accommodation" that many modern travellers were looking for.

A tray with a pot of tea, teacup, and a plate of scones sat untouched on the desk amidst a jumble of scarves, bags, hair accessories, make-up, and various other female paraphernalia. More clothing, shoes, and accessories were strewn across the rest of the room, but Poppy zeroed in on a large box on the bedside table. It was stuffed with various bits of rock-star paraphernalia, from signed posters and concert tickets to T-shirts and vinyl album jackets, and most of all—Poppy's eyes lit up—a colourful bandana hanging over the edge of the box. It looked very similar to the one that Rick Zova had worn to the party and she hurried across to pick it up. But Bunny rushed after her and snatched the box out of her hands.

"What are you doing?" she snarled, eyeing Poppy like a ferocious animal defending its young.

Poppy took a step back, holding her hands out in a placating manner. "Sorry... I just... Is that bandana from Rick Zova?"

Bunny looked cagey. "So what if it is?" she said, curving one arm protectively around the box.

"Well, I... um... I'm just really impressed that you have one. Where did you get it?"

Bunny gave her a suspicious look, then answered in a sulky voice: "I nicked it from his dressing room backstage years ago."

Poppy's heart sank at the words "years ago". How long ago? Would there still be any strands of hair left on the bandana by this time? She wanted to examine it, but she knew that she had to find a way to mollify Bunny first.

She forced a smile and said in a bright voice, "You know, I've never met a 'superfan' before—I'm not even sure what that means. So do you know all of Rick Zova's songs and everything?"

Bunny relaxed slightly and her grip on the box loosened. She puffed her chest out with pride. "Every one. I can sing them all—I know all the words by heart."

"Wow! And did you really go to every one of his concerts?"

"Most of them. There were one or two that I had to miss... but I even went when I had the flu!"

"I suppose, as Rick's 'superfan', you must know more about him than anyone else, huh? I mean, you could write a book on Rick Zova!"

"I could?"

Poppy nodded earnestly. "Oh, I'm sure now that he's died so tragically, publishers will be desperate to do a book about him. And I'm sure they'll need someone who is an expert on Rick... Someone like you!" she said, shamelessly laying on the flattery. "I'm sure no one understood Rick better than you. As his 'superfan', you're unique, and the publishers will be looking to you as the expert source of information. You could be Rick Zova's official biographer!"

Bunny's eyes sparkled and her face took on a faraway expression. "Yes... yes, I could," she murmured. "I know more about Rick than anyone else in the world."

"And it's brilliant that you've got some of his stuff too," Poppy added, indicating the box. "I mean, it's almost like a museum, isn't it? You've got genuine Rick Zova... um... artefacts and you know the stories behind them, the details about them that nobody else would know. I'll bet you could even host an exhibition or something! Other fans would be so grateful to you," she continued blithely. "How much stuff do you have in that box? Do you think it would be enough for an exhibition?"

Bunny put the box down and began taking items out eagerly. "Oh... oh, I think so! I've got things in here from back in the early 1990s, like from Rick's first concerts... I've got wristbands and promo stickers from his tours... I've got real 'Zova' key rings... I've got a copy of an itinerary that I stole from one of the tour buses..."

Poppy leaned over the box, pretending to watch Bunny with exaggerated admiration. "Wow! This is an amazing collection! How many years have you had these things? And did Rick wear this? Can I take a closer look?" she asked, edging her fingers closer to the bandana.

For a moment, she thought Bunny was going to snatch the bandana out of her hands, but then the other woman gave her a lofty smile and said, "Sure, but be careful."

Poppy picked up the bandana almost reverently and turned it over in her hands, her eyes searching desperately for any tendrils of hair that might have been caught in its folds. But she was disappointed to see that it was devoid of any strands. In fact, it looked so new and pristine that she began to have suspicions about Bunny's claims that the item belonged to Zova. She was just turning it over to check one last time when Bunny pulled a fistful of papers out of the box and thrust them proudly at

Poppy.

"Look at these! They're all the autographs I got from Rick... some of them even have a couple of lines, not just his name. See?" She showed Poppy one of the scraps of paper. It looked like the corner of a page torn off from a magazine, with some writing on the glossy paper which read: "*Live dangerously or don't live at all!*", followed by an arrogant scrawl which Poppy recognised as Rick Zova's signature.

"Er... that's great," Poppy said as she put the bandana back into the box and started to rise. Now that there was no hope of getting a DNA sample, she wanted to leave as soon as possible. She was beginning to find Bunny's "superfan" enthusiasm a bit creepy.

The blonde woman looked up from the pile of paper scraps and said, with a moue of disappointment: "I nearly got a new note to add to my collection at the party the other night. And it would have been amazing! A whole page of writing from Rick. I was going to take it but—"

Poppy froze in the act of getting up. "Wait... what note?"

CHAPTER TWENTY-NINE

Bunny looked at Poppy, surprised by her urgent tone. "The note from Rick. It was on the big desk in the study. I saw it when I was sitting there, when you went off to get me a drink..."

"And you're sure Rick Zova left it there?"

"Of course! I know his handwriting."

Poppy thought back to the night of Nowak's party. She had bumped into Zova coming out of the study, just as she was going in. He had said that he was looking for matches but now she realised that the rock star had lied. What had Zova really been doing in the study that night? Was this "note" connected to his murder?

"What did the note say?" asked Poppy.

"It was his song," said Bunny.

"What song?"

"Rick's song 'Blizzard Paranoia'." Bunny looked at her earnestly. "Don't you think it's got the most awesome lyrics?"

"Er... I don't know Rick Zova's music very well—"

Bunny gasped and clutched her chest. "You don't know it? Oh my God! It was the first song Rick released and I still think it's his best song ever!"

Poppy stared at her. It was strange sitting here watching a woman in her forties act like a teenager gushing over her first celebrity crush. There was something sad and tragic about it. It was almost as if Bunny had remained emotionally frozen in time, forever stuck with the shallow immaturity of a starstruck adolescent.

"You must know it," she insisted again. When Poppy shook her head apologetically, she sprang to her feet in consternation. "You have to know it! I'm sure if you heard it, you'd recognise it—listen, I'll sing it to you!" She cleared her throat, then assumed a pose as if she were holding an electric guitar and began nodding her head up and down, while singing in a loud, off-key voice:

Feel the rush in my head,
Ski the powder till I'm dead! Waiii—aiii—aiiieee!
Only she can take me there,
To snow-capped peaks and mountain airrrr...!
Gonna lose my sanity, gonna lose your trust,
When the lines of reality turn to dust...
Feel the rush in my head,

Ski the powder till I'm dead! Waiii—aiii—aiiieee!

Poppy winced as Bunny struggled to hit the high notes, and when the other woman started repeating the verses again, she began clapping manically, hoping to cut the impromptu performance short.

"That's great!" gushed Poppy. "Really good. You've... er... got a great voice."

Bunny beamed. "Yeah, I practise Rick's songs in front of the mirror—I know them all really well. But this one's my favourite! I recognised the lyrics as soon as I saw them."

"And the note just had song lyrics? There was nothing else? No message?"

"No."

"Was it addressed to anyone?"

Bunny furrowed her brow, then brightened. "Yeah, I just remembered—it said: 'To dear Dawn' at the top."

"Dawn?" Poppy stared at the other woman. This was the last thing she had expected. Why would Rick Zova have left a note for Nowak's PA?

"I don't suppose you've got the note?" she asked.

Bunny pursed her lips in annoyance. "No! I told you, I wanted to, but then this bald bloke came in and took it."

"Who?"

Bunny looked at her as if she were stupid. "The man who was having the party."

"David Nowak?"

She shrugged. "I dunno his name."

"What did he do with the note?"

"He read it and then he asked me if I knew who'd left it. I told him it was Rick and he looked kind of annoyed. Then he said it was probably just another stupid prank and chucked it in the fire. I was so mad! I wanted to add it to my collection!" She pouted. "After he left, I thought there was no point staying on at the party, so I left too."

"Did you tell the police about the note?"

Bunny looked at her blankly. "No. They never asked me about Rick's songs. I tried to tell that detective sergeant about my collection, but he wasn't interested."

More fool him, thought Poppy. Sergeant Lee had missed an important clue!

As soon as she left the pub, she rang the police station, asking to speak to Suzanne. To her chagrin, however, she was told that the detective inspector was out on another investigation.

"Is this about the Rick Zova case?" asked the desk sergeant. "Detective Sergeant Lee is in charge of that. I can transfer you to him—"

"Uh, no... that's all right," said Poppy hastily. "I'll try again later."

She hung up, wondering if she had done the right thing. Should she have spoken to Lee? After all, it was really the police's business to follow up this new lead. But she had nothing concrete to show and she had a bad feeling that Lee was unlikely to take it seriously. With Joe Fabbri already in custody, officially charged with murder, Lee would want to wrap the case up quickly and simply.

If only I had a copy of the note! thought Poppy in frustration. If only it hadn't burnt in the fireplace...

CHAPTER THIRTY

Poppy arrived back at Hollyhock Cottage with a heavy heart. She found a hungry ginger tomcat waiting for her by the front gate, loudly demanding food, and realised with a guilty pang that what with the storm damage and then Joe's arrest, she had completely forgotten to pop next door to feed Oren his breakfast that morning.

"Sorry, Oren!" said Poppy, hurrying to lead the way to Nick's house. "Come on, I'll feed you now."

When she walked into Nick's kitchen, though, she groaned in dismay to see the heaped bowl of cat food in the corner, untouched from last night. It looked like the ginger tom had turned his nose up at his special diet biscuit again. In fact, from the perfect symmetry of the mound in the bowl, it looked like he hadn't taken a single bite!

"Ohhh, Oren!" cried Poppy in frustration. "Why won't you eat your food?"

Oren padded over to the fridge and looked up at her hopefully. "*N-ow?*" he said.

"No, you know I can't give you anything else!" said Poppy, frowning at him. "You have to eat your diet food. I already shouldn't have given you that bit of chicken yesterday... Nick will kill me if he finds out."

She crouched down next to the tomcat and reached out to stroke his silky orange fur. "Come, Oren—please? Be a good boy and eat your diet food."

"*N-o-o-w!*" growled Oren, lashing his tail. He pawed again at the fridge door and looked at her expectantly.

Poppy sighed and went back to the untouched bowl of food, wondering what to do. *Should I just leave it here and hope that once Oren gets hungry enough, he might finally deign to eat some?* Other than the bit of roast chicken that he'd had yesterday, he hadn't eaten anything for days. *He's a big, strapping tomcat,* she reminded herself. *It won't hurt him to go a bit hungry.* But what if she came back tonight and the bowl was still untouched? And tomorrow morning as well? How long should she hold out for?

Poppy hesitated, then pulled her phone out and called Nick's number. After all, Oren was his cat and she didn't want to take responsibility for making the wrong decision. She wondered if Nick might be in the middle of a book-signing or some other event, and was relieved when he answered on the second ring.

"Poppy!" He sounded surprised. "Is something wrong?"

"No, no, everything is fine. Well, except that your cat won't touch his diet food," she said with a sigh. "He's been refusing to eat it for the last three days running and I don't know what to do. I'm worried he might starve."

"Chance would be a fine thing," muttered Nick. "The little beast is just being obstreperous on purpose."

"Do you think I can give him a bit of something else?" asked Poppy hesitantly. "He's obviously really hungry and keeps begging for food. I gave him a bit of sliced roast chicken from your fridge yesterday and—"

"What? No wonder he won't touch his diet food— he's holding out for the good stuff! Poppy, I told you that you need to be firm!"

"I know, I know," said Poppy, hanging her head. "But I feel sorry for him! That diet food looks so unappetising; it's just dry biscuits—"

"It's what the vet prescribed," said Nick. "We've got to follow orders. It's the best thing for Oren's health. You know overweight cats have a higher chance of getting things like cancer and diabetes. The vet said it can even lead to heart problems and arthritis, and things like bladder stones..."

Poppy sighed. She knew that Nick was right.

"Look, I'm hoping to be home tonight," said Nick,

his tone softening. "So just leave the food down and I'll deal with the bugger when I get home."

"All right," said Poppy. "But what will *you* do if he won't eat it? Hey listen, why don't you ask your father if he might be able to help? I'll bet Bertie could come up with a special sauce or something that we could add to Oren's diet food, so that it's a lot more appetising, but without adding any calories—"

"I'm not asking that crazy old coot for anything," growled Nick.

Poppy sighed again. She was beginning to think both cat and master were as stubborn and infuriating as each other!

"Is everything else all right?" asked Nick. "You sound a bit down."

Poppy paused, unsure what to say. Her childhood and early adult life of constantly moving around with her mother meant that she had never managed to make close friends. In fact, Nell was her closest confidante, but the older woman was more like a beloved aunt than a best friend. Since moving to Bunnington and meeting Suzanne Whittaker, Poppy had started seeing the detective inspector as a cross between an older sister and a friend. But when it came to some things, like the murder investigation, she knew that Suzanne's dedication to her job would always trump any bonds of friendship.

So what about Nick? Poppy still wasn't sure how she really felt about Nick Forrest. He was not quite an easy friend and yet also not "just a neighbour".

There were times when she wanted to thump him on the head and other times when she felt like he understood her better than anyone else in the world...

"It's... it's a bunch of things," she blurted in a rush. "My greenhouse has been completely destroyed and I don't know where I'm going to find the money to rebuild it... and Joe got arrested this morning, but I *know* that it can't be him; I know it looks like he has the perfect motive and I know his trowel was found at the scene of the crime, but he's not a murderer! It must be someone else... except that it can't be Bunny because she's got a solid alibi, and it can't be Geoff Healey either or Nowak, because they both have alibis—although Nowak lied about his but he was really with Dawn and then he said he saw Joe—"

"Whoa! Whoa!" said Nick, cutting her off. "Slow down, Poppy! I don't know what you're talking about. What's happened to your greenhouse? And what's this about Joe getting arrested? The last time I saw you, at the police station with Suzanne, no one had found Bunny yet and I thought Joe had no motive? And what was Nowak doing with Dawn?"

"Well, a *lot* has happened in three days," said Poppy wryly. Quickly, she recounted everything that had happened since he'd gone away.

"Okay, first of all, about the greenhouse—don't worry. I can help with the funds for rebuilding," said Nick.

"Oh!" Poppy was so surprised, she was almost struck dumb. "But..."

"It's no problem. I've got the spare cash and I'm happy to help. After all, your grandmother always let me come over whenever I was struggling with writer's block, and you've been kind enough to continue the arrangement... so think of this as a way to repay you," said Nick persuasively.

Poppy wavered. She was tempted, very tempted. As one of the country's bestselling crime authors, Nick could well afford to help her out, and it was true that he did enjoy free use of the cottage garden. But at the same time, something in her balked at the thought of borrowing money from Nick.

"I... thank you, that's really kind but..." She took a deep breath. "I can't accept. It just wouldn't be right."

"What do you mean—'it wouldn't be right'?" said Nick irritably.

"I mean... it's... it's not like you're family or... or anything. You're just my neighbour—I mean, sorry, I don't mean to be rude—I mean, you're a nice neighbour... but you're not..." Poppy stammered. "I just... I can't be beholden to you this way."

Nick was silent for a moment, then he said: "Poppy, I hope you're not following in your grandmother's footsteps."

"What do you mean?"

"Her stubborn pride and independence cost her in the end. There's no shame in accepting help when you need it."

Poppy swallowed. "Thanks, but... but I'll manage." She took a deep breath, then deliberately changed the subject. "This note that Bunny mentioned—I feel like it's important somehow, but it doesn't make sense. Why would Rick Zova leave a note full of song lyrics?"

"What was the song? Was it one of his own?" asked Nick.

"Yeah, it was something about skiing... and snow and mountains... it's called *Paranoid Blizzard* or something like that... no wait, *Blizzard Paranoia*."

"*Blizzard Paranoia...*" Nick mused. There was the sound of tapping on a keyboard, then he said, "Ah! Found it online. It was one of Zova's first songs." He paused, then read: "*Feel the rush in my head / Ski the powder till I'm dead! / Only she can take me there / To snow-capped peaks and mountain air! / Gonna lose my sanity, gonna lose your trust / When the lines of reality turn to dust...*"

"Yes, that's it!" said Poppy. "Only I had to listen to Bunny *singing* it and she's got the most awful voice. She kept trying to do all these sound effects too. It was like listening to a cat wailing!"

Nick didn't seem to be paying attention. Instead, he was muttering to himself, "Feel the rush to my head... ski the powder... lines of reality turn to dust..."

"What?" asked Poppy. "Do the lyrics mean anything to you?"

"Possibly..." said Nick slowly. "I think the song is about drugs."

CHAPTER THIRTY-ONE

"Drugs?" Poppy frowned.

"Yes. Cocaine, to be specific."

"Huh? How do you know?"

"Well, drugs were a huge part of the rock music scene—still are, I'm sure—but the Seventies, Eighties, and Nineties were legendary. A lot of the famous heavy users, like Keith Richards and Ozzy Osbourne, were big celebrities then. And cocaine, in particular, was popular with glam metal rock bands like Rick Zova's."

"Okay, but I still don't see—"

"It's the words: *powder, snow, dust, lines...* they're all slang terms for cocaine," Nick explained. "Plus the word 'rush' is a general term for a drug-induced high."

"But how do you know that's what he meant?

Maybe Zova really *was* just singing about skiing."

"Trust me on this one."

"Oh my God..." Poppy breathed. "I've just remembered something! Stuart—Nowak's executive secretary—told me the other day that Dawn is an ex-drug addict. She was recruited from the drug rehabilitation programme sponsored by Nowak's own charitable foundation."

"Well, that's a bit of a coincidence but—"

"No, it's not a coincidence!" Poppy cried. "The note was actually addressed to Dawn!"

"What? You didn't tell me that."

"Sorry, I missed that part. Bunny said 'To dear Dawn' was written at the top of the note."

"She's sure about that?"

"Well, that's what she told me. And now that I think about it, I remember Lena Nowak complaining to me that day I was at Chatswood House... She was complaining about Dawn's desk. I'd originally assumed that it was Nowak's desk—it's the bigger one—but his is actually the smaller desk by the window. So that means the desk that Bunny sat at, the desk that Rick Zova left his note on, was Dawn's desk!" said Poppy excitedly. "Maybe there's some connection between Dawn and Zova that we don't know of, some motive that hasn't been discovered yet! She could have—" Poppy stopped, deflated. "Oh, I forgot. She has an alibi."

"Provided by Nowak, according to you," said Nick. "I'm not sure that's worth much. Even if he was telling the truth and they really went outside to meet each other, he wouldn't necessarily know what she did after they parted. They didn't go back to the party together, did they? Nowak had to return via the wine cellar, which means that he wasn't watching her the whole time. What if Dawn didn't go straight back to the party?"

"Yes, yes," said Poppy, getting excited again. "Nowak told me that he could see Zova through the bushes from where they were standing. He didn't think that Dawn had seen Zova because she was facing the other way, but he could have been wrong. She might have caught a glimpse of Zova and instead of returning to the party, she went over to confront him. Then she could have thrown a stone into the wasp nest and fled the scene. Yes, it all fits! And it could explain those wasp stings I saw on Dawn's arms at the pharmacy too. She said they were from the day before but she could have just made that up quickly to cover up... Oh my God, Dawn could be the murderer!"

"Don't get too excited yet," said Nick dryly. "There could be a simpler explanation for the note."

"Such as what?"

"Well... Dawn could be a rabid Rick Zova fan and he left the lyrics as a gift for her, for example."

"Aww, come on—you don't really believe that! Isn't it just too much of a coincidence that the song was about drugs and Dawn is an ex-drug addict? There *has* to be a drug connection! Plus, even if she was just a fan, how would Zova have known about her?"

"She was at the party, wasn't she? Perhaps they bumped into each other. You weren't watching Zova all the time—you don't know every person he talked to that night. Maybe she told him that she was Nowak's PA and what a big fan she was, maybe *Blizzard Paranoia* was her favourite song... and he decided to be nice and leave her a gift on her desk."

"That's so far-fetched, it doesn't even deserve considering!" spluttered Poppy. "Zova wasn't that kind of 'nice guy'! Besides, if Dawn really was such a rabid fan, why did she leave the note behind? She wouldn't have—"

"All right, all right, calm down... I'm just playing devil's advocate," said Nick, chuckling. "You're incredibly easy to rile up, you know."

Poppy flushed. "Sorry," she mumbled with a sheepish laugh.

"But I'm not just mucking around," said Nick, his tone turning serious. "True detective work is about questioning every assumption, double-checking every lead, and only accepting conclusions backed up by evidence."

"Yes, yes, you're right," said Poppy, chastened as she remembered how often she'd criticised Sergeant Lee for jumping to conclusions. "Well, maybe Nowak can tell us more about the note—"

"I'm surprised he hasn't mentioned it to the police so far," said Nick.

"Bunny says he thought it was another of Zova's

stupid pranks. That's why he threw it in the fire."

"Hmm…"

"What?"

"Maybe he threw it into the fire on purpose. After all, if he was having an affair with Dawn and he realised that the murdered man had left a note addressed to her, he could have downplayed the note as a way to protect his mistress."

"Yes, but he couldn't have known at that time that Rick Zova was going to get murdered, could he?" Poppy pointed out. "When Bunny saw him chuck the note away, the murder hadn't happened yet. Besides, after the practical joke that Zova played when he first arrived at the party, it was probably reasonable for Nowak to think the note was just another silly prank."

"Maybe…" Nick didn't sound convinced. "I just wouldn't be surprised if Nowak *is* hiding something—oh, maybe not deliberately, but being emotionally involved can cloud your judgement. When I was in the CID, I saw several cases where people covered up for their romantic or sexual partners. You need to report this and then the police can question Nowak again."

Poppy thought of the conversation she'd had with Nowak yesterday, when the billionaire businessman had proposed a pact of silence, so that the police wouldn't know about his false alibi and his secret meeting with Dawn in the garden. It had made her uneasy at the time, but she had agreed because she knew that if Nowak revised his statement, he would have to mention seeing Joe behaving aggressively to Rick Zova and that would only add to the case against the old handyman. Now, she was faced with the same dilemma. *But the police already know that Joe confronted Zova*, she reminded herself. *He told them himself. So it's not making things that much worse if Nowak gives an additional witness account. At least this way, Dawn would be investigated...*

"All right—I'll call and speak to Sergeant Lee," said Poppy.

After hanging up, Poppy steeled herself for the conversation with the unpleasant detective sergeant. She knew that Lee would be sceptical and dismissive so she had to be prepared. She didn't want to flounder for information or struggle to recall details when she was arguing with him. Mentally, she went over the conversation with Bunny about the discovery of the note and her heart sank as she remembered how incoherent and emotional the blonde woman had been. She realised that Bunny would probably be considered an unreliable witness.

In fact, given that the police still didn't know that Nowak had lied about his alibi and still thought that he had been down in the wine cellar with Geoff Healey... if the billionaire businessman decided to stick to his original story and refused to admit that he had met Dawn outside or that he had seen a note with her name, it would be Poppy's and Bunny's word against his. And Poppy knew whose side the police would be likely to take. After all, who would believe a histrionic stalker fan over a respected businessman and philanthropist?

If only the note hadn't been destroyed! she thought with frustration. If she just had the note—or even a fragment of it—to show to the police, she knew that she would be in a stronger position.

Then she caught her breath. *Wait a minute!* Bunny had said that Nowak had chucked the note into the fire, so she had assumed that it must have been reduced to ashes. But what if it hadn't? What if part of it *had* remained intact? She thought excitedly of what Bertie had said yesterday, when he had burst in on her and Nowak. He had been rambling about his research on the flammability of different types of paper and he had mentioned that glossy magazine paper burns very poorly: *"...simply chars without burning at all"*—were his exact words.

If Zova had written his note on a page torn from a magazine—something he seemed inclined to do, based on all the samples that Bunny had collected— then it might not have been completely destroyed! It might only have burnt slightly, and there might still be remnants where the writing was legible. The note could still be in the fireplace in Nowak's study... *Hang on!*

Poppy thought of Bertie's visit to Chatswood House and the mayhem CLARA had caused while attempting to clean Nowak's study. In that tornado of vacuuming, the robot had left the fireplace completely spotless—which meant that if the note was anywhere, it was probably in a vacuum bag in CLARA's body, back at Bertie's place!

CHAPTER THIRTY-TWO

"N-oww? N-OWW?"

Poppy jumped and realised that she was standing in the middle of Nick's kitchen, staring into space. Oren was rubbing himself against her legs and looking up at her. Obviously, the ginger tom was still hoping that he could avoid eating his diet food and get a delicacy from the fridge instead.

"Sorry, Oren," said Poppy, giving him a hasty pat. "I've got to go. Be a good boy and eat your food, please? If you finish that bowl, I promise I'll give you a huge treat!"

Leaving the ginger tom with a disgruntled expression on his furry face, Poppy rushed out of Nick's house and hurried down the lane, past Hollyhock Cottage to the modest property beyond, which was Bertie's house. She knocked impatiently on the front door, and when there was no reply she made her way around to the rear, knowing that Bertie often left his back door open. Her hunch was right but, when she went in, she found the house empty. There was no sign of the old inventor or his little terrier anywhere.

Poppy paused in the middle of the sitting room and scanned her surroundings impatiently. Where had Bertie gone? He was normally very reclusive and hardly even went into the village. She looked around and noticed that CLARA seemed to be missing too. Had the old inventor taken his robot out for a trial somewhere?

She sighed and wandered back into the kitchen, which always looked like a cross between a chemistry lab and an eighteenth-century cookhouse. There was something simmering in a pot on the stove and when Poppy peered in and saw the congealed grey substance sticking to the edges and beginning to burn, she hastily turned the fire off. She was just lifting the pot off the stove when she heard a noise. She turned swiftly around.

"Bertie?"

Poppy took a few steps, then paused and listened.

Yes, there it was again... A muffled thumping. A floorboard creaking.

"Bertie? Is that you?" Poppy called.

She began making her way down the corridor at the rear of the house. She realised that there were more rooms back here—she'd forgotten that Bertie would have a bedroom and probably a guest room too. They were just beyond the bend of the corridor and she hurried around it, nearly colliding with someone coming the other way.

"Mr Nowak!" cried Poppy in shock.

"Ojej!" He jumped and clutched a hand to his chest. "Oh—Miss Lancaster, you scared me."

"What are you doing here?" she asked.

"I'm looking for Dawn. She sent me a note saying she needed to see me urgently, but she wasn't at Chatswood House when I returned from the office. Stuart told me that Dawn had mentioned coming to see Dr Noble, so I thought I'd come and see if I could find her here."

Why did Dawn want to see Bertie? Poppy wondered worriedly. Had she somehow learned that the old inventor might have a remnant of the note addressed to her? Had she planned to take it off him by force?

"Have you seen Dr Noble?" she asked Nowak.

'No. The front door was open when I arrived, but there was no one in the front rooms. I thought it was a bit odd so I was just about to check the bedrooms when I heard someone outside."

"That was probably me," said Poppy. She indicated the two doors at the end of the corridor. "So you haven't checked the bedrooms yet?"

Nowak shook his head. Poppy slipped past him and walked the rest of the way down the corridor with the businessman following. She paused outside one of the rooms, which had its door slightly ajar, and froze as her ears caught a sound. It sounded like a soft whine—a dog's whine.

"Einstein?" cried Poppy. She shoved the door open and rushed inside, then gasped.

Bertie was lying unconscious on the rug next to the bed, a nasty-looking wound on the side of his head. Einstein was crouched beside him; the little terrier looked like he had been injured too and was crawling weakly to his master's side, whining softly.

"Bertie!" Poppy cried.

She started forwards but, before she could take a step, someone grabbed her from behind. An arm like a metal band snaked around her body, holding her captive, whilst a hand clamped over her mouth.

"Mmm! Mmm…uunngh…mmmhh!" Poppy fought to free herself as she tried to scream through the hand covering her mouth.

But it was no use. Her captor was too strong. She wriggled harder, managing to turn her head slightly, and she bit down hard. There was a muffled oath and the hand jerked away from her mouth. Poppy gasped in relief. She drew a breath but, before she could scream, something hard came down on her head.

Blackness descended.

CHAPTER THIRTY-THREE

Poppy opened her eyes as she slowly came to her senses. Her head hurt horribly and she felt sore all over, but nothing seemed to be broken. She struggled to raise herself. Looking hazily around, she realised that she was half sitting, half lying on the rug next to the bed. Bertie lay unconscious next to her, and Einstein was curled up by his master's head. The normally feisty little terrier looked weak and dazed. He kept trying to lick Bertie's face, whining forlornly, but the old man lay completely still.

Poppy's heart lurched. *No!* She leaned over Bertie, looking frantically for signs of life, then let out a breath of relief as she saw the faint motion of his chest rising and falling. He was unconscious but alive.

A sound on the other side of the room made her jerk her head around and her eyes widened as she saw David Nowak standing in the corner, bent over a tangled heap of metal. He was muttering to himself, cursing and smacking the contraption in front of him. It was CLARA, Poppy realised. The cleaning robot had been flipped upside down, with its cash-register head bent sideways, its scrubbing brush arms flailing in all directions, and its wheels spinning uselessly as Nowak lifted it off the floor and shook it violently.

"Come on... come on...!" he said, jiggling the robot up and down. "Why don't you open up?"

"*I am suspended,*" said CLARA.

Nowak poked and prodded various buttons on the robot's body, then raised it higher off the ground and shook it hard again. "Open up, you stupid piece of junk!"

"*I am suspended,*" said CLARA.

"AHHH SHUT UP!"

Nowak dropped the robot with a crash and seized a piece of metal piping. For a moment, it looked as if he was going to start smashing CLARA to pieces, but then he caught sight of Poppy and turned towards her instead.

"Don't... don't come closer!" Poppy cried, scrambling backwards. She was shocked to hear that her voice was hardly more than a croak.

Nowak paused in surprise, then looked down at the metal pipe he held in his hand and back up at her. "Oh, I didn't mean to hurt you—I just didn't want you to scream," he said, almost conversationally. He gave her a reproachful look. "You bit my hand, you know."

"It was *you*," Poppy said hoarsely, staring at him in horror. "You killed Rick Zova!"

She shrank away and came up against Bertie's inert body beside her. She looked down at the injured old man, and suddenly she wasn't frightened anymore. She was bloody furious.

She whirled back to face Nowak. "What did you do to Bertie?" she demanded.

Nowak looked bewildered. "I just hit him on the head."

"What do you mean, 'just'? You worm!" cried Poppy, outraged. "Attacking a defenceless old man—does that make you feel good?"

Nowak looked at her blankly. "I had to get him out of the way while I looked for the note," he explained in a matter-of-fact voice.

"That story about Dawn looking for Bertie was just something you made up, wasn't it?" said Poppy.

"Well, of course. I had to give a reason for being in Dr Noble's house. It wasn't Dawn looking for him—it was me. Ah, perhaps you can assist me, Miss Lancaster!" Nowak looked at her with anticipation and indicated the robot in front of him. "I don't suppose you know how to open up the compartment with the vacuum bag? Women are always so much better at these things. My wife tells me that I'm useless in the home, you know," he added with a chuckle.

Poppy stared at him. Was the man totally mad? He was acting as if they were making polite conversation over afternoon tea. Still, she reminded herself that this was better than him being aggressive and violent.

Taking a deep breath, she forced herself to say in a cajoling tone: "Dr Noble really needs some medical attention for his head. If you let us go, I can take him to hospital and leave you in peace to work on the robot."

For a moment, she thought Nowak was going to agree and her spirits rose, then the businessman shook his head regretfully and said:

"Oh no, I can't let you go. You know too much now. I really didn't want to do it but now that I think about it, I'm afraid I will have to kill you, after all."

He still spoke as if they were exchanging pleasantries at a garden party and Poppy felt her skin crawl. She changed her mind. The excessive politeness and creepy understatements were somehow scarier than violent and abusive behaviour.

"You... you can't kill us," she said hoarsely. "People will find our bodies. Someone will remember seeing you come here. It will all be traced to you—"

"Oh, I don't think so," said Nowak complacently. "You see, I noticed quite a lot of dangerous and flammable chemicals in the kitchen when I came through the house. Really very foolish to leave so many lying around, especially when one is a bit elderly and absent-minded... I'm sure nobody would be surprised if there were an explosion and the house went up in flames. By the time they find your bodies, you will be burnt beyond recognition and it will be hard for any forensic evidence of murder to be discovered."

"No...!" said Poppy faintly, staring at the man in front of her in horror.

There was no point reasoning with Nowak, she realised. For all his demure appearance and pleasant manner, he *was* a psychopath, after all, with no capacity to feel remorse or empathy. Their only hope was to escape. But she was still weak and shaky; she didn't know how well her legs would hold her if she tried to stand up, never mind tried to run. In any case, she didn't have the strength to tow an unconscious Bertie with her and there was no way she was leaving the old inventor behind.

So, trying to escape was out of the question. And she was scared that if she started screaming and calling for help, Nowak might try to choke her again. That left disabling him as the only option.

Poppy eyed Nowak warily. The businessman had turned back to CLARA and was muttering to himself once more as he began to wrestle with the robot. He yanked and prised and pounded and shook, doing anything he could to try and force the central compartment open. Screws rattled and fell out, sections of the machine broke off, and pieces of equipment flew in all directions as he shook the robot violently. Three rags, a feather duster, and a scrubbing sponge were ejected from CLARA's torso, followed by a large squirt of stain remover.

"AAAGGHH!" cried Nowak, angrily wiping the blue liquid out of his eyes. "You stupid machine!"

He smacked CLARA against the wall, causing several pieces of rubbery material to fall out of the robot's joints. A chunk of pink rubber came loose from under the robot's right armpit and an alarm sounded.

"*Attention: armpit breach detected,*" came CLARA's mechanical voice. "*Armpit breach alert.*"

Nowak stopped and looked at the robot quizzically. "What the—?"

"*Insulation damage. Electrical grounding malfunction. Armpit hazard.*"

A wild idea came into Poppy's head as she stared at the pieces of insulation rubber littering the floor around Nowak. She eyed the distance between them, mentally calculating how far apart they were, then she grabbed the edge of the rug that she and Bertie were lying on and flipped it over. It had a thick, non-slip rubber backing. She glanced back up, her thoughts racing. Could it work? She wasn't sure they were far enough away to be safe, but she had to trust the rubber lining on the rug to protect them. There was no choice. This was their only chance...

"I... I think I know how to open the robot!" she croaked.

Nowak stopped and glanced over his shoulder at her. "Eh?"

Poppy licked her lips and tried to assume a helpful expression. "There's a... a special button," she said. "It's sort of like a... um... factory reset button. If you press that, it should unlock all the compartments in the machine."

"Really?" Nowak's eyes lit up. "Where is it?"

"You have to turn CLARA right side up first."

He lifted the robot and flipped it over, setting it upright on the floor. Lights flashed from CLARA's cash-register head, then the words "GRAVITY RESTORED... STANDBY MODE" moved across the screen.

Poppy pointed. "If you look under the robot's right armpit, there should be a gap between the metal plates...can you see it?"

"Yes... yes..." said Nowak excitedly, ducking his head to look.

"Okay, the button's in that gap. You need to insert a finger in there and press hard," said Poppy, keeping her own fingers crossed.

She held her breath and watched as Nowak eagerly stuck his right forefinger into the crack between two metal plates.

There was a sudden crackling sound, then an explosion.

Poppy recoiled, cringing against Bertie's body as a shower of sparks lit up the room. Nowak cried out. His body jerked convulsively, then he collapsed in a twitching heap on the floor.

A few more sparks flew, then the smoke cleared

and Poppy released the breath she had been holding. She felt a sense of elation. Her idea had worked! Nowak had been electrocuted by the exposed wiring in CLARA's armpit and the rubber backing on the rug had insulated her and Bertie, and kept them safe from any live current on the floor.

She breathed a huge sigh of relief, then peered at the crumpled figure on the other side of the room. Was Nowak dead? She was about to go a bit closer when he stirred and groaned. Poppy jerked back, scared. Visions of horror movies she'd seen where the monster could never be killed filled her head. Was Nowak going to get up again?

"*Foreign object detected,*" said CLARA suddenly.

A familiar probe appeared and a blue light scanned Nowak's body.

"*Commencing a new cleaning cycle.*"

One of the robot's remaining arms shot out and began industriously scrubbing Nowak's bald head with a toilet brush. The businessman yelped and attempted to get up, but he was pushed to the floor and pinned in place by another robot arm wielding a mop. Poppy sat back again, her body going limp with relief.

"*Ruff! Ruff-ruff!*" said Einstein suddenly, his head up and his ears pricked as he stared at CLARA.

Poppy followed his gaze and burst into giggles as she watched David Nowak, murderous businessman and philanthropist extraordinaire, get his bald head buffed to a high shine.

CHAPTER THIRTY-FOUR

"The doctor's in there at the moment, together with Dr Noble's son," said the nurse. "I'm afraid no other visitors are allowed."

Poppy glanced at the closed door of Bertie's room, then sighed, thanked the nurse, and turned away. It had been a long night. First the anxious hours in the Emergency waiting room as the doctors treated Bertie, taking scans of his head and dressing his wound; then the long wait in the Intensive Care ward, dozing off on the hard plastic seats, as she hoped for news that the old inventor had regained consciousness.

Suzanne Whittaker had come by a few times, in between seeing David Nowak (who was being treated on the same ward for electrocution burns), notifying Nick about his father's condition, and organising for

Einstein to be taken to a veterinarian. Poppy had been grateful that there was someone else to take care of everything. Now that she was safe and the ordeal was over, a deep sense of exhaustion had engulfed her. Everything felt distant and dreamlike, and even the simplest actions required a massive effort of concentration.

The doctors had examined her head and pronounced her lucky to have escaped concussion. They told her to go home and rest, but she hadn't been able to bear the thought of leaving Bertie alone in the hospital. Somehow she must have fallen into a fitful sleep, because when she finally awoke, it was the next morning. Someone had laid her flat across several chairs and tried to make her comfortable, with a folded towel under her head and a jacket draped over her like a blanket. She'd guessed who that "someone" was when she sat up and saw that it was a man's jacket. It had smelled faintly of a familiar male aftershave. *Nick had come back!*

Poppy had sprung up and hurried eagerly up the corridor to Bertie's room, only to be met by the nurse outside. Now she retraced her steps back down the corridor and paused at the doorway to the waiting room. She couldn't face sitting down in there again. Instead, she decided to go for a walk to stretch her legs. She had only gone a few steps, however, when she looked down a different corridor and saw a police constable standing guard outside a room.

David Nowak must be in there, she thought with a

quickening of interest. She had barely given the businessman any thought since the police and ambulance had arrived at Bertie's place the night before, but now she found herself walking towards his room, as if she couldn't help it.

As she neared the door, she heard a familiar voice coming from inside, and she saw Nowak sitting up in bed, propped up by pillows, facing a stern-faced Suzanne Whittaker, who was obviously questioning him about the murder.

"I'm sorry, miss, but you can't be here—" the constable by the door started to say.

Suzanne looked up and saw Poppy hovering in the doorway. She smiled and waved, calling out: "It's all right. Let her in."

Poppy joined the detective inspector at Nowak's bedside and looked down at the man who had tried to murder her and Bertie. He looked charming and affable again, and he smiled at her as if last night had never happened.

"You had a lucky escape, Mr Nowak," Suzanne was saying. "The doctors tell me that you only suffered minor electrocution burns and don't seem to have had any internal organ damage. But that doesn't mean you're going to escape the law so easily. You're under arrest for the murder of Rick Zova and you will also be charged with the assault and attempted murder of Dr Noble and Miss Lancaster. However, it will be easier on you if you cooperate and give us a full confession."

A thin, bespectacled man, who had been standing unobtrusively in the corner of the room, cleared his throat importantly and came forwards. "As Mr Nowak's lawyer, I must protest against this unseemly harassment of my client in his hospital bed—"

"It's all right, Whitby," said Nowak, waving a hand. "I'm not afraid of their questions." He turned back to Suzanne and looked at her expectantly.

"So you admit to killing Rick Zova?" said Suzanne.

"I had no choice—he was blackmailing me!" said Nowak, sounding like a defensive child in a playground saying: *"He started it!"*

"Blackmailing *you*?" Poppy blurted. "What on earth could he have to blackmail you about?" Then she recalled the note with the song lyrics and stared at Nowak even more disbelievingly. "Surely *you're* not doing drugs?"

"No, not anymore but... I did, once," said Nowak, looking a bit sheepish. "It was a long time ago. I was young and stupid—it was what you did to have a good time then, you know? Rick got me into it. He used to take me to these crazy parties, with girls everywhere and drugs on tap."

Suddenly, Poppy recalled the night of the party and the exchange between Nowak and Zova when the ageing rock star had first arrived...

"Rick... that really wasn't a nice thing to do."

Zova rolled his eyes. "Oh, lighten up, for God's sake! It was just a joke!"

"There are some things you just don't joke about."

"Bollocks! What's happened to you, David? You used to be fun. You used to do all sorts of crazy things! Yeah, that important businessman act might fool others but it won't work with me... We were lads together, remember? I know about all the things you used to get up to."

She looked down at the man in the bed and realised that the answer had been there in front of her all along, if only she had known to look.

"Sir!" the lawyer said, looking alarmed. "I don't think it's a good idea to discuss your past—"

"Oh, I was never an addict," said Nowak airily. "And I never did heroin! Just cocaine and marijuana and a bit of ecstasy..."

The lawyer looked even more horrified and began protesting again, but Nowak ignored him.

"I thought you were anti-drugs," Poppy said, thinking of Nowak's high-profile press releases and public statements condemning the drug culture in the UK.

"I am!" said Nowak, sitting up straighter in bed. "I got clean and I realised how drugs can destroy people's lives, and I wanted to do something about that. In fact, ever since I've been able to, ever since my company started becoming successful and I was financially in a position to do so, I have supported the fight against drugs in any way I could. I even started my own charitable foundation helping ex-addicts get back on their feet. My foundation has paid for temporary housing, training workshops, equipment, counselling..." He turned to Suzanne. "Surely you can see how much good I've done?"

Suzanne folded her arms. "That doesn't change the fact that you've committed murder."

"But it was necessary!"

"*Necessary?*"

Nowak gave her a contemptuous look. "Don't you understand anything? I'm standing in the parliamentary elections in a few months; I have a strong chance of winning, of becoming an MP for this constituency and having the power to make a real difference—but one sniff of a drug scandal and it will all be lost! The media love a bit of mud; image is everything, as my wife keeps saying."

He turned to Poppy, saying in an aggrieved voice: "Do you think it's right that I should be punished now for a small mistake I made in my youth? After all the amends I've made, all the good I've done since—and more importantly, all the good I can *still* do if I were to be elected—is it right that I should lose that chance, just because of a selfish, greedy bastard who never did a kind thing in his life?"

"It... it doesn't make murder right," said Poppy.

"It wasn't murder—not really," argued Nowak. "I just disturbed the wasps. It wasn't as if *I* stabbed him with a knife."

"But you knew about Zova's allergy, you knew a sting was likely to be fatal for him," protested Poppy.

"It was tantamount to murder—"

"What was I supposed to do?" demanded Nowak. "He was going to expose me! He left me that sick note in my study—"

"The note was for *you*?" said Poppy in surprise. "But how come Bunny said it was addressed to Dawn? Oh—I get it! It was the handwriting. Bunny must have read it wrong. It was addressed to '*David*'! A 'v' and a 'w' can look very similar, especially if everything is written in a scrawl... So the note was for you all along! But why did Zova put it on Dawn's desk, then?"

Nowak shrugged. "I suppose he assumed that it was my desk. It was the bigger one."

"Wait, what note?" interrupted Suzanne. "What are you both talking about?"

Belatedly, Poppy realised that the police still didn't know about Nowak's false alibi, his meeting in the garden with Dawn, or the note that Rick Zova had left in the study. She stood back and listened as Nowak recounted everything, ending with: "Rick left me that note as a reminder of his demands."

"A reminder?" Suzanne raised her eyebrows. "Had he contacted you before the party?"

Nowak nodded. "Several months ago. That's when it first started. At first, I did everything he wanted. I paid Rick what he asked for. But then he started demanding more and more each month. He said he had photos he took during the parties—photos of me doing lines of cocaine—and he was going to send them to all the news outlets if I didn't pay up. Everyone would find out... Even my wife would find out about the drug-use in my past!"

Poppy thought wryly that the businessman looked more terrified of his wife learning the truth than anything else.

"Did you expect Zova to come to your party?" asked Suzanne.

"No! Of course not—did you think I'd invite him? In fact, I'd decided the month before that I wasn't going to be intimidated by him anymore, so I didn't send him the usual payment. He didn't respond at first and I thought... I thought maybe he'd given up, now that I'd called his bluff." Nowak frowned. "Then he turned up at the party, swaggering around, jeering at me, leaving me that note... I tried to reason with him, but he just wouldn't listen! When I met Dawn outside, I looked over and saw Rick through the bushes with that old handyman chap. I thought at first that he was going to get a good thumping and I was delighted! But then the handyman left without doing anything and Rick was just standing there again. Smoking a cigar. As if he didn't have a care in the world... while my world was falling apart!" Nowak clenched his fist. "I felt so angry, so furious! Why should he be allowed to do this? I have so much to offer—so much good I can do for this country—but he was going to take it all away from me, just because his music was no longer selling and his last tour was a failure, and he wanted some easy money... It wasn't right!"

"That may be so, but it didn't give you the right to assault him," said Suzanne.

Nowak gave her a disgusted look. "I told you—I never laid a finger on him. I never even went near him."

"But what about the wasps?" said Poppy. "You had to have done something to disturb the nest."

"Oh, that was easy." Nowak gave a modest laugh. "I played a lot of cricket in my younger days—I was the star fielder for my school team. I've got brilliant aim and I can hit the stumps from thirty metres away. It didn't take a minute to find the right-sized stone and lob it into the wasp nest from a safe distance. I have to say, though, it was brilliant luck that the opening to the nest was facing my way. It would have been much harder to rouse the whole nest if I hadn't got a stone in. I really needed them to swarm and overwhelm Rick before he could get away."

Poppy recoiled at his heartless manner. "Did you stay and watch?" she asked in a horrified whisper.

The businessman wrinkled his nose in distaste. "Certainly not! I left as soon as I'd thrown the stone. For one thing, I didn't want to risk getting stung by any wasps. I was pretty far away but you can never tell, once they start to swarm. And for another, I had to get back as soon as possible to establish my alibi. Luckily, Geoff was still down in the wine cellar when I climbed back in and he didn't ask any awkward questions. By the time we found the bottle of wine and returned to the orangery, all hell had broken loose. You and that crime writer chap had come running in from the terrace and there were wasps everywhere—nobody even noticed that I'd been away."

He glanced at Suzanne and said with a complacent smile, "When your officers questioned me, I just told them that I was down in the cellar with Geoff. I knew I could persuade him to go along with the story—after all, it was giving him an alibi too. And I knew I was safe with Dawn. She'd never tell the police that we had been outside together. She'll do anything I ask her to." He grimaced. "It was just a shame that that bloody handyman had to get mixed up in things. If he hadn't come to have words with Zova and dropped his trowel, the police might never have suspected foul play and then the whole thing would have been written off as a tragic accident!"

"Don't be so sure. We would have traced things back to you at some stage, Mr Nowak," said Suzanne grimly.

"Oh, I doubt it," said Nowak loftily. "There was nothing connecting me to Rick, except that stupid note that he left me, and I would have found it and destroyed it... if *this* hadn't happened," he said, gesturing to himself. Then he gave Poppy a grudging smile. "You were smart, Miss Lancaster. You might think I'd be resentful but I'm not. I like resourceful people who can think quickly under pressure—in fact, you're exactly the kind of person I'd like to hire for my company."

"Er... thanks," said Poppy, thinking it was the weirdest compliment she had ever received. She couldn't quite believe that the man was still acting like he was running a multi-billion-pound corporation, rather than someone who was about to go to prison for murder.

"But the point is, you didn't destroy the note, Mr Nowak," said Suzanne impatiently. "The police have retrieved it from the robot's vacuum bag now, and it will used as evidence in your trial."

Nowak made a sound of irritation. "I should have been quicker! When I came to Hollyhock Cottage that day to see Miss Lancaster and met Dr Noble, I realised my mistake."

"It was Bertie—I mean, Dr Noble, talking about how different types of paper burn that alerted you, wasn't it?" asked Poppy.

"Yes, that's when I realised that the note might not have burned completely, after all. It had been scrawled on a page torn from a glossy magazine, exactly the type that Dr Noble had described. I rushed straight home and checked the fireplace in my study, but it was empty. Then my wife told me about Dr Noble's robot and I realised that the note could have been inside his infernal machine!" Nowak shook his head. "I should have done something that night, instead of waiting until the next day. It could all have been so different. No one would ever have known it was me..."

He's right, Poppy thought as she left the room a few minutes later. Nowak's charming, affable demeanour had completely blinded her—and everybody else—to his real character. It was slightly disturbing to realise that "nice guys" could be murderers too.

"Poppy—wait!"

Poppy turned back in surprise to see Suzanne hurrying out of the hospital room. The other woman held something out and Poppy felt a small plastic item being slipped into her hand. She looked down to see a transparent Ziploc bag containing a clear glass vial. Inside the vial was a cotton swab. Puzzled, she looked back up at Suzanne.

"I hope I'm not breaking a dozen laws doing this," said Suzanne wryly. "The swab contains a DNA sample taken from Zova's corpse. Enough for you to do a comparative test on."

"Oh!" Poppy stared at the other woman in surprise and delight. "That's... that's really kind of you. Thank you so much."

Suzanne smiled. "I hope this helps... and gives you the answers you're looking for."

Poppy looked down at the plastic bag in her hands after the other woman had returned to Nowak's room. She should have been happy. She had lost the opportunity to get a DNA sample when she had failed to find any of Zova's hair in Bunny's collection, but here was a second chance, a way at last to get definite answers.

And yet she found herself feeling queasy as she thought of Suzanne's words: *"...gives you the answers you're looking for..."*

Poppy swallowed. *What was the answer she was looking for?*

CHAPTER THIRTY-FIVE

A gust of wind tore through the cottage garden, whistling through the tree branches and scattering the dead leaves that Poppy had spent the last half an hour painstakingly raking into a pile.

"Oh bugger!" she cried in annoyance, watching the red and gold leaves swirl tauntingly around her.

She sighed and was just about to start raking all over again when she heard her name being called. Turning, she saw a man enter the front gate and come up the garden path. As he got closer, Poppy was surprised to see that it was Hubert Leach.

"Cousin Poppy!" he said with false joviality. "You're looking well!"

"Hello, Hubert," said Poppy coolly. This was the first time she'd seen him since David Nowak's cocktail party and she wasn't inclined to be friendly.

"Have you come to apologise at last?"

"Apologise?" Hubert forced a laugh. "Aww, come on, now... there isn't really anything to apologise for, is there?"

"Nothing... to... apologise... for...?" spluttered Poppy. "You dragged me to that party under false pretences, forced me to take part in a lie, then abandoned me there without even—"

"Ahh, that's a bit unfair, don't you think? I gave you the chance to attend an exclusive, high-society event; I even paid for your outfit! And all right, I might have been bending the truth slightly when I asked you to go as my girlfriend, but it was only a little white lie—bloody hell, it wasn't as if I asked you to betray your country or something! You just had to adopt a glamorous alias for one evening. Surely that wasn't so much to ask?"

"*A little white lie?*" Poppy's voice was shrill with outrage. "You *used* me to deceive David Nowak. You used me to provide a fake testimonial for your company. It's completely immoral and—"

"Does he know?" asked Hubert quickly.

"What? Does who know?"

"David Nowak. Did you tell him about... you know..."

"Well, I had to tell him that I was really your cousin—not your girlfriend. I'm sure he worked out the rest. He's not stupid," said Poppy dryly. "But no, we didn't discuss you in detail, Hubert. We got distracted by a murder investigation, among other things."

Hubert rubbed his hands together, muttering to himself, "Good... good... then the deal is still safe..."

"Nowak is in police custody and is going on trial for murder," said Poppy. "I hardly think he'll be negotiating any property deals in the near future."

"Not to worry—his wife will be taking the reins," said Hubert.

Oh, good luck with her, thought Poppy with an inward smile. Somehow she didn't think Hubert was going to have as easy a time with the property deals as he thought.

"Anyway, I came over to see how my favourite cousin was doing," Hubert continued.

"I'm your *only* cousin," muttered Poppy.

"I heard that your greenhouse was damaged in the storm at the weekend?"

Poppy looked at him suspiciously. "How did you know about that?"

"Oh, I have my sources. I hear it's a total write-off. You're probably better to rebuild it from scratch than try to repair the old structure."

Poppy sighed. "Well, I'd love to have an entirely new greenhouse, but I just haven't got the funds. I don't even know how I'm going to afford simple repairs, never mind a complete rebuild."

"Ah, well, that's where I come in," said Hubert, shifting his weight. He cleared his throat. "I... er... might be able to help you there."

"What do you mean?"

He fidgeted, not meeting her eyes. "You know, the greenhouse. I... er... I can give you the money needed for the work."

Poppy wasn't sure she had heard him correctly. "Pardon?"

"Look, you don't need to worry about the money to rebuild your greenhouse, okay? I'll sort it out."

"You mean... you mean you'll lend me the money?"

Hubert shifted even more uncomfortably. "No. I mean, *give* you. It's not a loan. The money's yours."

Poppy gaped at him. This was the last thing she had expected, the very last thing she had ever imagined happening.

"Are you serious? Are you having me on?"

"Of course I'm serious!"

"What's the catch?" asked Poppy suspiciously.

"No catch, no catch..." Hubert waved a hand.

"You mean..." Poppy eyed him incredulously. "You're just offering me the money... without any conditions? Without expecting anything in return?"

"Yes."

Poppy stared at him, still unable to take it in. She had been convinced that her cousin was a greedy, self-serving rat and yet here he was, making an incredibly generous and kind offer. Could she have misjudged him? Could all her instincts have been wrong?

"Why are you doing this?" she asked at last.

"What do you mean? We're family, aren't we?

Family have to help each other." Hubert gave her a cheesy grin. "So... what do you say, coz?"

Poppy still hesitated. She knew she shouldn't have been looking a gift horse in the mouth—she should have grabbed Hubert's offer with both hands and thanked whatever strange compulsion had caused his sudden display of charity and compassion. But she just couldn't shake off the sense of unease. If past experiences had taught her anything, it was that her cousin couldn't be trusted. She had already been burnt once and had regretted putting herself in his debt... did she really want to do it again? He might say that he wanted nothing in return now, but would he stick to his word?

On the other hand... Poppy glanced towards the rear of the property, where the damaged shell of the greenhouse was just visible through the shrubbery. Here was an unexpected boon, a chance for her to get back on her feet and fight for her dreams, without having to sell out or give up the cottage garden nursery. It would be crazy and stupid for her to pass it up. After all, what Hubert had said was true—he *was* family. If you couldn't accept help from family, then what did you have left?

And perhaps I've wronged him, after all, she thought, turning back to look at Hubert. *Maybe he does have a heart and isn't as bad as I thought he was...*

Swallowing her misgivings, she took a deep breath and smiled at Hubert, saying hesitantly, "Thank you.

It's… it's incredibly kind of you. It's—it's like a miracle… I never imagined… I don't know what to say."

"Well, if you decide to say yes, then let me know. In fact, if you get a quote for the building work and then call up my secretary and give her the details, she'll make sure that the money is transferred to your account."

Poppy stood staring after him long after Hubert had left. She couldn't believe how quickly things had changed that morning. She had gone from deep despair to excited elation. She was suddenly full of ideas and plans for the new greenhouse. Dropping her rake, she rushed into the house to tell Nell the good news. When she walked into the kitchen, however, she was brought rapidly back down to earth when she saw Nell sitting at the kitchen table with a worried look on her face.

"Have you heard anything new about Bertie yet?" Nell asked.

"No." Poppy's high spirits vanished in a flash as she thought of the old inventor who was still in a coma in hospital. It had been three days since that fateful evening when David Nowak had attacked them and Bertie still hadn't regained consciousness.

She glanced down at where Einstein the terrier was curled up at Nell's feet. He had been treated at the vet for minor injuries and then brought home to stay with them, but it was obvious he was pining for his master. He showed little interest in food or play, and spent most of the time lying morosely with his head in his paws. Even a visit from Oren earlier that morning had done nothing to rouse the normally feisty terrier, and the orange tomcat had left again in a huff.

Poppy crouched down next to Einstein and stroked the terrier's ears. He touched his cold nose to her hands, then sighed and laid his chin down on the floor again.

"Poor Einstein..." said Nell, watching him. "I tried to get him to eat something this morning but he wouldn't touch anything. Do you think the hospital would let you take him in for a visit? I'm sure it would be good for Bertie too. They say people in comas can still hear things around them and I'm sure it will do him good to feel that Einstein is nearby."

"I wish I could, Nell, but Bertie is in intensive care. It's a high-risk ward. They'd never allow it." Poppy gave Einstein a final pat, then stood up decisively. "But I'm going to pop over to the hospital now. They never tell me much when I call—I might get more news if I go in person. Besides, Nick is probably there and I might be able to speak to him."

The Oxford Infirmary seemed even busier than usual when she arrived, with the ICU ward, in particular, full of activity. Several new patients had been transferred to intensive care that morning and Poppy found a crowd of anxious friends and relatives congregating around the reception desk. She hovered uncertainly at the back of the group for a few minutes, before deciding to make her own way to Bertie's room.

She arrived to find a distinguished-looking man wearing scrubs and a stethoscope standing outside, surrounded by an entourage of junior doctors, medical students, and nurses. *This must be the consultant neurologist making a ward round*, thought Poppy, eyeing the doctor with respect.

Nick was standing beside him and the two men were in deep discussion. The crime writer looked like he hadn't slept much: his clothes were rumpled, his dark hair tousled, and his eyes slightly bloodshot. Poppy was touched to see that despite his outward antagonism towards his father, Nick had obviously been maintaining a vigil by Bertie's bedside. As she drifted closer, she caught a snatch of the men's conversation and realised that they were discussing Bertie's prognosis.

"...difficult to say. Coma cases can be unpredictable. The good news is that the scans show no sign of significant brain injury and it's encouraging that he's able to breathe on his own without the assistance of a ventilator. He's just unresponsive to any attempts to wake him," the consultant neurologist was saying.

"How long do you think he will remain like this?" asked Nick.

The consultant sighed. "I really don't know. Comas can last a few days to a few months, or even longer. The brain is a complex organ. It can be difficult to tell how head injuries can affect a person. Some think a coma may be nature's way of allowing the brain to rest and recover."

"Is there a chance he may not awaken?" asked Nick grimly.

The doctor hesitated. "As I said, it is impossible for me to tell you for certain..."

Poppy barely heard anymore. Her heart had lodged in her throat at the thought of Bertie never waking up. She squeezed past them unnoticed and slipped into the room. Slowly, she walked over to the bed and looked down at the old man. He looked so vulnerable lying there against the white sheets, still and silent, his usual childlike exuberance gone. Poppy had to resist the urge to reach out and pick up Bertie's hand, lying so limply on top of the sheets. Instead, she shoved her hands into her pockets.

Something hard pressed into her right palm and she groped around in her jeans pocket, pulling the item out. It was a small, round, flat tin. Poppy stared at it in puzzlement for a moment before she realised what it was: the tin of stinkhorn mushroom salve that Bertie had given her for her wasp stings. With it being so small and flat, it had remained unnoticed in her favourite jeans' pocket all this time. She felt overwhelmed by a wave of sadness as she remembered Bertie's infectious enthusiasm when he had talked about his plans for the stinky fungus. As she turned the tin over, she caught a faint whiff of the horrible, putrid smell, and she gave an involuntary chuckle as she recalled telling Bertie that the foul odour was strong enough to rouse a corpse.

Then she froze. Poppy looked from the tin to the unconscious old man in the bed, then to the tin again. She glanced over her shoulder, where, through the open doorway, she could see the crowd still gathered around Nick and the consultant neurologist. Nobody was paying her any attention.

What do I have to lose? she thought. Holding her breath, she unscrewed the tin, then leaned over the bed and waved it under Bertie's nose.

The old man's nostrils flared.

He stirred and inhaled deeply, then shifted in the bed, his nose twitching spasmodically.

Suddenly Bertie jerked up in bed with a cry, coughing and gagging.

Poppy gasped and fell backwards, just as there was a commotion outside the door.

"What is it? What's happened?" cried the consultant, rushing into the room, followed by Nick and his entourage. "Who are you?" he demanded of Poppy. Then he stopped short and stared at Bertie, who was sitting up in bed, blinking at everyone around him.

"Dad?" said Nick.

Bertie turned and beamed at him. "Ah, Nick! What are you doing here, son? And why am I in hospital?" He looked around. "Poppy, my dear! How nice to see you here too. Do you know... I have been having the strangest dream. You were in it... and CLARA too...

and an unpleasant bald man wielding a metal pipe—
"

"Oh my God, what is that horrible smell?" cried one of the junior doctors, putting a hand up to cover her nose, whilst a medical student behind her gagged and another sneezed uncontrollably.

Belatedly, Poppy remembered the tin and quickly screwed the lid back on. The consultant looked suspiciously at her for a moment, then turned back to Bertie.

"Dr Noble—you were in a coma. We couldn't wake you. How are you feeling?"

"Me? Oh, never better, never better..." said Bertie jovially, making a move to get out of the bed.

"Remarkable..." said the consultant, watching the old man stand up and stretch his arms. Then he turned back to Poppy in bewilderment and said: "What did you do?"

Poppy smiled at him. "Oh, it wasn't me—it was *Phallus impudicus.*"

CHAPTER THIRTY-SIX

Poppy straightened and looked around in delight at the huge sheets of glass around her. Late autumn sunshine streamed in through the sparkling glass panes, filling the area with light and warmth. She raised her head, looking up and admiring the soaring space above her, the gleaming glass roof surrounded by a solid new wooden frame. She would never have believed that so much could be achieved in the space of a week, and she would be forever grateful to the team of builders and carpenters who had worked so hard to complete her beautiful new greenhouse so quickly.

Turning back to the long wooden workbench, which had been unearthed undamaged from the fallen debris, Poppy gazed with satisfaction at the new trays of seedlings and plug plants which had just been delivered that morning. She was having to start again and it would certainly set her back several weeks, but she wasn't feeling defeated. In fact, looking at the dainty little seedlings now, green and lush and bursting with life, she felt a renewed sense of hope.

Gardening is all about failing and trying again, she reminded herself with a smile. And her smile widened as her gaze went beyond the trays to a potted plant standing at the other end of the workbench. She went over and picked it up, holding it up to the light to admire it: her little gardenia, which had miraculously survived the falling tree in one piece and been rescued from the wreckage.

She took it over to a new ledge that had been built beside the greenhouse walls and placed it up where it would receive the full benefit of the sun's rays warming the glass. Poppy was pleased to see no more yellow leaves on the plant—in fact, there were fresh, new green leaves and shoots appearing at the tips of the stems. Then, as she rotated the pot to adjust its position, she caught sight of something nestled against the glossy green leaves.

Oh! Her heart skipped a beat and she felt a wave of delight as she stared down at the creamy-white flower. It was an exquisite gardenia bloom, its snowy petals clasped in the shell-like green corolla and arranged in a perfect whorl. Somehow, this bud had held on when all the others had fallen off, and now it was opening to yield its sweet perfume. Poppy leaned down and pressed her nose to the velvety petals, inhaling the rich, sultry fragrance.

Then she stood back and smiled as she looked at the sunlight playing across the gardenia leaves. Any doubts that she might have had about whether she had done the right thing yesterday were gone now. She had been surprised when Lena Nowak had called to renew her husband's offer. She would have thought that the last thing Nowak's wife would be thinking about now was business. But it seemed that Lena was not going to let a small thing like her husband's murder trial interfere with her plans for expansion. She had doubled her husband's proposal, making Poppy's eyes nearly pop out with the amount of money being offered, and added pressure for a quick answer.

It had been one of the hardest decisions in her life and Poppy had winced at the thought of being beholden to Hubert in some way, once more. But in the end, she had listened to her heart and rejected the offer. She wasn't Mary Lancaster's granddaughter for nothing and she wasn't ready to give up her independence yet—especially not to a boss like Lena Nowak!

The sound of her name being called roused her from her thoughts and Poppy walked out of the new greenhouse into the rear garden. She was surprised to see Joe Fabbri coming down the garden path from the front of the property. He was carrying a large wooden plaque, which he thrust at her.

"For me?" Poppy looked down in surprise. She realised that it was a handmade wooden sign—beautifully hewn, sanded and lacquered, with writing engraved across its surface. It said:

"HOLLYHOCK GARDENS & NURSERY"

It was almost identical to the old sign currently hanging on the stone wall next to the front gate. Then she caught her breath as her eyes fell on some smaller words engraved underneath—words which were not on the old sign:

"Proprietor: Poppy Lancaster"

A rush of emotion swept through her, and Poppy felt her throat tighten. She looked up to see Joe regarding her with a rare twinkle in his eyes.

"Old sign past it," he said, jabbing a thumb towards the front of the property. "Time for new one."

Poppy gave him a tremulous smile. "Thank you, Joe. This is... Thank you so much! You don't know what this means to me."

He gave a nod and turned away, looking as if he would head off on his silent way again. Then he paused and turned back to her.

"No. Thank *you*. For believing in me," he said. Then he grinned and added, "Six new greenhouse cleaning jobs this week. Could do with an assistant...?"

Poppy made a face and laughed. "Can't wait!"

She accompanied him back to the front gate and watched him walk away. She was about to hang the new sign when the village postman came past on his bicycle.

"Morning!" he said cheerfully, handing her a bundle of leaflets and envelopes.

Poppy thanked him, then looked down absent-mindedly at the mail in her hands. Her heart skipped a beat as she saw the business logo "*MyDNAnswers*" stamped in the corner of the top envelope. Slowly, she put the wooden sign down and laid the rest of the mail on the stone wall. She stared down at the envelope in her hands. Her mouth felt dry and her fingers shook slightly as she tried to tear the flap open.

Here, at last, was the possible answer to the biggest question of her life, the nagging mystery she had lived with ever since she was a child. For as long as she could remember, all she had ever wanted was to find out who her father was. But now that the chance for truth was in front of her, she found that she was reluctant to take it. Perhaps it was silly and naïve of her, but she had always held on to a fairy-tale fantasy of her father. She had always been sure that he would be a wonderful man, a quintessential knight-in-shining-armour who would be kind and wise and, above all, honest and decent. Now, faced with the possibility that her father could have been a drug-abusing, womanising, self-serving shark, who had resorted to plagiarism and blackmail to get ahead, it made her question whether she really wanted to know the truth, after all.

Do I really want to find out? Isn't it better to live in ignorance than to have all my illusions shattered?

Poppy took a deep breath and slid her finger under the flap, then paused. She didn't want to do this alone. She thought about finding Nell; it would be good to have moral support when she confronted her demons.

But when her legs began moving, she wasn't walking back into the cottage. Instead, Poppy found herself heading up the lane to the elegant Georgian house next door. Standing on the doorstep, she hesitated for a long moment before ringing the bell. She wasn't sure why she had come, and when the door was flung open to show a scowling Nick Forrest, she wondered if she had made a terrible mistake.

"What?" he snapped.

Yikes. Obviously she had come at a bad point in his writing routine. "Never mind," said Poppy, taking a step back. "I... it's not important..."

She started to turn away, but Nick caught her arm to stop her. His tone softened slightly as he said:

"Poppy, what is it?"

Poppy licked her lips, holding the envelope up for him to see. "Um... the DNA test result... I just received it."

Nick frowned. "DNA test?"

"To compare Rick Zova's DNA with... with mine,"

Poppy explained. "I asked Suzanne for a sample. I sent it off for a private test. He had a tattoo, you see. It sounded just like a tattoo my mother described in her journal."

"Ah." Nick looked at her for a moment, then said abruptly, "Come in. I've been staring at the same bloody paragraph for the last hour—I might as well take a break."

It was hardly the most gracious of invitations, but Poppy followed him gratefully into the house. When she walked into the kitchen, however, she stopped short at the sight of Oren with his head in a bowl of dried cat biscuits. The loud sound of crunching filled the room.

"Are those...?" She pointed disbelievingly. "Oh my God—is he eating the diet food?"

Nick gave her a wry smile. "Miracles do happen."

"How did you do it?"

Nick cleared his throat gruffly. "Well, actually... uh... I asked my father for some help. He came up with a zero-calorie, salt-free, fat-free, sugar-free flavour enhancer that can be sprinkled on the food."

Poppy frowned. "If it doesn't have any salt, fat, sugar or anything, how does it make the food taste better?"

"Well, apparently your sense of smell is closely linked to your sense of taste—did you know that? It's why when you have a cold and your nose is blocked, you can't taste anything properly. Bertie created a formula which uses highly volatile compounds that stimulate the olfactory senses in such a way that it tricks the taste buds. In other words, Oren is smelling something which makes him think he's tasting delicious roast chicken," said Nick, grinning down at the ginger tomcat.

Poppy shook her head in disbelief. "Bertie never ceases to amaze."

"And infuriate," muttered Nick under his breath.

But Poppy smiled to herself. Somehow, she had a feeling that Nick's hostility towards his father was becoming less genuine and more of an act. As she leaned against the kitchen island, she cast a surreptitious glance at the paper model of the miniature apartment, thinking how lucky it was that she had managed to glue the broken items before Nick had come home. By the time she had finished meticulously sticking everything together, it had looked as good as new.

Oren jumped up suddenly and strolled across the island to her. He passed the model on the way and paused to rub his chin against one flimsy paper wall.

"Careful!" Nick said, hastily picking the model up. Turning to Poppy, he added, "One of my fans made this—can you believe it? Incredible attention to detail! I've received all sorts of fan mail, but I've never received fan art like this. It's marvellous." He gave the kitchen island a rueful look. "Although I suppose I really shouldn't leave it in here. It's so delicate and easily damaged... In fact, I'm surprised Oren hasn't done anything to it yet."

"*N-ow?*" said Oren, his yellow eyes wide and innocent.

When Nick had left the kitchen to put the model in his study, Poppy leaned over and placed a finger against her lips as she looked at the ginger tom.

"*N-ow?*" said Oren again.

"Shhh!" said Poppy, grinning. She gave Oren a wink. "It'll be our secret."

Nick returned a few moments later and indicated the gleaming coffee machine on the kitchen counter. "Fancy a latte? Cappuccino?"

"Just a cup of tea would be great, thanks," said Poppy.

She perched on one of the kitchen stools and watched as he boiled the kettle, then filled two mugs and handed one to her. She took her time adding milk and sugar, and stirring things vigorously. She knew she was just stalling, but the more she thought about it, the more she was scared of opening that envelope and finding out the answer.

"Would you like me to open it for you?" asked Nick at last in an amused voice as she started stirring her tea anticlockwise.

Poppy bristled. "I can do it myself."

Still, Nick's teasing had pricked her out of the nervous paralysis she had been feeling and she was secretly grateful. She took a deep breath and picked up the envelope, then tore it open and extracted the single type-written sheet inside. She held her breath as her eyes scanned the neatly typed paragraph.

"It's not Zova," she blurted. Her shoulders sagged in relief and she let out the breath she had been holding with gusto.

Nick looked at her curiously. "You seem very relieved."

"Wouldn't you be?" Poppy demanded. "Imagine if you had a self-centred nutter for a father."

"I don't need to—I already do," muttered Nick.

"Aww, come on! Bertie is nothing like Rick Zova! He's wise and kind and sweet and thoughtful!"

Nick regarded her silently for a long moment, then he said at last, in a measured tone:

"My father isn't the harmless, sweet old man you think he is. He has done things—questionable things, hurtful things... Don't forget, greatness always comes at a price. And he wasn't always the one who paid it."

Poppy stared at him. It was the closest Nick had ever come to talking about the reason for the rift between himself and his father. She wanted to ask him more but something in his expression made her hesitant. Instead, she refolded the letter and stuffed it back into the envelope, then drained her mug and took it over to the sink.

"Well, thanks for the tea... I think I'd better go," she said.

"*N-ow?*" said a plaintive voice and she looked down to see Oren sitting by her feet. He tilted his head and looked up at her, his yellow eyes enormous.

Poppy laughed and bent to scoop the ginger tom

up in her arms. "Yes, Oren, now. I'm going back to do some stuff in my new greenhouse."

"How do you like it?" asked Nick casually.

Poppy turned a shining face to him. "Oh, it's fantastic! It's got a wider roof that lets more light in and a sturdier frame and more space for everything..." She shook her head, laughing to herself. "I still can't believe Hubert made such a generous offer. It seems totally out of character for him! But I suppose I must have misjudged him in the past."

Nick gave a small smile. "Perhaps."

"Anyway, I was thinking—I'd like to give a small party this weekend to celebrate. Would you... um... would you like to come?" asked Poppy, looking at him shyly.

Nick's smile widened. "Of course." He glanced at Oren in Poppy's arms. "And I suppose the big orange monster is invited too?"

Poppy chuckled. "Oh, he's the guest of honour. Who else is going to knock the first terracotta pot off the bench?"

CHAPTER THIRTY-SEVEN

When Poppy returned to the cottage, she found Nell energetically scrubbing the kitchen sink.

"Didn't you clean that yesterday?" Poppy asked, puzzled.

"Have... to... get... rid... of... this... mould..." Nell panted, shoving the scrubber into the corner between the sink and the kitchen wall, and moving it aggressively back and forth.

Poppy could see dark patches embedded in the surface of the wall and in the seam between the edge of the sink and the counter.

"It's a real bugger! I've done the basic sugar soap and now I'm tackling it with bleach..." Nell set her mouth in a hard line. "And I'm not stopping until I get it all out!"

"Why don't we get CLARA to come and clean it for

you?" suggested Poppy. "You know, Bertie's new cleaning robot. She can be programmed to focus on specific types of dirt, like mould, and she could probably—"

"Ohhh no!" said Nell. "I'm not letting some new-fangled contraption into my kitchen—"

"She's not a 'contraption'," Poppy said. "She's really high-tech. She has all these special sensors and multiple cleaning modes and fancy attachments—"

"No machine can clean better than a human!" declared Nell. "Cleaning is a complex skill, you know. You have to understand dirt, to respect it and meet it on its own terms."

"Er... right," said Poppy, her lips twitching. "But Nell, I think CLARA *does*. Understand dirt, I mean. She has an advanced GDS and she can also—"

"*No* robot is setting foot in this house while I'm here," said Nell, folding her arms.

Poppy gave an exaggerated shrug. "Well, I suppose if you feel threatened by—"

"Who said anything about being threatened? I'm not scared of a stupid machine!" said Nell indignantly. She rolled her sleeves up. "Fine! Bring her in here and we'll see who can scrub a sink better!"

Ten minutes later, Poppy wheeled CLARA nervously into the kitchen, wondering if she had started something she was going to regret. Bertie had offered to come too but she had put him off, thinking that having to deal with both the eccentric old inventor *and* his robot at the same time would be too much for Nell's nerves. Now, though, she almost wished that Bertie were here to give her moral support.

She found Nell waiting, dressed in her best rubber gloves and cleaning smock, and brandishing a mop with a dangerous gleam in her eye.

"Er... here she is," said Poppy, pushing CLARA forward.

Nell eyed the robot up and down. "Is that it?"

"Well, I haven't powered her up yet," said Poppy, hastily going to the back of the robot and trying to remember the instructions that Bertie had given her. She turned a knob, pushed a few buttons, then stepped back.

There was a whirring noise and multicoloured lights flashed all over the robot. The words "*READY FOR CLEANING*" blinked in CLARA's cash-register display head.

"Hmm..." said Nell, not looking impressed.

Poppy directed the robot towards the sink and watched hopefully.

"*Commencing scan...*" said CLARA. The robot emitted a ray of blue light which moved back and forth. "*Kitchen butler sink and draining board. Circa 1960. Fire-clay ceramic. 600mm long, 460mm wide, 250mm deep. Signs of wear and tear from excessive scrubbing.*"

Nell bristled. "Excessive? I'm not excessive!"

A siren sounded suddenly and the robot said: "*SGS Alert! Serious Grime Situation!*"

"Serious grime?" cried Nell, outraged. "How dare you!"

"*Contamination by fungal spores detected. Mould Removal Protocol initiated.*"

CLARA rolled forwards and began attacking the sink with multiple arms brandishing scrubbers, sponges, steel wool, and steam cleaners. Nell watched, slightly stupefied, as the robot blasted the sink with a jet of steam, fogging up all the kitchen windows and raising the temperature in the room by several degrees. When the vapour finally cleared, the area around the sink was pristine, with not a speck of mould in sight.

"Wow!" said Poppy. She looked eagerly at Nell. "Isn't that amazing? Aren't you impressed?"

Nell compressed her lips, giving the sink a grudging look of approval. "Hmm... It's a good effort, I suppose. She missed a spot there... and there..." she added, pointing behind the taps.

"Aww, come on, Nell! You *have* to admit that CLARA did a good job! And so quickly too—"

"She has no imagination," said Nell, sniffing disdainfully. "It's all done without any sensitivity, without any real appreciation of the process."

Poppy rolled her eyes in exasperation. "Who needs imagination to scrub a sink? Seriously, wouldn't you rather sit back with your feet up and a cup of tea, and watch a robot do your cleaning for you?"

"Certainly not!" said Nell, looking scandalised. "Doing cleaning yourself, by hand, is a priceless activity. It's mind-soothing. It's character-building. It's—"

She was interrupted by a volley of excited barking, and Einstein the terrier rushed into the kitchen from the back door. He had obviously been running through the boggier parts of the garden, still wet from the recent rains, and now left a trail of muddy pawprints on the kitchen floor as he scampered in.

Nell and CLARA emitted simultaneous shrieks of horror.

"It's just a bit of mud," said Poppy. "No need to get so worked up."

Both the robot and Nell stopped and swivelled their heads to give her a beady glare (or "*%$@#!!*" on the display in CLARA's case). Then they turned back to the muddy terrier as one.

Poppy watched, dumbfounded, as Nell leaned down, peering over her spectacles, then held out a rubber-gloved hand to CLARA.

"Scrubber. Scissors. Floor mop," she said tersely, whilst the robot obediently produced each implement and handed them to her, in the perfect imitation of a surgical theatre nurse.

This is mad... I'm living with a bunch of complete nutters, thought Poppy, struggling not to laugh as she watched them.

What with Nick and Oren... and Bertie and Einstein... and now Nell and CLARA... it was like being in the middle of a bizarre, madcap family!

Then a slow smile spread across her face.

Poppy looked back at Nell and the robot with new eyes. She thought of the brooding crime author next door with his bossy, talkative cat... and the eccentric old inventor on the other side with his feisty little dog and his mushroom teas and crazy inventions... and the taciturn village handyman with the heart of gold... and the elegant detective inspector with her sisterly concern and affection...

Poppy took a deep breath. Maybe she would never find out who her father was... and maybe it didn't matter. Maybe she didn't need to know who her real family was. After all, she had the perfect family right here.

FINIS

ABOUT THE AUTHOR

USA Today bestselling author H.Y. Hanna writes British cosy mysteries filled with humour, quirky characters, intriguing whodunits—and cats with big personalities! Set in Oxford and the beautiful English Cotswolds, her books include the Oxford Tearoom Mysteries, the 'Bewitched by Chocolate' Mysteries and the English Cottage Garden Mysteries. After graduating from Oxford University, Hsin-Yi tried her hand at a variety of jobs before returning to her first love: writing. She worked as a freelance writer for several years and has won awards for her novels, poetry, short stories and journalism.

A globe-trotter all her life, Hsin-Yi has lived in a variety of cultures, from Dubai to Auckland, London to New Jersey, but is now happily settled in Perth, Western Australia, with her husband and a rescue kitty named Muesli. You can learn more about her and her books at: **www.hyhanna.com**

Sign up to her newsletter to be notified of new releases, exclusive giveaways and other book news! Go to: **www.hyhanna.com/newsletter**

ACKNOWLEDGMENTS

This book has taken longer than usual to write and was a struggle to complete, with constant interruptions and delays due to family illness and the situation with Covid-19. I would never have managed it without my wonderful beta reading and editing/proofreading team. So thank you to: Kathleen Costa, Connie Leap, Basma Alwesh and Charles Winthrop, for their invaluable insights and patience with all my questions, as well as my editor and proofreader for being so flexible about fitting me into their schedules.

A special thank you also to Billy Huang and Theresa Chen, for helping me brainstorm the plot and work through writing blocks.

Finally, to my wonderful husband who, as always, has been the most understanding, supportive and encouraging partner a writer could ask for.